The
CITADEL

The
CITADEL

Written by Dave Bailor

Illustrated by Jason Clifford

Copyright © 2012 by Dave Bailor.

Library of Congress Control Number: 2012913304
ISBN: Hardcover   978-1-4771-4973-7
                Softcover   978-1-4771-4972-0
                Ebook   978-1-4771-4974-4

All rights reserved. No part of this book may be reproduced or transmitted in any form or by any means, electronic or mechanical, including photocopying, recording, or by any information storage and retrieval system, without permission in writing from the copyright owner.

This is a work of fiction. Names, characters, places and incidents either are the product of the author's imagination or are used fictitiously, and any resemblance to any actual persons, living or dead, events, or locales is entirely coincidental.

This book was printed in the United States of America.

To order additional copies of this book, contact:
Xlibris Corporation
1-888-795-4274
www.Xlibris.com
Orders@Xlibris.com
96806

ACKNOWLEDGEMENTS

Many, many thanks for the countless hours my friend and editor, Chris Canter, put into the project. His untiring effort, dedication, patience and professionalism are greatly appreciated.

No work by a married man can be truly claimed by him. This book would not have been completed without the encouragement and the behind-the-scenes work by my amazing wife, Donna.

When an artist is discovered that can interpret the storyline and 'sees' the same scenery as the author, a valuable commodity has been found indeed. A special thank-you is extended to Jason Clifford for the creation of the fine illustrations that help bring the story to life.

Finally, my undying gratitude to my English teacher, my moral compass, and someone I have grown to admire in every facet of her life—my Mom.

CHAPTER ONE

"This is great!" David announced as he excitedly paced back and forth across the large family den. His trek appeared to be contained between the low footstool at his father's feet and the lone end table next to an over-stuffed easy chair. He was holding a newsreel in his hands and, from time to time, stopped pacing long enough to re-read another piece of an article.

"Another significant achievement that will have an enormous impact on our city, the country, and eventually, the entire world" David quoted from the newsreel. He continued pacing across the room, once again muttering to himself.

Darren, David's older brother, shook his head with derision. A sardonic chuckle escaped his lips before he broke into his brother's sporadic commentary. "Eventually, the entire world will be able to use this technology! Yeah, right. As if our esteemed Mayor Kourei will let us employ it anywhere except in his 'approved' communities."

Darren and David's father spoke up, "My, my, aren't we negative, today. Remember, this is a 'significant achievement'. There is even going to be a ceremony conducted in our honor. Not only did we come up with an efficient method to harness solar energy, we have already employed the technique in such a way that saves the general populous thousands in energy payments. Kourie will HAVE to allow us to construct the discs throughout the city. Do you have any idea what kind of rioting would occur if the people found out our illustrious Mayor was keeping something like that from them?"

David looked up from the newsreel. "Riots? That's just what we need, more riots. Everyone is angry these days. What now, a transport strike?"

Darren and his father looked at one another for a moment before they ruefully shook their heads. It really didn't matter, though. David's attention had already shifted back to the reel. They settled back into their respective over-stuffed loungers to wait for David to eventually rejoin the rest of the family.

"Did you see these power predictions? Ha! They are not even close!" 'Someday, we'll get that kind of energy production', David quoted from the article. "We are generating that kind of power now! We should be able to generate more than enough power for the new city." David was still talking out loud.

"NEW city? What new city? Oh no, this was the last project. There is no new ANYTHING! You are all heroes, now. That's what you wanted, right?" Jocelyn Kendal eyed the two brothers with increasing alarm. "I thought you were done!" Jocelyn whirled towards the older of the two brothers, "Darling, you said you were finished. What's this about a new city?" Although the question was directed towards her husband, she managed to send a frosty glare towards her father-in-law across the room.

The sharp voice pulled David to a stop in mid-turn of his pacing. He glanced quickly first towards his brother, then his father, completely avoiding the person for whom the voice belonged before David hastily buried himself into the newsreel.

Mr. Kendal flinched; his broad, powerful shoulders tensed and he suddenly found a great interest looking down at his calloused hands. Robert Kendal was a big man and has often been mistaken for someone in the service of athletics or agriculture. His brawny build had assisted him many times in the boardroom as he very successfully sold his ideas, inventions and practical application of those inventions to the York-City officials. The dark, appraising brown eyes were shadowed by bushy, graying eyebrows that seemed to provide balance to his square, clean-shaven chin.

The overall impression was that he was a big, strong, teddy-bear type of a man that would do anything to protect and absolutely nothing to harm anyone. So, now, with Jocelyn going into one of her infamous tirades, Mr. Robert Kendal was diligently attempting to blend into the surroundings.

Darren looked towards his wife and let out a long sigh. With a rueful shake of his head he began, "Jocie, you know this is not about fame and fortune. This is truly a device that will help people. All we need to do is properly employ it. What better way than to start with the new city? Now, Dad has this idea-"

"Do you honestly believe you have to create a new CITY? We *have* a city. We have plenty of power, energy and whatever else you think needs to be created. It won't make a difference to those people out there", Jocelyn waved vaguely at nothing in particular, "WHAT you do to 'help' them." Jocelyn continued her attack, "They don't care. They'll just find something else to complain about. You said this was the last project. 'We can get out of the engineering nightmare and just live out our lives'. Isn't that what you said?"

Darren looked at her with exasperation and furtively glanced at his father with not a little embarrassment. Jocelyn Marie Kendal was an attractive woman with finely carved features that could have easily placed her into the entertainment industry had she had any inclination to work in the services. She did not. Jocelyn, Jocie to VERY few people and by her permission to NO ONE, had come from a well-established family. There had never been a need for her to apply for a service and the idea to do so had very likely never even occurred to her.

"We are not done with this project", Darren continued. "All we have accomplished so far is the creation of an invention and a small show-case to display how it works". Darren's voice grew sterner and the temperature in the tone of his voice dropped a few degrees as he continued his attempt to deflect his wife's anger. "We will be 'done' with the project when the people in our city are no longer slaves to the energy companies. We will be 'done' when the people can live their lives without having to riot to survive!"

Jocelyn was obviously not swayed by her husband's remarks. She settled back into her easy chair and deliberately crossed her arms across her breasts before launching into her next argument. "You ARE done. You have created your Solar Discs and you have shown the world how the discs work. It was a great achievement—congratulations!" The sarcasm was really beginning to flow from her words. "Now, let THEM-"

"Oh, man!" David suddenly exclaimed. "This is a green tie affair! Did you see who is invited to the ceremony? This is going to be GREAT!" David looked up from the newsreel to meet Jocelyn's icy stare. The temperature in the room had been steadily dropping these past few minutes but David had been blissfully unaware. Now his face was flushed from the cold. In panic, he quickly looked over to his brother, then to his father, for help.

Mr. Kendal piped up in an attempt to rescue his youngest son from his somewhat opinionated daughter-in-law. "This will be bigger than the banquet the city put on for the liquid purification beam you two came up with last year. There will be plenty of dignitaries at this one. After all, every Vision station will be transmitting coverage of the event to the farthest reaches of their broadcasting zone."

Robert Kendal glanced quickly towards his oldest son hoping for a comment and further assistance.

"That's right", Darren quickly picked up on the conversation. "First, we added an optical guidance system to the transports. THAT was a good idea, using optical scanners to analyze objects to create an auto-guidance system. We got plenty of publicity out of THAT one. Fewer people killed in transport accidents, HA! There were fewer accidents, period".

"Not that there are that many transports in use", Jocelyn sarcastically tossed out her comment.

"Then, the purification beam", David hastily chimed in. David was careful to avoid any eye contact with his brother's wife. "We abandoned the entire physical straining technique in favor of using a particle beam that lanced through the liquids and were programmed to block specific debris. It was faster, cheaper, and could purify liquids at a much greater rate than what the City could do. I thought THAT one would save people LOTS of credits since they no longer would need to buy York-City-purified water."

"It didn't quite work out that way, though." Darren finished the thought with a quick, downcast look towards his father.

As she entered the room where the three were debating, Maxine glanced for a moment at Jocelyn expecting a response, then, turned to Darren as she picked up on the conversation, "Oh, the BEAM worked FINE. It just didn't save the people any credits. The beam needed power and the Power Venders made sure everyone had to pay for it."

Jocelyn rewarded David's future wife with an acid look. She opened her mouth to give another retort but Mr. Kendal successfully cut her off.

"I enjoyed the 'Vision Optical' idea the best", Mr. Kendal quickly said. "We had fun with that one." Robert Kendal leaned forward in his chair as he warmed to the new turn of the conversation.

Jocelyn sighed audibly as she settled more deeply into the overstuffed easy chair. She had come to the realization that they were going to talk around her. Eye contact with her was not likely to happen any time soon. Jocelyn's temper was quite flammable and it was obvious to everyone in the room (even David), that she was not, yet, finished with her topic of discussion.

"You know what? It really was fun converting signals from the optical analysis into a vision beam. We were having fits with the formulas but-"; Darren was interrupted by his father's sudden laughter.

"Ha! Engineers! Only an engineer would have fun playing with the formulas! I'm talking about the images we created! Max, you should have seen the first tree Darren created for us!" Mr. Kendal shook his head and chuckled at the memory.

Darren rolled his eyes and crossed his arms across his chest in a classic 'pout'. "Okay, okay, so I forgot to reverse the opticals . . ." Darren was trying to defend himself but now that his father had opened the topic, David was not about to let the opportunity pass by. He quickly joined in the ribbing of his older brother.

"Reverse the opticals . . ." David mimicked. "It was upside-down, all right. But that was the strangest 'tree' I had ever seen!" David turned to Maxine and, still holding the newsreel, became very animated trying to demonstrate while explaining his brother's 'tree'. "It had branches and a trunk, but it was hard to focus on anything. All the pieces of the tree moved and flowed like a nest of slow-moving snakes. I don't know what happened to the leaves and", David started laughing, "and then this bird flew within optical range . . ."

Mr. Kendal was laughing, now. Darren had abandoned his pout for a more defensible 'just a poor, misunderstood engineer' pose. But now, even he was laughing.

David continued, "You see, the opticals just added the bird to the tree. When was the last time you have ever seen an upside down tree with wings and feathers?" David laughed!

Maxine was enjoying the friendly persecution of her soon-to-be brother-in-law. Jocelyn, however, was completely unmoved by the story. She merely sighed, crossed her legs and wriggled her foot with annoyance.

"I corrected the formulas!" Darren exclaimed with feigned indignation.

"Yes, yes", David said soothingly while patting his brother on the shoulder. "You make very pretty trees, now."

Darren took a quick, playful swing at his little brother, and David, with apparent years of practice, deftly ducked out of the way.

Darren Kendal took after his father. He had a strong, fairly powerful, athletic build. He was slightly taller than Mr. Kendal with a thick, barrel chest similar to his fathers' but lacking the broad shoulders. Darren had always preferred a 'clean-cut' look. His blonde hair was close-cropped and he had never sported a beard. When he bothered to have one, he would grow a very short, almost militaristic mustache. Usually, though, he had forgotten that he had started one and it was shaved off before anyone noticed the attempt.

David, however, appeared as though he had come from an entirely different family. He stood several inches shorter than Darren with fine, dark hair. David had never worn his hair long, but he didn't like to keep it as short as Darren and his father. He had grown a mustache ever since he was twelve years old. He grew a beard, faithfully, every fourth cycle of the year. He said it was to keep his face warm while he was 'in the field' but, truthfully, he kept the beard too short for it to provide much protection from the elements. David had a much leaner build than his sibling, which probably explains his quickness for moving out of target range of his older, larger brother.

Darren redirected the attack towards his father. "Engineers?" A hint of a mocking tone could be heard as a small smile tugged at his lips. "Tell me why, Mr. 'Engineer of York-City', you think it is humorous that I 'have fun' playing with formulas. Who was it that couldn't stop talking for an entire cycle about the mathematics needed to apply the opticals in the transports?"

Mr. Kendal shrugged his shoulders and raised his hands up in the air as if to indicate that he had no idea whom his son was talking about.

"Just be glad that he IS an engineer", David piped in. "He could have been a Y-CR like Max."

A 'Y-CR'; a representative of the York-City Resources Service, had the dubious privilege of placing residents in need of employment into a city service opportunity as quickly as possible. It was an honor only because people needed employment to survive. All York-City residents were educated in accordance to the current or foreseeable service needs of the city. Many, if not most, of the people within the city were employed within services for which they were qualified only because of the education they had received. Nowhere in the city's charter was it stated that the citizens must have any interest in or any aptitude for the service. As long as there was a service need, a person need only to have been properly trained for the service—they didn't have to like it.

Max was an attractive woman of medium build and height. She was not necessarily considered beautiful although that word had been used to describe her. She was . . . 'striking'. Her brownish-blonde hair accentuated the intelligent blue eyes and fair skin. Her features were well balanced, proportioned—even powerful. One would think that she could have done very well indeed within the Athletic Services. Many citizens of York-City, however, were grateful that she had been placed into the city Resources service instead. Her ability to analyze and foresee the service needs of the city and her compassion to place people into the services that they not only excelled in but actually enjoyed had earned her several city awards and the gratitude of many of its residents. David would tell anyone who would listen to him that he would not be able to explain which of her features he enjoyed contemplating the most. Intelligent, compassionate and beautiful—as far as he was concerned, everything about her was perfect!

The overall goal of the Resource Service was to ensure unceasing, educated service that administered to the needs of the city. Even though Max was considered an excellent Y-CR, her success had come with a price. Maxine's dedication to her service was to the populous of the city rather than to the Employment Administration Board. Her 'misguided' dedication had not endeared her to the top executives. Most of the people who were placed into the Resource Services could earn a decent living, but there was the ever-present knowledge that there were plenty of other people in the city with similar credentials that could replace them at a moment's notice. The termination of anyone in any service employment placed that resident back into the non-servicing pool. It had been fortunate for Maxine that there had been very few failures within the pool of people that she had placed into the services. For many of the other Y-CRs, those types of people had been the exceptions.

Darren laughed again, "Dad? A Y-CR? Now THAT would have been a sad turn of affairs! Max has the best track record of any Y-CR that I have ever known. But Dad, I would bet you that he would have been released into the pool within two cycles!"

Mr. Kendal had been fortunate to be in the right place at the right time at the right age. Nearly fifty years ago York-City needed architects and engineers and that was precisely during the timeframe that a very young Robert Kendal was eligible for education. Mr. Kendal had excelled as a practical engineer and was given many projects for which he was able to turn into credit-producing services. He had become so well respected within the city government that he was allowed to guide his sons' educational opportunities in such a way that the boys were able to choose their own profession. It was to his great satisfaction that they had chosen, and enjoyed, the service of practical engineering.

Mr. Kendal shook his head, "Do you really think I could have lasted two cycles? Maybe, in another world, I would have been the Y-CR and Max would have been the engineer!"

Now it is Maxine's turn to laugh. She chimed in, "I wouldn't have survived a single cycle before the City would have turned me loose. Hmmm, maybe I could have been a transport mechanic". She turned to David and ran her fingers through his hair. "I'd come home from work with trans-oil on my hands and-."

David leaned back to escape her grasp, reached up and snared her hand. He pulled the hand out of his hair while telling her, "Fortunately for me, you are a Y-CR." He carefully inspected her hands then continued, "Whew, no trans-oil. For a second there I was worried!"

Everyone was laughing. Well, almost everyone. Jocelyn was still sitting in the plush chair in stony silence. She took the pause in the conversation as an opportunity to revive her argument.

"Maxine does not need to work in the services. NONE of you would have to continue to provide service if you would just sell the rights to your inventions. York-City would pay enough credits to last us several lifetimes." Jocelyn looked around the room for a moment before continuing, "We could all retire, move out of these holes, get a nice, city-staffed mansion and be comfortable."

Silence hung in the room for a few uneasy moments. Maxine broke the quiet with a change of topic. "Would anyone like another drink?" She pointed to the tray of refreshments that had been brought into the room and placed on the table during the conversation.

Jocelyn sniffed unappreciatively at the tray of drinks. Darren deliberately took a small, half-filled drink from the tray and sipped it with satisfaction. David selected two drinks. He handed one drink to his fiancé with a mock bow of servitude and brought the other to his father before returning to the tray and selecting one other drink for himself.

David took a healthy drought from his goblet, looked slowly around the large, well-furnished den and sighed. After another, smaller sip, he announced, "I like it here. This 'hole' is plenty nice enough for me. I certainly have more here than I will ever need". David may get distracted and heaven knows he enjoys a good joke or prank, but he has never played political games or shied away from confrontation. He deliberately looked into Jocelyn's dark eyes, "I like it here. I am comfortable here."

The controlled face that Jocelyn had been wearing quickly faded away. "Fine, be 'comfortable' here. We'll just leave and be comfortable in OUR York-City provided hovel! Darren?" Jocelyn looked expectantly at her husband as she jumped to her feet and prepared to leave.

Darren took a measured sip of his drink before answering. "You go ahead, Jocie. Dad, David, and I are going to go to the office for a while. I would like to take another look at the schematics Dad has for the new city."

Jocelyn stopped moving towards the door, frozen for just a moment, turned and appraised Darren for a moment. "You are not going to go there, tonight, are you? I mean, there have been riots all over the city, today. Haven't you been paying attention to *anything?* Those people that you are trying so hard to help don't know who you are. You'll just be another big shot in a transport. Look, you want to talk about the new city? Fine! Let's talk about the city. But we will either stay here or we are going home."

Darren was beginning to look distinctly annoyed and somewhat embarrassed. It's one thing to have his wife argue with his family, but he had never appreciated her tendency to order him about. He deliberately eased out of the comfort of his chair and gestured with his drink towards her. "We-"

Maxine unexpectedly interrupted Darren, "She's right, you know."

"What?" David, Darren and Mr. Kendal said all at once. David and Mr. Kendal spun around to stare at Maxine in disbelief.

Surprise played across Jocelyn's face only to be replaced by annoyance that someone had felt the need to defend her.

Maxine shrugged her shoulders and calmly continued, "She is. The rioting has been going on for the past week, you know that." She looked pointedly at David. "Today has been the worst, by far. These people are not working, they are living in squalor, they cannot receive education unless York-City allows them and, then, they don't get to learn and do what interests them. They won't know who you are and they won't care who you are. If they target you . . ." Maxine hesitated while looking at David.

Jocelyn completed the thought, "They will destroy anything. It's a mob mentality." She looked at her husband and this time there was genuine concern in her voice. "Let's just go home."

Darren turned his head towards Maxine for a moment and gave her a quick wink. Then, he cocked his head challengingly at his wife. "No, Jocelyn", he spoke quietly but firmly. "We won't be gone long." Darren softened his tone before continuing, "Besides, Brennan will avoid the crowds so you won't have to worry about us."

Jocelyn stared coldly at her husband for a moment before she whirled about and stalked out of the room. The word, 'no', and the name, 'Jocelyn', are not often used in the same sentence.

There was another awkward moment of silence before Darren slowly let out his breath between pursed lips. "There will be Hell to pay, tonight", he muttered. He looked over towards his father. "Let's get out of here. She may be right but I am NOT going to give her the satisfaction. Still, we probably shouldn't be in the city very long, tonight."

Darren's father got to his feet and patted the shoulder of his oldest son. "Don't worry. This will blow over. She just wants to make sure that she has some security for you, herself and Sunis. He's getting older and you know what the price tag is for bringing up children these days, don't you?"

Mr. Kendal turned his head towards a view screen and called softly, "Brennan? Would you bring the transport around to the front of the house, please?"

A well dressed man appeared briefly on the screen and gave a short nod of his head before speaking clearly into the audio, "Right away Mr. Kendal." The screen automatically returned to its previous setting as Brennan turned away.

Mr. Kendal looked back at Darren. "You are right, though. This cannot be one of our long discussions, tonight." Now he looked at his youngest son with a smile. "David, get your kiss so we can get going." He abruptly turned and crossed the room to exit through the same door that Jocelyn had stormed through just moments before.

Darren poked his little brother in the ribs as he turned to follow his father. "Get a couple of 'em", he muttered, "I don't think that I will get any for quite some time." Darren followed his father out of the room.

David gave Maxine a close hug and slow kiss. "You heard them. We won't be gone long. Will you be here when we get back?"

"Oh no", she exclaimed with mock exasperation, "I know how you are whenever the three of you are together. It might be days before I see you again. I'll give you an audio, tomorrow." Maxine gave David another kiss before taking him by the shoulders and turning him around. "Now, get going, and remember, don't be gone TOO long. It looks like it is going to be a long night for Darren and there is no use making it any worse for him!"

David walked out of the room and through the large, double-door front entranceway. With a quick glance around the property, he spied his father and brother and began walking to where they were waiting for the transport to arrive.

Mr. Kendal grinned, turned to Darren, and said, "Pay up!"

Darren looked at his younger brother with a grimace, "He said you would be here in less than two minutes. His face changed to a 'this-isn't-my-day-today' look and muttered, "I thought you loved the girl more than that." With that statement as an explanation, Darren pulled out his wallet and handed over some credits to his father.

Mr. Kendal happily pocketed the credits, looked up, smiled, and said, "Perfect timing!"

A soft, throaty rumbling grew only slightly louder as Brennan cruised up the drive in a sleek, dark transport. Brennan guided the transport to a stop and settled onto the pavement. Before he could disembark, Darren reached out and opened the passenger area door. With a low bow and a wave of his hand, he gestured for his father to enter first. As David stepped forward to follow his father into the transport, Darren cut in front of him, "I don't think so", he remarked with mock indignation. "You just cost me 30 credits!"

David paused and glanced back towards the house and spied Max framed by the window in the den. Even in the dim light the concern on her face was visible. A smile brightened his face and he raised his hand to wave.

"Don't worry", his father, grinning, told him as he nudged him into the rear area of the transport. "You'll see her again."

With that comment lingering in the night air, the small, trim, transport lifted from the pavement and began to coast smoothly away from the Robert Kendal Estate.

CHAPTER TWO

David had always enjoyed the trips made using his father's transport. The city had provided him a brand-new, fresh-off-the-assembly-line vehicle that had been outfitted with the newest innovations for the private use of one of their top civilian engineers. The sleek, modified hover-craft could operate like the old-fashioned automobiles from the past when necessary but its real lay-to-fame was its ability to follow the contours of the land in a low-flying altitude without the need for roads or expressways. The travel was always much more smooth when the guider followed the paved 'ways' and, once the high-rise portions of the city had been entered, it was essential that the low-flying craft follow the designated roads and boulevards.

Brennan guided the vehicle down the manicured lane and out of the estate. Once the transport had cleared the wrought-iron gates, he flipped several override switches and entered commands into a console. A series of holographic images appeared between the two front seats. A violet blip moved slowly through the maze of thoroughfares and transport-ways. Brennan keyed a few more commands into the console and the holographic image began to shift and become more crowded as more information was relayed from the optical analyzers.

"There seems to be a lot of activity on the ways tonight, sir", Brennan announced to the senior Kendal.

"Do the best you can, Brennan", Darren Kendal called back to the guider before his father could respond. "I do NOT want to give Jocelyn the satisfaction of being right, is that understood?"

Brennan flashed a quick smile to Darren. "I absolutely understand, sir." Brennan reduced the speed of the transport and entered more commands into the console. The holographic display shifted and the guider adjusted the transport to a path contrary to the most direct course to the office building.

The city was heavily intersected with small transit corridors that allowed access to service-centered areas, parks and businesses. To reach the larger businesses, government buildings and medical facilities, multi-lane arteries were constructed above the smaller corridors to expedite travel through the heavily congested areas of the city. The ways were wide and usually clear of obstacles so that the persons being transported had a fast, efficient route to any key destination within York-City.

Usually there was very little foot traffic since the City residents were efficiently located as closely as possible to their service-area. On this night, however, there appeared to be an abundance of people as well as miscellaneous articles in the thoroughfares. It was most unusual and Brennan was not taking Darren Kendal's order lightly. He continued to enter overriding commands into the console and kept a careful watch on the rapidly shifting holographic images.

"She's just a little high-strung, tonight, son. It will pass. She's worried, that's all."

Darren looked up at his father. "I would like to believe that, I really would. But, she has this . . . control thing. Sometimes, it drives me crazy!" He gave a rueful shake of his head before continuing. "There are things that I want to do, that I want to get done. I don't want her telling me what to do like she does Sunis."

"Ah, Sunis", his father mused out loud. "Now, there's a bright boy. He may do just what Jocelyn tells him to do. But, then again, he may have just enough of his father in him to drive his mother crazy, instead!"

"He has a mind of his own, I'll give you that", mused Darren. As much as David and Darren had followed their father into the engineering world, Sunis had not shown the slightest inclination or interest. Instead, he had a head for numbers and profit, very much like his mother. It had been a sad awakening for Darren when he realized that the examples shown to him by his father that had encouraged him had absolutely no effect on his own son. On the contrary, he had to back off any guidance towards engineering and allow Sunis the opportunity to find his own niche.

Darren continued, "I have a feeling that he and Jocie are just too much alike. Jocie has always had a tough time disciplining him. I sincerely doubt there is anything that Sunis could do that would ever bother her."

"Don't get me wrong, I am not advocating rebellion. Sunis doesn't like to be controlled any more than you do. But, there will come a time when your son tells his mother 'no', and you know how well that will go over."

Darren smiled at his father, shook his head before he looked up, frowned, and addressed the guider, "Uh, Brennan? Just where, exactly, are we going?"

Brennan had been constantly overriding the transport controls. Even now the guider appeared to be lost in concentration as images were continually transmitted to the holograph. The ways would appear to be clear for a moment, then clouds of pinpoint lights appeared in the holographic image. The guider would immediately override the controls and guide the craft to another thoroughfare. "Sorry, Mr. Kendal", Brennan said with just the briefest of an apologetic smile. "We'll get there, sirs. But, like I said, there is a *lot* of activity out here, tonight."

Mr. Kendal shrugged his shoulders, stretched out his legs and looked over at his youngest son. David was, once again, lost in the newsreels. He nudged Darren to take a look. Darren looked over to the far side of the passenger area to see David contently devouring articles displayed on the transport's vision-port. Darren winked at his father and spoke loudly enough to cause the guider to smile despite Brennan's navigational problems while causing his brother to grimace. "He must be reading some pretty interesting stuff. I don't think he even remembers that there are other people in here."

David scowled at the two men, "No, I haven't forgotten that you two are here and, yes, this is pretty interesting '*stuff*'." David turned his attention back to the newsreel. "According to this, it's no wonder Brennan has his hands full. There are service shifts from all over the place that have just walked out on their contracts! Look! Look at this! The Bursal Building is on fire! And here, Posin's security has blockaded the 140th Way trying to keep the rioters away from the power structures!"

Mr. Kendal hastily entered commands into his console and an overhead vision-port came alive. David shut his personal port down and all three men watched the short segments of chaos the newsreels were spewing to the transport community screen. The rioting and chaos was, indeed, spreading throughout York-City. Even though the Mayor had deployed his security forces throughout the major industrial areas, they were not prepared for the concentrated attack from people who were becoming more and more desperate.

The Bursal Building was really an administrative complex tasked to provide medical treatment to families that were currently in-service. The growing unemployment within the services and, therefore, the growing number of people that could not receive medical treatment had been a major point of contention within the city for quite some time. The situation had, quite obviously, gotten worse. The angry residents that had been denied medical treatment had been sent away with annotations to their service files. Those black marks in their records would put them into a larger rotation cycle for the next available employment service which would make it even more difficult to land their next job. It was understandable that the people were upset and concerned, but to set fire to the very medical facility that was needed to treat them was certainly not a rational course of action. But, then again, since when are mob members rational?

Darren and David continued to gesture and comment as different sections of the city were depicted on the vision-port. Every once-familiar scene within the city was accompanied with fire, destruction, and a host of angry people. In an attempt to keep the looting and destruction down to a minimum, additional security troops with drawn weapons had been positioned across several main thorough fares. The government-controlled media showed the line of young men as they bravely stood their ground against the senseless crowd. Although no violence was displayed, numbers were almost casually bannered across the bottom of the screen stating injuries and fatalities among the service and governmental employees. Those numbers were climbing rapidly.

It was Mr. Kendal who first came to the realization that they may very well have embarked on an ill-advised trip. "Brennan, I am sure you have been thinking this all along, but, have pity on three engineers. Why don't you just turn this thing around and get us out of here."

Brennan gave the senior Kendal a tight smile before responding, "Right away, sir." Then muttered under his breath, "This place is . . . bad . . . tonight!" The guider immediately issued commands that would cause the transport to slow in preparation to turn about. The transport, instead, veered sharply to the right. "Oh man. Where did THEY come from? They are already right on top of us", the guider shouted excitedly!

A large group of angry people had suddenly broken away from the buildings on the edge of the way. When people are hungry, unemployed, and left without the means to care for their families, they can become anxious, upset, frustrated, sometimes frantic to the point that the smallest of catalysts can cause a concerned group of people to quite suddenly transform into an undisciplined mob.

Indeed, people who had always been considered decent, law-abiding citizens of the city were suddenly enraged at the sight of the transport, an obvious symbol of wealth and station. Darren and David shrank away from the view ports as faces within the crowd, livid and unreasonable, became more distinct and were quickly moving closer to the now almost stationary vehicle.

The transport's opticals had immediately interpreted the people as objects to avoid. Despite the guider's commands, the vehicle had automatically reduced its speed and slid to the right-most part of the way.

Brennan was furiously entering commands into the transport's console, quickly attempting to encourage the vehicle to move further from the approaching mob. He felt the transport begin to shift its position while he watched first with trepidation, and then relief, as the cruiser began to negotiate the many moving obstacles. The vehicle had managed to bypass the mob without incident by turning hard to the left, away from the crowd, then slowly moving forward again. The guider breathed a brief sigh of relief while he once again returned to study the display for the next best route back to the estate.

Darren ran his hand across his face, slick with sweat, then patted his console lovingly, "Good Opticals. Nice Opticals."

Brennan was still uneasy. The transport had not picked up much speed yet, and they were still on the far side of the Way. He would feel a lot more comfortable when the craft was traveling faster and utilizing the middle of the ways where both he and the craft could 'see' more clearly. There were so many people out tonight and it seemed that every one of them was looking for a fight. "It looks like we may have a clear path up ahead", he announced over his shoulder. "We just need to get clear of this next service area . . ."

The transport slowed to negotiate the intersection Brennan had indicated. As the sleek craft smoothly glided around the corner, the holograph suddenly lit up. The transport shuddered and hesitated. There are people everywhere. The opticals could not immediately negotiate a path without endangering an obstacle and had quite sensibly issued commands to shut down.

The vehicle had slowly settled onto the crowded thoroughfare surface and the angry throng of people quickly surrounded it. These people were already primed and ready for trouble. They were carrying torches, clubs, sections of pipe—anything they could wield to cause damage, and damage they were certainly causing. The muffled sounds of splintering wood and the dull ring of metal filled the air as the mob attempted to smash open the transport. The voices of the mob were indistinguishable from inside the transport but their intent was very clear.

David sat stiff and immobile with shock and horror. The color drained from Darren's face as he distractedly patted his console again and muttered, "Bad, bad opticals."

David stared at his brother in disbelief before he shouted out to the guider, "Brennan, get us the Hell out of here!"

"Trying, sir!" He yelled back while frantically trying to get the transport to respond.

Men and women, their faces distorted with rage, were just as frantically trying to reach the occupants of the seemingly dead craft. These are the very people that Mr. Kendal had spent much of his life trying to help. These were good people that had been pushed too far and now, for the moment, their violent actions were beyond their own comprehension.

The sound of power suddenly filled the compartment as the commands entered into the console finally brought the transport back to life. Despite the power once again pulsing through the transport, the crowd remained encircled about the craft. Brennan was able to coax the beleaguered vehicle to very slowly lift off the smooth surface. He desperately attempted to maneuver the craft through and away from the mob.

The frustrated people were determined to not allow the transport and its captive occupants to escape. They attempted one last assault on the vehicle. Bottles and stones as well as verbal debris pelted the transport but the final, reckless attack seemed futile. The transport slowly shouldered people out of its way while their ineffective weapons pounded unsuccessfully on the outer structure of the craft.

The crush of people seemed interminably dense with no openings available to the determined guider when the mob suddenly thinned. Brennan skillfully guided his vehicle through the small openings that briefly appeared within the crowd. Amid cautious sighs of relief from his passengers, the guider commanded the transport to take a sudden, wide gap made available by the separating mob. A small, dark object appeared, briefly, in the forward view screen before everything turned a bright, sizzling white. Then their world turned suddenly dark.

CHAPTER THREE

The Piersur building was not the closest medical facility to the incident but it was the nearest functioning facility since the Bursal building was no longer in operation. Fires had been set on the premises of nearly every accessible industrial complex. City security had their hands full trying to keep rioters from getting any closer to the government buildings.

Chaos reigned within many sectors of the city. Many good, law-abiding citizens had smashed the windows and were in various stages of looting stores along the main thoroughfare. Many of the department and grocery stores had long since been emptied of their goods as entire families had grabbed items off the shelves and had greedily taken their prizes back to their small, cramped apartments.

Security units had been dispatched throughout the city trying in vain to quell the riots. Medical crews had been sent to the most desperate of situations and, in the confusion, both the injured rioters and city executives were being rescued and brought to safety.

Displayed on every view screen within the hospitals, executive offices, and, eventually, the public housing areas was the well-groomed face of the Honorable Mr. Kourei; Mayor of York-City. He had calmly made an appeal to the people to stop the unwarranted violence and destruction. He had pledged that a thorough investigation into the claims of discrimination and poor treatment would be made and that their problems would be solved. They were good words. Unfortunately, the populous had heard those words before and too many of the promises of this administration, as well as from many of the previous ones, had not been kept.

While the Mayor was being interviewed by the city's view stations, once again discussing the deplorable and unfortunate situation of the general populace, another weary security team brought in six more bodies. Two of those bodies were routinely re-routed to the morgue while the other four were sent immediately into the already over-crowded surgery rooms. The emergency communication links were nearly full with security agents notifying families but there were still a few units available for this latest crew to use.

"Try that unit and call about those two", ordered the team leader as he pointed to the other end of the COMM links. "I'll contact . . ." he looked at his clipboard, "Mrs. Kendal."

Several of his crew trudged down the hall while the rest of his team plodded wearily down in the hallway before leaning heavily against the nearest wall.

"I'll never get used to this", he mumbled to himself as he prepared to notify the next family of the latest people he and his team had brought into the facility. Communications were spotty at best, with COMM links down all over the city. The violence, once begun, had spread like radiation throughout the city. He and his crew had just left a small fire fight where nearly two dozen recently released servicemen had tried to abduct a doctor from the Bursal building with the hope of ending a children's virus that was rampant in one of the unemployed sectors.

He and his team had ended the ill-planned attempt without as much as a scratch or mark on anyone. But, since they were one of the closest units, they had been summoned to a transport disturbance on the ways. They arrived at the site within minutes of the explosion and as they disembarked from their military-style transports, they could hear the screams and cries from the injured as well as the shouts of anguish and anger from the survivors.

Scattered sections of the once-stylish transport were burning, sending oily plumes of smoke above the crowd. There were bodies strewn about the transport in grisly poses that told the crew chief that there was very little reason to check them for life. He signaled for his team to activate their shields and begin advancing towards the ruined transport. The most immediate danger was from the scattered but still enraged members of the mob that were still looking for an outlet for their frustration. Bottles, trash and threats were thrown at the crew as they moved cautiously forward amidst the burning debris and broken bodies. Wailing sirens hailed the approach of other security teams and the dispirited crowd began to show signs of nervousness. It wasn't until the next military transport arrived that the crowd began to disperse, shrinking away from the carnage and deaths of their friends both known and unknown.

"Yes, I need to speak to Jocelyn Kendal. Yes, this is very important. No, I am sorry to disturb her but . . . yes, I will wait." The security agent sounded like he had had a very long day. His uniform was smudged from the smoke of at least one fire and the perspiration stains under his armpits were clearly evident on his uniform and the uniforms of his crew lounging close by. He had laid his crumpled cap on top of a ruined jacket in the empty chair next to him and his hair looked tousled and singed.

The security officer suddenly sat up and spoke carefully into the audio, "Ms. Kendal? I am Officer Kiese. Your husband has been in an accident. He-."

There were short pauses between words while the officer attempted to answer questions and explain the situation, "No, he is in surgery", "three hours ago", "we just got him here", "we did the best-", "very severe-", "no, he's lost a lot of blood, I-", "No, the Piersur buil-", "Piersur", "yes . . .", "no . . .", "We-", "I-." The officer stared at the audio for a moment before replacing the device into its holster. He looked at his team members leaning against the wall and said sarcastically, "Well, *that* went well." He looked over to other team members and asked, "Did you have better luck?"

"I reached someone at the Kendal estate. She is already en-route. I think she will be here fairly soon since another security team is providing an escort", the other officer replied. "She didn't ask questions; she just wanted to get over here. I figure we can fill her in when she arrives."

The team leader's eyebrows shot up in surprise. "Forget that!" he said in horror. He pointed to his audio and said, "I don't want to be anywhere near here when the lady I talked to gets here! The incident has been logged", he began to tick the items off on his fingers, "we've informed everyone of the accident, and we've delivered the casualties to the hospital." With finality in his voice he continued, "Let the Investigators sort it out!"

With that, he gathered his hat, jacket and clipboard, turned abruptly away from his team and walked shakily toward the exit. The team members hesitated for only a moment before they obediently followed their leader out of the complex.

* *

David awakened to the soft hum of machinery. His vision was blurry and any desire to move about was hampered by the bandages on his body and the slings draped about to hold his arms and his leg immobile. He blinked his eyes hard a few times to clear the cobwebs. Still, the view that eventually came into focus is one that he had not witnessed before.

The room was small and every conceivable section of wall space had been filled with machines and monitors. Short, quiet beeps could be heard from a number of devices scattered about the room and the soft burning sensation on his left wrist told him that he had an I.V. There was a small chair crammed as far out of the way as possible in one corner of the room. That, too, was filled, with Max!

He was just trying to figure out how to spit out the oxygenator from his mouth when a tired-looking nurse dressed in a light blue uniform stepped into his view.

"You mustn't become agitated, Mr. Kendal. You'll get me into a lot of trouble if you start bleeding, again." She looked tired, but, the smile was genuine and her words seemed to make a lot of sense under the circumstances.

Again, David attempted to remove the mouthpiece but the nurse put her hand up to his mouth and said, "Leave it in. You can talk through it."

David gazed sleepily past the nurse and spoke weakly through the oxygenator, "Max."

The nurse gave David a tired smile and a short nod before she turned to the young lady collapsed in the only piece of furniture in the room. She walked over to the partially reclined chair and placed her hand lightly on her shoulder. The gentle shake from the nurse was hardly necessary, "Ma'am?"

Instantly Max was awake. She looked up with alarm, first at the nurse, then towards her fiancé. The nurse moved deftly out of the way as Max struggled awkwardly out of the chair. Despite the wires, tubes, bandages and medical equipment, Max was able to maneuver quite close to his side.

There is too much concern in her eyes, David thought to himself. What did I do *this* time? With as much energy as he could muster he asked, "Hi, Sweetie, what happened? Did I fall off the slide-board again?" His words were slurred and sounded strangely metallic through the oxygenator.

Maxine stared at him for a moment. *The bruising on his face and arms looks worse than it did when I nodded off,* she thought. Her mouth opened but no words came out. Instead, tears began to flow freely from her blue eyes.

David glanced over at the nurse but she was suddenly engrossed changing the controls to one of the many monitors. The fog was still heavy in his mind and David's face was etched with concentration as he tried to piece together what had happened. "I remember . . .", his voice sounded flat through the oxygen device, "leaving the house in the transport . . ."

Max reached over and touched his cheek, "Don't even think about it right now. You should just sleep."

David could see that she was worried, but there was something else, too. He closed his eyes in concentration, "We were watching news-reels . . . the Bursal building was burning . . ."

"Honey. Stop. Not now. Just sleep", Max murmured while she adjusted his pillow and blankets.

"There were lots of people . . . We decided to turn back . . . Brennan was having trouble . . . the light!" His eyelids suddenly shot wide open. "What happened, Max? Where are Dad and Darren?"

Max leaned in closer and, drawing in a deep breath, started to fill in some of the lost time. "They believe that Brennan was killed instantly", she started, thinking that she probably needed to try to use short sentences. "Someone must have thrown a device at the transport", she paused, then continued again, "and it exploded directly in front of him." She paused again as she watched David carefully for his reaction. "No one is really sure if your injuries are from the transport dropping from the explosion or from the explosion itself."

"Dad?", he weakly asked. "Darren?"

"Darren's and your father's injuries were definitely from the blast", Max answered carefully. David's face was lined with concentration as he tried to recall the events as Max very briefly explained them to him. "Darren was in the surgery room right next door until just this morning . . ."

David closed his eyes feeling the shock. A sigh of relief slowly escaped through the oxygenator as he asked, "Darren is out of surgery? So, he's okay?" He opened his eyes and attempted to focus on Maxine. *Oh, this doesn't look good at all*, he thought. "What about Dad?" It seemed to David that his voice was beginning to sound higher in pitch. Maybe it was the oxygenator.

The door to the med-room abruptly opened and a man from the Investigation service unceremoniously entered into the room. He took in the distress on Max's face and the concern and confusion on David's. The nurse started forward to intercept him but he squared his shoulders, brushed her aside and introduced himself, "I am Lieutenant Macy, from Investigation services. I am glad to see you are awake."

"I don't think . . ." Max started to speak as the lieutenant glanced down at his notepad.

"Your father was pronounced dead on arrival", he continued. "And your brother died this morning. The medical team was unable to stop the bleeding. It seems that you were the lucky one." With his duty apparently finished, the officer gestured to the bandages and tubes and with a sudden moment of personality commented, "They weren't so sure that you were going to make it either."

Maxine and the nurse stared in disbelief at the man.

"Can someone sign this, please?" Obviously, the officer was merely performing his duty, but Maxine was rapidly preparing to cause this investigator some serious, bodily harm.

"Dad's dead?" David said in disbelief.

Max immediately turned back to David. She leaned in close so that she was the only person in his line of vision.

"Darren died?" David was trying to focus. "But you said . . . I thought . . ."

The nurse had abruptly shouldered herself around the Investigator and began fussing with the medicinal stream being administered into David's body. "Now, just try to get some sleep Mr. Kendal." She nodded towards Max, "Your fiancé will stay the night with you while you sleep."

David was still shaking his head in disbelief while the nurse changed the topic. "She also told us that there was nothing to worry about—that you had an appointment at the marriage grounds in a couple of weeks, remember? She said that you were never late to important engagements."

David still appeared confused but the change in topics seemed to be working.

Maxine's cheeks reddened but a look of defiance crept across her face. She leaned over and looked into David's eyes (which were beginning to get blurry, again), "I'll let you be late for this one, mister. But, don't think you can make this a habit, do you hear me?"

David sighed weakly and faded into a medicated sleep.

The nurse turned to the two visitors, "You two should leave. He is going to be out for awhile, now." She looked at Maxine, "This will be a good time for you to get some rest. He will want to see you again and he is going to have to hear that all over again." Then, she turned to the Investigator. "You've delivered your message", she said icily, "I don't doubt that you've already written it in your log. If he doesn't remember any of it, *she* can tell it to him." She opened the door and gave a firm arm gesture indicating that he was certainly welcome to exit the room.

The Investigator appeared a little uneasy but resolute. "It's not part of the job that I enjoy, but it *is* part of my job." With that, he turned to leave. As he pivoted around, his elbow bumped into a small vase of flowers. With deft hands, he caught the vase and returned it to the stand next to the door. The card that was leaning against the vase had fallen to the floor.

Maxine picked up the card as the investigator left the room. It was from Jocelyn. The card only read, "Get well, soon."

CHAPTER FOUR

"Mother, I've told Uncle David that it is time to leave but I don't think he is listening to me."

The voice was not quite a whine nor was it a complaint. The speaker was merely offering information back to the requestor. And yet, somehow, the voice managed to be annoying. Sunis was going to be tall like is father. He had the same long legs and angular face but had neither the thick chest nor the look of strength that seemed to be a character trait within the Kendal family. Even at the young age of twelve, Sunis Kendal seemed to resemble a used-transport dealer.

Jocelyn Kendal was not satisfied with the report. She gave a quick, impatient look at the front room timepiece before getting to her feet. The look of impatience quickly left her face as she looked down at her son. "Well, then, let's both of us encourage your Uncle David to leave. I don't want us to wait here any longer than we have to." With that announcement, Jocelyn turned Sunis around and, together, began to walk back towards the den. The look of impatience had already returned.

David was limping absent-mindedly around the den. He would stop and stare at a visio-graph for a moment, then move on. He stopped again, this time in front of an awards cabinet. Inside the glass cabinet were visio-graphs of David, Darren and his father accepting congratulations from York-City officials. There were numerous awards for the liquid purification technique and citations of achievement for the interior dome formulas that had allowed for the construction of the new, spacious, column-free York-City office buildings.

Here was an award for one of their first achievements together—the 'Flex-Stone'. Now THAT was an achievement! The accomplishment wasn't amazing just because of the engineering techniques that had been utilized, nor the complex formulas that went into its creation, but that the father and two sons had, together, been able to survive their first notable creation.

His father had needed to learn to not trample his sons' enthusiasm while encouraging his sons to challenge themselves. The sons needed to learn to thrive under their father's leadership while retaining their own identity and initiative. There were many times that the 'partnership' appeared to be dissolving as quickly as the failed attempts to create a flexible building material. The result was a bond between the father and sons that was as strong and enduring as the 'stone' that was created from their efforts.

'Flex-Stone' supported the interior dome while utilizing architectural principles that Darren had formulated. The 'stone' itself was a chemically created brainchild of David's. A flexible building product was a need foreseen by Mr. Kendal. Not only was Flex-Stone the perfect building material in which to create the spacious domes used more and more throughout York-City, it was also the perfect material to build dams, sky-reaches, and other edifices that needed to be able to adjust to high tension, high pressure situations.

There was a newly cleared area on the second shelf for their latest award—the solar disk. Oh, being able to reuse solar power had been around for a long time. Their disk allowed the transfer of energy without the use of the cumbersome batteries and cables. The disks were quite simple to install and, except for the particle transfer device and software, were fairly inexpensive to manufacture.

David knew that his father had not cared a whit about the awards. Mr. Kendal was really only interested in what the technology could do to help raise the standard of living among the residents of the City. Flex-Stone and the liquid purifier would enable more efficient housing at a much more affordable cost to the residents. The crowning achievement, however, was the solar disk. The disk enabled the residents to have their own power source—something they pay dearly for in their present circumstances.

With a heavy sigh, David moved on to a holograph that lit up a corner of the den. Robert Kendal's genius had been put to use to create a near self-sufficient community. The dome structure was used to create massive athletic arenas as well as simple and efficient homes. Flex-Stone was used to create the structures, even a dam for hydroelectric (albeit backup) power and the water necessities of the community. The solar disks had been strategically deployed to supply the entire community with enough energy for all of their practical needs.

The community seemed perfect. The York-City officials apparently believed it to be so, too, because no sooner was the community created and was proven to function without the power grants of the City, did the officials commandeer and immediately transfer their offices and private residences into it. The community was now cordoned off from the residents of the City. Only security-obtained government officials via transport access were allowed to and from the Kendal Enterprises created community.

With a slow shake of his head and another heavy sigh, David turned away from the holograph. It was at that moment that Jocelyn and Sunis entered the room. Sunis was already pointing at his uncle as if to say, "*See? I told you!*"

"At least you are dressed", Jocelyn quipped. "The way Sunis described it, you were sitting in one of these chairs sound asleep!"

Jocelyn appeared the 'perfect' widow. She was dressed in a long formal if not elegant black dress that managed to convey grief without sacrificing the lines of her figure. She had the traditional dark veil but it was set back on her head (it would be lowered at the proper time). She also wore ebony gloves that covered her arms to the elbows with matching, black shoes. She wore no makeup; it would not do to have her face showing lines when she cried. Everything about her was in absolute harmony of a bereaved widow.

"I didn't say he was asleep. I said he was not listening to me", Sunis defended himself. He vaguely waved his hand towards David and said, "It looks like he is ready to leave, now."

Maxine walked into the room and with only a brief pause, she squared her shoulders and approached them. "Good morning Jocelyn, Sunis." Max stopped in front of Sunis and gave him a grave look. With great solemnity she shook his hand. "This must be a terrible day for you. How are you holding up?"

Sunis looked up at Max before he spoke words that contradicted the look in his eyes, "Sure. I'm okay."

Maxine held Sunis's gaze for a moment longer before she stood up to face her grieving soon-to-be sister-in-law. Max stepped forward and gave Jocelyn a hug. "This is a terrible day for everyone, Jocie", she whispered.

Jocelyn returned the hug for the moment then pulled away. With a tight, practiced smile she replied, "I'm getting by. It's still hard to believe that Darren is gone—that they are both gone." Jocelyn narrowed her eyes at David for a brief moment. "This should never have happened—and, it's JOCELYN."

David quickly broke eye contact, "I wish it hadn't happened, Jocelyn. You will never know how much I wish this hadn't happened."

Maxine walked over to David and kissed him on the cheek. "It wasn't your fault, honey, you know that."

David looked up at Maxine and shrugged his shoulders, "I guess it really doesn't matter, now, does it?"

A young man entered into the room and announced, "Sirs? Ladies, it is time for me to guide you . . . to . . ." He broke off the sentence uncomfortably.

Jocelyn glanced back up at the timepiece and sighed, "Yes, it's time. Sunis? Let's go."

David walked over to the young man, "And you are . . . ?"

"I have been assigned as your guider", a fairly young man stepped smartly forward and shook David's hand.

"Well, young man, this is my fiancée, Maxine Kacey. The young lad is my nephew, Sunis Kendal, and my sister-in-law, Jocelyn Kendal. We are pleased to accept your services as our guider. You have some large shoes to fill—Brennan was an excellent guider and our friend." David gave the room one last look, "And, as Mrs. Kendal has already said, it's time to go."

Jocelyn and Sunis had waited in the foyer for the guider to open the front door to the house before they exited. Mother and son walked quickly to the transport while David and Maxine followed more slowly behind them.

The new guider hurried past them to open the passenger door. It was too late. Already Jocelyn had folded her arms and was impatiently tapping her toes on the driveway. Once the silver transport was loaded, the passengers were made as comfortable as possible under the strained circumstances. The new transport operator lifted the craft and coasted smoothly away from the David Kendal Estates.

The funeral was perfect. All the correct words were spoken; all the correct emotions were displayed. Sometimes, it is difficult to imagine someone else's funeral. A person may consider the words spoken at their own funeral; the wonderful achievements, how much they will be missed by their loving family and how the community, nay, the entire world had benefited by their very existence. But what person ever dreams about someone else's demise?

The funeral of a family member is the absolute worst event to attend, especially when the death was unexpected and much too soon. Robert Kendal still had other dreams to follow, ideas to initiate, and plans to pursue.

Darren had already shown great promise as an extraordinary engineer. The city executives were hoping that he might prove to be more cooperative than his father and develop cost and energy saving devices that could help make their lives that much more comfortable. Instead, the careers of the two most promising men to service the city had been cut short.

It was expected that the rioters and protesters may find this unhappy event to be an ideal setting to cause mischief and chaos. The funeral of a highly revered city executive could be a perfect time to command attention by airing their grievances. Instead, there seemed to be a truce among the residents and the security forces. Both the wealthy and the poor seemed to recognize that the untimely deaths of these two men were a tragedy that should not be exploited.

The Vision network crews, however, had no such limitation. They seemed to be everywhere filming the crushed and dispirited family members and friends. Many of York-City's finest officials were in attendance and several of the highest ranking of them were scheduled as speakers at the service. Impromptu interviews were set up and taped for airing at another time or, perhaps, as a campaign commercial. Long before the services were set to begin, throngs of people had filled the small chapel and had begun to line the walkways outside.

The Mayor of York-City was not only in attendance, but was one of the principle speakers. The tension among the city residents began to build as the Honorable Posin Kourei made his way to the audiophone but any fears of reprisals from the crowd quickly vanished as the distinguished politician uncharacteristically limited all his remarks to Robert Kendal's engineering achievements and how they had brought prosperity to the City. Mr. Kourei described the humble beginnings of the City's most respected engineer and, how through hard work and determination, was able to carve his name into the history books of one of the largest cities on the planet. To David's surprise, the Mayor even stressed that Mr. Kendal's achievements were always implemented with the welfare of the residents of York-City in mind.

Two of the Kendal Enterprise's board members spoke next. Asman Kennedy and Jonathon (Skip) White took turns discussing the life and work of their good friends and fellow engineers. It was these two men who emphasized that, although Mr. Robert Kendal was a gifted practical engineer, he was also a caring father who was able to guide his sons, work with his sons and even inspire those young men to help him design and create some of the greatest inventions that York-City has ever known. No sooner would Asman Kennedy describe a Robert Kendal achievement than Skip White would step up to the audiophone and explain the part played by Darren Kendal that was needed in order to develop and complete the invention. Asman and Skip took turns speaking to beautifully describe the mentor and student, engineer and architect, dreamer and creator relationship that existed between the father and son. Asman and Skip stressed that the deceased two engineers always had one joint goal in mind: to help enrich the lives of the residents of York-City.

There were other speakers, more words, and a lot of emotions on display but, to David, it was all a blur. When the last words were spoken, there was a moment of silence and a prayer offered by Robert and Dona Kendal's long-time friend, Minister Paul Thompson. The Minister's quiet voice spoke of Robert finally being reunited again with his beloved wife and, while the accomplishments of this life are important to those left behind; their family accomplishments were of greater importance in the world to come. Their love had truly helped to raise two fine sons who have been a blessing to the community and city. He spoke of Darren's lovely wife and son that are still here while Darren has moved on to be with his Father in heaven.

For all the words uttered during the proceedings, David held fast to those spoken by the minister. His tears freely flowed as he tried to acknowledge that he may not see his father and brother again for a very long time.

At the resonant sound of the word, "Amen", the network crews quickly began to load their equipment in order to depart for their next assignment. Slowly the crowd began to disperse until there were only small groups of people left in the chapel. Some of the City's officials and many of the family's friends and co-workers remained gathered around the grieving Kendal family for a time to offer their sympathy and condolences.

Finally, only the closest of friends and family remained. Even Jocelyn and Sunis had taken their leave; the stress and emotion of the day had clearly taken their toll on them. A long, dark transport had slowly carried them past the cameras and away from the crowd after Jocelyn completed a brief interview for the evening's Vision broadcast.

Minister Thompson led the last of the grievers to a somewhat small, but comfortable counseling room for privacy. He embraced David once more and paused as if to say something more but, sometimes, there are no more words to be said. Finally, only Asman, Skip, David and Maxine remained seated in plain but comfortable chairs around a small glass table.

Silence ruled the room. It seemed clear that everyone's minds were still occupied with the day's events. Asman looked up at Skip for a moment. Skip, catching the glance, offered a short nod to his peer. Asman cleared his throat and, after a moment, attempted a conversation. "This is not the best time, I know. Hell, I don't know if there IS a 'best time' but-", again he glanced at Skip. With only the faintest signs of encouragement from his fellow board member, he placed his hands on the table in front of him and suddenly blurted out, "David, what now?"

David looked up from staring at his hands with a blank, startled expression, "What?"

Asman looked uncomfortable but, now that he had finally started the topic, he knew he would need to finish the conversation. "What are you going to do, now? I mean, you've had time to think about it. There is not much time left if we are going to at least START the project . . ."

Maxine stared with amazement at their friend. Annoyance and anger competed one with another across her face; anger won as she shot Asman a quick retort, "You are right. This is NOT the best time!"

Skip leaned forward in his chair, "Max, we're sorry but, well, there just really isn't much time left."

She started to get out of her chair when David spoke out loud to no one in particular. "They are right, Max. I need to decide, 'We' need to decide. Has she already begun, then?"

Asman stood up and began to pace across the small the room. "Oh yes. She has begun all right. She has already retained attorneys. We", pointing to himself and Skip, "know that she is nearly ready to file. If she gets into the courtrooms before you do, you won't have to decide anything. It will be over." He looked directly at David, pointed his finger at David and Max before continuing, "You two would stand to receive a LOT of credits. Jocelyn, of course, would be set for life."

Maxine, with a look of surprise, asked Asman, "Can she really have the inventions turned over to the City? Does she really have that kind of authority?"

Skip gave a short, derisive laugh, "The wife of one of the deceased, maybe. With York-City Officials wetting themselves to get a hold of the rights, definitely! But, if *you* file *first*, David, then you will have the first rights. As the only son and brother of the deceased, that would be enough."

David looked first at Asman Kennedy, then Skip White. Finally, David searched his fiancée's face before he slowly shook his head. "I believe, lady and gentlemen, there is really only one thing we *can* do." David looked back to his two friends, his fellow engineers. "Would you two, please, ask the other board members to join Max and me at the estate tomorrow morning? If everyone is willing, we all have documents that need to be signed," David winked at Maxine, "and a city to build!"

* *

"Thank you for seeing us on short notice, Your Honor", the tall, lean man glibly stated. It was merely the proper thing to say, not that it made much difference to him or to his companion. The other lawyer was nearly a carbon-copy of the first man, a couple of inches shorter but he wore the same style dark suit, striped tie and freshly-pressed white shirt. They both carried identical-looking synthetic-leather brief cases and they wore the same ingenuous smiles.

"My pleasure, gentlemen", replied Posin Kourie. The same ingenuous smile graced the lips of the Mayor of York-City. "Please, take a seat." The Mayor had not bothered to come around from behind his massive desk to shake the hands of the lawyers and the two men had not bothered to offer.

"Tell me", the Mayor began without preamble, "what does she plan to offer?"

Without a moment's hesitation, four loud snaps were heard as the briefcases were quickly opened and two identical folders were laid on the Mayor's desk. The taller of the two men began to explain the content of each folder while the shorter lawyer completed each sentence.

"Ms. Kendal has compiled a summary for each of the inventions and patents", he gestured towards the two folders, "that originated from both Mr. Robert Kendal-".

"—and from her husband, the late Mr. Darren Kendal."

"An asking price has been assigned to each article. However, we have been instructed to inform you—"

"—that the amounts are only marginally negotiable."

"Please understand that she will not consider a court date until all items of interest have been agreed upon."

The second lawyer appeared momentarily surprised that he was not given the opportunity to complete the sentence. In an effort to reassert himself into the presentation, he began the next stage of the explanation, "She expects that you are aware that the selling of these patents and inventions", he also indicated the two folders, "will be very likely—"

"—contested by Mr. Robert Kendal's surviving son, Mr. David Kendal", completed the first lawyer with a smug grin.

The Mayor was not amused by the presentation, nor was he impressed with the conditions of the sale. His brows furrowed in a moment of disdain before he slowly stood up, which called an end to the brief conversation. With a slight nod of his head to invite the two men to leave, he routinely stated, "Thank you for the information, gentlemen. My lawyers will be in touch."

Jocelyn Kendal's two lawyers quickly rose and turned to exit the room. The first lawyer paused for a moment before he turned back to ask, "Is there a time-frame that she may expect your response?"

Without bothering to make eye contact, the Mayor replied, "My lawyers will be in touch", with a dismissive wave of his hand. He had already sat back down into his plush executive chair to continue with more important work.

CHAPTER FIVE

"Look, we know we can get this to work. We have nearly everyone on the council behind it. We have the finances and we have the technology. We can *do* this", David was performing his characteristic pacing, albeit with a limp, while talking out loud to Maxine.

"Sure, we can do this—IF no one tries to block it. You KNOW she is going to put up a fight. Has she ever NOT fought for what she wants or believes that she deserves?" Maxine knew that she was being used as a sounding board. She also knew that David was just trying to get his thoughts in order for the inevitable showdown.

Maxine was sitting comfortably in one of the many chairs surrounding a conference table centered in a room that could easily accommodate twenty people. An old-fashioned marker board, showing signs of wear and age, was attached to the wall across from the doorway; a large, over-stuffed easy chair was set just to the right of it. The doorway was exactly centered in the stark white wall across from the still usable marker board. A large newsreel monitor was attached to the wall to the right of the doorway. The only sign of vegetation was half-heartedly displayed to the left of the doorway, a designer's touch to a room that was, obviously, meant for business transactions. The leafy plant was set in a vase on a small bureau that added a small splash of color to an otherwise drab and business-like environment. Six monitors were attached to each of the other two walls. Fairly uncomfortable-looking extra chairs lined the walls below the monitors. No one else was in the room besides David and Maxine and every monitor in the room was dark and lifeless.

"Oh, yeah. She'll put up a fight, but for the life of me I don't understand why. She has everything she needs. She received more insurance credits than most people receive after a lifetime of service. There is no need to stop the city from being built. There has GOT to be a way to get through to her!"

David stopped and looked up as the image of their new guider, dressed to fit the role of the transport operator of a respected leader of the community, suddenly appeared in one of the monitors. "Ms. Kendal has arrived, sir. I will escort her inside in just a few minutes." The edginess in his voice made it obvious that Ms. Jocelyn Kendal had already made quite the impression on the newest member to the Kendal Estates.

"Thanks for the warning", David said with only a hint of sarcasm. "We are probably as ready as we are ever going to be. Please, escort her in." David drew a deep breath and looked over at his new wife as the screen went back to its lifeless state.

Maxine smiled lightly. "It's show time!" she said as she gestured David towards the end of the conference table where a large easy chair, reserved for the director, was patiently waiting.

David acknowledged Max's show of bravado with a wry grin and walked over to the designated chair. With a hint of reluctance, he took his father's place at the table.

David only had a few moments to get comfortable before the conference room door burst open. The guider quickly slid past Jocelyn as he entered into the room and stepped swiftly to the right and out of the way. He began to introduce Jocelyn, "Ms. Joc—".

"Well, you certainly look comfortable", Jocelyn snapped as she strode past the guider and into the room. "It's beginning to look pretty obvious, now, why I cannot get anywhere with the legal department. You must figure this is YOUR show now!"

Maxine covered her mouth with her hand, smiling at Jocelyn's choice of words.

Jocelyn had continued to walk across the room toward David, not bothering to acknowledge Maxine and certainly not bothering to notice the guider's swift departure. She stopped halfway across the room to where David was sitting and directly across from Maxine, set her dark briefcase down and leaned menacingly on the polished table. "I want to make this as clear as I possibly can; I want this ridiculous nonsense stopped. I want the patents sold and I want *my* share of the family estate. I do NOT want to worry about my next meal, where I am going to live nor do I want to worry that my son may financially struggle. You lost your father, but I lost my husband and Sunis's father. We deserve to be compensated." Jocelyn straightened up and lightly pressed her hands against the waist of her suit jacket to smooth away imaginary wrinkles. "I think these are reasonable demands. All I have to hear from you is your plan of the time-table as to when I can expect my first payment."

With a lofty air of expectancy, Jocelyn nonchalantly slipped into one of the conference chairs. She caught Maxine's eye for a moment and lifted an eyebrow as if to say, *There, See? I am being perfectly reasonable.*

David stared at Jocelyn for a moment before he sadly shook his head. "I do not understand why you are taking this stance, Jocie. You may well be one of the wealthiest persons in the City and yet you want more."

Jocelyn stared icily at David as she straightened up in her chair. She opened her mouth to begin her retaliation but, before she could say anything, David continued, "I will make sure you receive your compensation. You and Sunis will want for nothing so long as I have anything to do with it."

Jocelyn smiled at David and nodded her head in satisfaction. "Good. The patents should bring a pretty price. I have made a list of companies that are already interested in them and, of course, the York-City Officials will pay whatever it takes to acquire them." She reached down and deftly pulled a large bundle of legal papers from her briefcase. She set the papers on the conference table and nudged them towards David a few inches before oozing back with satisfaction into her chair.

"You misunderstand me, Jocelyn. The patents will not be sold—they are mine to use and I intend to use our inventions just as my father and brother would have me use them. I said that you would be compensated. I promised that I would take care of you and Sunis. I have had the legal department draw up a schedule of payments dependent upon our success." With that announcement, David reached out and set a sheaf of papers on the conference table and pushed them towards Jocelyn.

At first, Jocelyn did not move. When she did move, it was to slowly stand and place one hand on the stack of documents David had left for her. Her eyes never left David's face, "You . . . will 'take care of me' . . . so long as you are successful?" Jocelyn's voice became venomous, "Take 'CARE' of me?!"

Maxine leaped quickly into the conversation, interrupting Jocelyn before she could further marshal her thoughts, "Look, Jocelyn, it's not that you need taking care of. We are only trying to reassure you that you won't have to worry about where or how you live. You and Sunis will have all the financial security anyone could want. You—"

"We?!" Jocelyn snarled. "So, David is only a puppet, is he? *You* are going to control *MY* compensation? I don't think so, 'Mrs. Kendal'!" Jocelyn shifted her attention back to David. "You are *nothing* without your father! You are less than nothing without your brother!" Now she looked squarely into Maxine's eyes, "And you are nothing without *my* credits!"

Suddenly, Jocelyn looked back at David and smiled; a coiled, venomous snake ready to administer its poison. "I will take this to MY lawyers. You will pay, oh yes, you will pay me. And I will make your life a living hell until I get what is mine!"

Jocelyn glared at Maxine for a brief moment before turning to David one last time. A slow smile once again appeared on her lips but the warmth never made it to her words, "Thank you, Mr. and Mrs. Kendal, for seeing me on such short notice. You will be hearing from my lawyers." Jocelyn turned and, with a nonchalance belied by the tone in her words, confidently exited the conference room.

David punched a button on his console and only had to wait for a moment before the face of a very nervous guider appeared on the same monitor as before, "Sir?"

"Please inform me when Ms. Kendal has left the property."

"Yes, sir", he replied tight-lipped. The screen immediately went dark.

Maxine smiled wryly at her husband, "That went well, don't you think?"

David let out a deep sigh, "It went about as well as it could, I suppose. I just don't see why--"

Images of a transport leaving the property appeared on the guider's monitor. A relieved voice was heard in the background, "Ms. Kendal has left the premises, sir."

"Thank you. That was a tough way to start a new job, eh?"

"I . . . it wasn't . . . she . . . , um, will there be anything else, sir?"

"No thanks. Why don't you take a breather?"

"Yes, sir", a tired voice intoned before the screen, once again, went blank.

There were a few moments of silence in the room as David moved around the table to sit next to Max. After getting comfortable in the conference chair, David abruptly asked no one in particular, "So, what did the rest of you think? Are you still 'in'?"

Nearly all at once the monitors in the room quickly came alive.

"What a witch! Yeah, I am still in!"

"For a minute there, I thought you WERE going to give her everything! How are we going to—"

"I'm in!!"

"Me, too!"

"I'm out."

"I'm . . . what?"

The room grew quiet. All eyes turned to the third monitor. Ironically, the voice came from the screen directly across from where David and Maxine were now seated. "I'm out." A young face with haunted eyes was looking only at David. "You said that if we didn't like the outcome, then we could choose to get out. No condemnation. No blame." Those eyes swiftly scanned the other members of the council for any signs of disapproval. "I'm out."

David nodded his head before replying, "We completely understand, Alican. We would be pleased to keep you on the council, if you wish to remain." Alican nodded her head with evident relief. David continued, "Ladies and gentlemen of the board, this topic will not be discussed with Alican. She will remain the point of contact for business-as-usual events. All other matters will be attended to with professionalism. Are there any questions?"

Without a moment's hesitation, the remaining members of the council ratified David's announcement. There were words of comfort and understanding given before, with obvious relief, Alican signed off. The remaining members switched to the corner monitors so that their discussions could be better seen as well as heard.

It probably did not surprise anyone that Carol Brunson was the first person to speak. "So, there are six of us. We've all had some time to go over the schematics and plans that Robert and Darren had been working on. What are your thoughts?" With the practice of many discussions concerning new projects behind her, she simply asked, "Ladies and gentlemen, how are we going to do this?"

Carol's face nearly filled the display on the monitor but that is exactly how she liked to present herself to an audience. If truth be told, she spent a lot of time with her facial presentation. Her auburn hair was perfect, not a single strand was out of place. Her make-up was precisely administered to ensure balance as well as tone and color compatibility. However much time she spent ensuring her face was perfect, she would spend a minimal amount of time and energy on the rest of her. Carol was a little on the heavy side with a penchant for wearing baggy, sometimes called 'frumpy', clothes. She *always* looked striking on the monitor screens and people were always surprised when they actually met Ms. Brunson face-to-face. She took whatever time was necessary to be presentable for whatever meetings and conferences she had to attend in person, but certainly did not waste any other effort for 'non-priority' issues. Carol was really only interested in her most current project. Robert Kendal's extraordinary project organizer would spend tremendous amounts of time and energy on any project for which she had been assigned.

Carol Brunson had worked quite a few projects with the elder Kendal and her role had always been to receive the information, analyze the project, and keep the project successfully headed in the right direction. Carol didn't get sidetracked. Carol didn't get distracted. She also didn't have the 'vision' to initiate a project. She would ensure that the project was completed, within a budget, on time, and according to a plan, but Carol never came up with a plan. That was what Carol was asking for now . . . a plan.

Asman and Skip looked at one another through their monitor screens for a moment, then, Asman cleared his throat. "Carol, we know the plan is to build a city. We know 'how' to build a city. We have everything we need to build it." Asman pressed several controls on his console and a hologram of the city-to-be was suddenly displayed over the conference table. "We know what to build and we know how to build it. I think, given that Jocelyn is going to do everything in her power to stop the construction, the question now is, WHERE do we build it?"

Asman Kennedy was a pure engineer. When Robert Kendal recruited Asman into his council many years ago, it was with the vision that as problems became apparent within a project, Asman would always find a solution. He was a tireless man who searched for flaws and ways to correct them. Robert Kendal and Asman Kennedy had become close friends as their mutual respect for one another had continued to grow. Asman saw this city as his last opportunity to work on a project that Robert would have wanted completed.

Where could the city be built that Jocelyn would not be able to stop its construction? This was definitely a problem. But, Asman merely saw it as a problem that needed to be solved. He had sincere hopes that there would not be any problems that would stop the completion of THIS project—not if he had anything to say about it. "You know that no matter where the site is chosen for the city, Jocelyn will do whatever she can to block its approval through the York-City directors." The short, wiry engineer turned to David, "As soon as she even hears a rumor concerning the construction of this city, she will put all of her considerable energy and resources into stopping its progress." Asman shook his head in derision, "She is not going to let us build this."

"Well, then. The solution is easy!" Skip White's voice boomed in from his monitor. "All we have to do is build the city without her knowing about it!" His voice sounded light and easy but the sarcasm was unmistakable. "Maybe we can send her away for the next twenty years or so?"

Skip White was Robert Kendal's right-hand man. There was not a member of the council that was in closer confidence to the late director. Oh, Robert Kendal confided in his sons, but Skip White was the man that Mr. Kendal always looked to when he would get his newest idea. Skip could shoot holes in an idea in a way that would only further Robert's determination to ensure it would become a reality. Robert and Skip had never quarreled; they were able to communicate at a level that other people needed to study to obtain. Skip was easy-going, yet sarcastic. He had an athlete's build similar to Robert Kendal's, but he did not present himself in such a way. Instead, Skip appeared as the consummate businessman, sharply dressed, shoes cleanly buffed, hair always in place, and sometimes when he saw the need, he would appear at a presentation or publicized meeting sporting a white cane. Arrogant? No. Confident? Definitely. His demeanor, now, was cheerfully sarcastic. He, too, wanted to complete the project of his former director and friend. Unfortunately, he was confident that he would be able to find the flaws in anyone's suggestions for a city site. He was also fairly certain that no one in the council would be able to offset his criticisms with the antidotes needed to keep the city alive. "So, Trish, where are we going to put a city?"

Trish Vonner smiled at Skip and pressed buttons on her own console. "Well, Skip, if you are looking for suggestions, let's see what real estate options are available." The city-to-be hologram was pushed off to the far edge of the conference table and a new hologram appeared in its place. The three dimensional object was easily recognizable to everyone in the room; a miniature York-City had been constructed right before their eyes, complete with the ruined Bursal building. Trish reset the controls to further shrink York-City and added the nearest outlying areas that surrounded the city to the conference room table. "Tell me where to put it, Skip", Trish called out, "and I will hook it up for you." She continued to press console buttons that gripped the city-to-be and moved it around York-City. She caused it to stop in a desert area, a wide, flat tract of unusable land far north of York-City. "There", she announced, her face lit up with triumph, "How's that?"

There was a moment of silence before the monitors suddenly erupted with muffled laughter.

"Oh, right. Perfect. The soil is still tainted from the radiation wars, there is no water, no foliage, and, if I am not mistaken, the average temperature is 105 degrees! Great choice!" Skip's voice fairly dripped with sarcasm but there was no real edge to it. He was merely stating the facts in his own charming, light-hearted fashion.

The 'Radiation Wars' was not, of course, the name of the conflict referenced in the history books. Even though the history of York-City and the former United States of America had been rewritten a number of times, 'Radiation Wars' continued to be how the populous chose to remember how the world had changed in the not-too-distant past. New York City had always been a proud city with a grand history. The Empire State Building and World Trade Center were not just famous buildings but historical landmarks and the city boasted a center of industry and economy that rivaled capital cities anywhere on the globe. This was a city that had survived floods, terrorist bombings, famine and, yes, the radiation wars.

There were other names given for the nation-changing conflict; the Second Civil war, the Oil War, and the Islamic War. But those names merely described the major problems that led up to a solution that ended in global bloodshed—and the indiscriminate use of nuclear weapons. Rich oil fields in Iraq and Iran were turned into vast, uninhabitable stretches of land that truly glowed from the satellite pictures broadcast back to Earth. The island countries of Great Britain and Japan existed only as memories and notations on maps. Large heaps of rubble protruded from the ocean where millions of people used to live on what used to be islands of paradise. Immense portions of Europe and Asia had been devastated as missiles created paths of destruction launched by people who had either nothing to lose or by religious zealots who believed they had everything to gain.

The United States had fared no better than the other, once-mighty nations of the world. The cities of Atlanta, Richmond, Austin, Colorado Springs, Salt Lake City and New York City had survived the holocaust that was unleashed upon the former U.S.A. There were other, smaller cities that had also survived the initial bombing but the radiation that was unleashed into the atmosphere had eventually obliterated all life covering vast tracts of land and seas. The enormous metropolis of New York City HAD survived, but only as an unsteady shadow of its former life. The name of the city had been cut short—more simply called 'York-City'. The name had become shortened like the life span of the people who now lived there. It is situated a number of miles south of where its name-sake once stood and the people that had eventually made their way from the surrounding devastation to their new home had long-since stopped arriving.

"Oh, is it too hot for you?" Trish's face changed into a pout that would have done Sunis proud. "Well, maybe if you had some water . . ." Rapid tapping was heard as Trish deftly entered new coordinates for an alternative location for the city-to-be. The holograph dematerialized from the northern area of the conference table, only to reappear well east of the city. Once again Trish transformed her face into a look of triumphant satisfaction. An impish grin crept into her features as the city once again solidified in its new location. "There!"

Asman grunted into his speaker, "Yes, technically that IS water . . ." Asman worked his controls to bring a close-up of the inland sea into the conference room. York-City was swept from the room as a dark body of water was brought into focus. The liquid seemed to appear . . . heavy. There were long, undulating waves on the slick, oily surface but there was no froth or foam. There were no birds flying above the dull, cheerless waves and there was no plant life growing on the shores. Somehow, the existence of the sea, even though only a holograph, brought a foul odor into the room. The stench of decay seemed to invade the conference room as each long, rolling wave of gray matter pounded the featureless shoreline.

"I think—", Maxine started to speak but was immediately over-ridden by the other members of the council.

"Well, that is MUCH better." Skip's sarcasm boomed into the room.

"C'mon, let it go!" Trish was trying to remove the holograph from the room but Asman had locked the image.

"No, wait. Look, the location has to be far enough away from York-City in order for Jocelyn to leave us alone, right? There IS water there, sort of, and the temperature is between ninety and one hundred degrees during all four cycles." Asman did not look very enthusiastic but apparently he was trying to consider the area as a possible solution.

"I think—", Max began again, but this time it was her husband who impatiently interrupted her.

"This is just wasting time", David groaned. "We need a viable location." With a sweep of his hand toward Skip's monitor to acknowledge his input, David continued, "Yes, we need water and, yes, the conditions must be tolerable." He, then, placed both hands in front of him, gesturing towards Asman's monitor, "And, yes, we need to, somehow, find an area that Jocelyn cannot interrupt our efforts. But we cannot relocate halfway across the continent! We need a REAL location! If we cannot come up with real estate that actually has potential, then we might as well follow Alican and give up the whole idea!"

David attempted to manipulate his controls to display other areas surrounding York-City, but, his displays kept colliding with Asman's image of the dead inland sea. With growing exasperation, David spoke with a flat, annoyed voice, "Asman. Do you mind?"

The inland sea quickly vanished from view. Although the smell of decay was not really in the room, the air seemed to clear as soon as the foul image and sound disappeared.

There were long moments of silence as David displayed one area after another over the middle of the conference room table. No words were necessary, although an occasional grunt or groan would escape from one or more of the council members. The locations were always either missing a key ingredient or there was an over-abundance of some very undesirable element. It seemed that not all life had ended in the radiated areas outside of the boundaries of York-City. Even Jocelyn was preferable to some of the creatures that had survived the brutal environmental conditions of the past few decades.

Maxine chose this moment to try again, "I have an idea", she quietly stated.

David looked toward his wife in surprise. Maxine cocked her head to the side and one eyebrow raised a fraction of an inch. Someone muttered into the speaker, "Oh, he is going to pay for that one . . ."

A wry grin took over the tight-lipped look that Maxine had used to stop David from speaking another word. With just enough ice to her tone, she casually asked her husband, "May I have the city, please?"

David shook his head for a moment and a smile of his own slowly grew on his face before he responded, "Oh, you want the CITY . . ." With a few, swift, keystrokes, the holograph was released into Maxine's care.

Maxine moved the city-to-be off to the side for the moment. With short, quick keystrokes, York-City was once again created over the conference room table. She moved the city to the west; nearly off the conference room table. As the city shrank to the edge of the conference table, a large canyon came into view.

Again there were mutterings heard over the monitor's speakers, "The other side of the canyon? We will still have the same problems. No water. The land is radiated. Don't you think York-City is a bit too close?"

Maxine ignored the comments as she brought the new city back onto the conference room table. She maneuvered the city directly over the canyon, then, carefully moved the city into the vast canyon until it was entirely invisible from view.

"I think", she began, "we could build our city IN the canyon. We could build a dam to provide us an uninterrupted supply of water and maybe use the dam's construction to conceal the construction of the lower portions of the city without interruption."

The seriousness on Asman's face froze the laughter before it escaped Trish's lips. She turned to Maxine and asked, "IN the canyon? Isn't the canyon part of York-City?"

Asman had not moved. He was still staring at the image Maxine had created. David was staring quizzically at Maxine while Skip was rapidly typing into his console.

"No, it is not part of the City. York-City's boundary extends TO the canyon but not INTO the canyon. But, it *is* rather close to the City, don't you think?" Skip addressed the question to Max, but his sarcasm was missing. His voice was quiet but firm. He had merely stated a fact, but, *what in the world was Maxine thinking?*" Skip thought to himself.

"Okay, so, technically, the canyon is not part of the city, but it IS right in Jocelyn's back yard. Just because she can't SEE it doesn't mean she won't know we are building it", Trish was beginning to sound annoyed. "This really IS a waste of time."

Carol frowned towards Asman's monitor, "We could try to construct an underground city. She wouldn't be able to see it from her house, but she will surely know we are building something." She reluctantly moved her gaze back to Maxine.

Maxine and Asman appeared to be in communication with one another. They were both typing into their consoles and, from time to time, the other members of the council would hear small snatches of their musings.

Finally, Asman looked out to the conference room from his monitor and, with a slightly embarrassed sound to his voice, announced, "It could work. This could really work."

David sighed loudly and with only a slightly patronizing voice asked, "All right. I'll bite first, 'what' could work?"

Asman grinned up at David, "Here, we'll show you. Max, move the city a little more east, would you please? Yes, just past that bend . . . Good. Now, if we put a dam right here, we can gather a fairly large body of water." Asman created a holographic dam that spanned the canyon at the narrow point just north of the city-to-be. "We can sell the idea to the city that we want to create a reservoir as an emergency water supply and a recreational area. While we build the dam . . ." a flurry of keystrokes caused the groundwork of a massive structure to appear south of the dam, overlaying part of the city Maxine had placed into the canyon.

Skip White was watching the holographs with interest, but, now his interest was beginning to wane. "Anyone paying any kind of attention at all will know that THAT structure," he circled the massive ground level of the city with a red, holographic marker, "has nothing to do with a dam."

Asman looked towards Max, "Your turn."

Max grinned for a moment before erasing Skip's marker. She expanded Asman's image of the ground level as she spoke, "The nice thing about bureaucrats is that they see whatever is in the blueprints. This . . ." Maxine brought Skip's red marker back into view, "is an underground reservoir. As we construct it, we will bury it and start the next level." She turned to David with a smile and asked, "How long will it take to create something this size?"

Before David could answer, Skip boomed in, "Eight, maybe ten years. Why-?"

Maxine cut into Skip's question, "Hmm, we will have to do better than that. How long would it take to build, say, seven or eight of them?"

Skip's eyebrows went up as Maxine continued to construct the levels ensuring that the sections closest to the dam were completed first. The holograph of the levels continued to overlay the original city placed into the canyon. The canyon was being filled with the new city from east to west. Each level, however, grew smaller at the southern end so that the new city, once completely buried, appeared as a very large, descending, terraced hill within the canyon.

Trish shook her head with irritation. Sarcasm was etched deeply into her voice as she exclaimed aloud, "And NO ONE is going to notice that we placed trillions of tons of flex-stone inside that miniature mountain?"

Maxine smiled again as she released the controls back to Asman. "It's not that anyone will notice. The fact of the matter is that no one will CARE. Asman . . ." With that declaration, Maxine leaned back into her plush chair and linked her fingers behind her head. *If the council doesn't buy THIS part, then this really WAS a waste of time.* The thought settled into her mind as Asman took up the next part of the plan.

"Jocelyn won't care about what we put under here", Asman circled the newly built up section of the canyon, "because she will be too busy trying to stop us from building a city up *here*!" Asman placed a holographic image atop the buried city. "This is the city that Jocelyn will be trying to stop us from building. These underground 'reservoirs' will be for the use of the city, at least, that's what they will think. That's why, even though Jocelyn will do everything in her power to try to stop us, York-City will make sure that we complete each and every level. Every step of the way, Jocelyn will be trying to stop us from creating this built-up area. Why? Because the new city, the city she does not want, will be built on top. No one will care what we are building underneath—they will just be looking for the new city, on top. But the REAL city, the city that *we* care about, will be down here, underground."

Trish's jaw was not even on the monitor screen any more. The entire idea seemed preposterous! An entire city constructed while the York-City officials not only watched, but actually ensured the successful completion? Impossible! And yet . . . Trish began to type figures and calculations into her console. "This . . . may be . . . possible", she muttered out loud.

A laugh boomed out over the audio system. "Possible? I suppose it could be done. But answer me just ONE question." Skip was, obviously, unconvinced. "Why? Why would York-City allow us to build ANYTHING? There is absolutely no reason to think that York-City officials will even consider the idea. There is *every* reason to believe that they will save Jocelyn all the trouble and just tell us 'No'. Why would they let us, let alone ENCOURAGE us to build another city?"

Maxine and Asman looked at one another but neither one spoke. *We lost*, thought Max. *We came close, but we lost.*

"I think they will be more than pleased to allow us to build it", David spoke up, unexpectedly. Asman and Skip looked at David in surprise. "No, really. Just think. We are creating a recreational reservoir. Who is going to get the most use out of it? The York-City officials will. We are creating, what *they* think, are underground reservoirs. Who is going to use them? The officials of York-City will. We would be building above and between radiated layers of soil and using property that has been considered unusable for years. York-City officials would be able to expand their presence without risk of contamination. And, when the new city is completed, whom do you think will run it? Us? Puhlease! I have every belief that the York-City officials will proclaim it as their new base of operations and move out of their 'old' York-City buildings and homes, probably before we even have it built!!"

The council members politely listened to David as he attempted to explain the possibilities. But, there was still strong doubt that the York-City officials would want to extend their boundaries into the canyon. David cautiously winked at Maxine and, with an innocent voice, he casually asked his wife, "May I, please, have the city?"

Maxine furrowed her brow for a moment, "Oh, now *you* want *my* city?" With a few swift keystrokes, the control of the city was released back to David.

"It would seem that each level of *our* city must be buried as we start constructing the new level", David continued. He used Skip's red marker to outline each level. "Where does all the fill soil come from? After all, we are attempting to fill in part of a canyon, remember? If we take the ruined soil from around the city, even the soil on the other side of the canyon to use as our fill soil, York-City would be able to, naturally, expand its borders and its elected Officials would be considered futuristic planners for providing new living and business space while creating service opportunities for out-of-service residents. The 'new city' built on top of *our* city would not even be considered another city—it would be annexed as part of York-City!"

David leaned back in his chair and, mimicking Maxine, laced his fingers behind his head while waiting for Skip to shoot holes in the plan. Trish's jaw was still off-view of her monitor. Asman was looking VERY pleased and Skip, well, Skip was rubbing his jaw while trying to think of a flaw that he could expose.

The new city was circled in red above the conference room table. Asman was adding touches to the holographic display. The reservoir had small boats in the wide expanse of clear water. Trees and foliage were sprouting up along the banks. Ever the engineer, Skip began dotting the walls of the dam with solar disks to provide power to the under and above ground cities.

Finally, Skip's laugh boomed out once again across the room, "Ladies and gentlemen, it appears that we are NOT going to build a city. We are going to build TWO!"

CHAPTER SIX

Standing at the edge of York-City and facing the radiated desolation of the land towards and beyond the canyon, it was difficult to imagine why anyone would be interested in building anything out there. The entire region outside the line of civilization of the city, amidst the shimmering heat waves and rolling hills of contaminated earth, everything appeared to be desolate and completely devoid of life. Well, not all life. There were always the annoying, pesky if not downright dangerous creatures that somehow, even without apparent shelter, food or water, continued to survive the effects of the slowly diminishing amount of radiation.

The northern-most boundary of the immense canyon was composed of an imposing, sheer granite wall that was virtually unbroken except by a small fissure, a mere crack in the stone, that allowed an impressive outpouring of lifeless, gray water. The austere waterfall could have appeared beautiful if there had been some change in the background. Perhaps the presence of rock formations or foliage could have provided a visual counterpoint to the harsh, gray liquid spewing from the canyon wall. There were no trees, brush or vegetation of any kind to adorn this particular entranceway into the canyon. In days long past, there must have been a torrent of water flowing from the rock outcropping in order to cut the vast gorge that guarded the city's eastern border. Now, only this small waterfall escaped the confines of the stark, naked stone to create a churning, narrow stream that was immediately lost from view amid the bleakness of the surroundings. The flow of water appeared to die at the base of the cliff only to reappear further south as a shallow, slow moving river that wound its way disconsolately away from the city as the canyon slowly widened.

Despite the availability of water, there was not the slightest sign of anything growing within the canyon. The airborne particles that had contaminated the soil around the city had settled in the lowest region—the canyon. As city personnel continued to find contaminates within its borders, the particles were removed from the city environment and sent to an area that was not likely to ever be productive again—the canyon.

Very few people had demonstrated the desire to leave the relative safety of the city to visit the canyon, let alone actually want to find a way down into it. Nor were they likely to have found a way down into it had they tried. The canyon bottom was virtually inaccessible for nearly hundreds of units beneath the edge of the sheer rock walls. The tainted earth outside the city borders made it difficult to bivouac anywhere close to the canyon and the defilement of the ecosystem became more intolerable as the distance lessened to the canyon's edge. It was nearly impossible to enter into the canyon from any direction other than from the south. The canyon continued to widen and the walls grew less menacing and more manageable as it stretched further south and away from the city. The closest, alleged, southern egress into the canyon was only recently disclosed to the public and the distance from the city to the supposed entrance was so great that it had ensured that no one would likely bother to dispute the discovery.

The despoiled environment, the uselessness of the land, and the wretched conditions made the sudden appearance of work crews and the construction effort within the canyon walls a sensation to the city's populace. An enormous effort appeared to be underway on the canyon floor and nearly all the Vision stations were broadcasting from every possible view from the eastern edge of the canyon walls of the apparent construction to their customers. Immense earth moving equipment had been air-ported to the canyon floor and large tracts of radiated soil had already been cleared. A small but growing settlement was being built a short distance south from where the canyon walls appeared to be at their most narrow point. Servicemen, clad in environmental suits, were seemingly everywhere as the desolation and inhospitable climate of the canyon was encountered, endured, and slowly conquered.

Already foundations for who-knows-what were being poured and placed, sometimes miles apart, within the confines of the canyon. Although a great section of the canyon seemed to have been invaded by the City's construction service-people, the largest concentration of activity was centered along a structure beginning to span the base of the canyon at its most narrow point between the sheer walls.

It was possible that there were some curiosity seekers, most likely unemployed or very bored, that had taken the arduous journey from the city to the canyon walls to see for themselves the construction effort but the trip was hardly necessary. Dozens of Vision station service crews had been deployed as close to the crevasse as was possible in an effort to interview anyone entering or leaving the site.

The citizens of York-City were treated to quite the spectacle at the Vision crew's expense. There was no lack of fuel for humor since the usually well-dressed anchor-persons were wearing antiquated environmental suits provided by the city. These ancient vintage suits had hoses that stuck out at odd angles and face shields that provided a fairly limited peripheral view to the wearer. The outmoded material of a number of the suits had been recently patched and was apparently quite heavy as was evident by the make-up crew continuously trying to repair the damage the rivulets of sweat had caused to their spokespeople.

Asman was still wearing his environmental suit but his helmet had been removed now that he was no longer in the canyon. The environmental suits worn by Asman and his servicemen were not city-provided but, instead, had been engineered by Kendal Enterprises. These protective suits were incredibly lightweight, fairly comfortable, and allowed a respectably large range of motion and versatility. The latter was quite important for the safety and efficiency of the construction workers more so than for David Kendal's elite engineers. Not that it mattered; the entire board wanted the safety and comfort of the service-people to be a priority of the highest level before the construction effort even got underway. Of course, that didn't mean David had to share his suits with the other services.

Asman was speaking with Carol Brunson and Trish Vonner. "Look, Carol, I know you are responsible for the functionality of the Citadel, but you have to let me build it first!" He sounded exasperated but his smile told them that he was really only joking with her.

"I just want to get as good a jump on the project as I can", explained Carol. "Just give me your general thoughts and figures so I have SOMETHING to work with. That's all I am asking."

"Besides", Trish joined the conversation, "Are you going to be able to build *anything* with her always hanging around?" Trish had been assigned the arduous task of keeping track of the wife of the late Darren Kendal. With a nod of her head she indicated Jocelyn Kendal and her dedicated band of protesters standing as close to the canyon's edge as they possibly could without accidently (and suddenly) joining the work crews far below.

Asman and Carol looked to where Trish had indicated and observed the antics of a small, but loud, group of demonstrators. However, they also noticed that several small Vision station crews had broken away from their interviews with several of the construction foremen and were trudging their way in their awkward suits to join their group. Carol nudged Asman with her elbow and pointed towards the nearest Vision crew. With a rueful shake of her head she said, "We'll talk to you later at the office. There is no way we want to be part of that!" With that short declaration, the two ladies deliberately moved away out of camera range even as the first reporter approached them.

The York-City Vision station crews had been interviewing everyone they could find that had recently returned from the canyon floor. As soon as word had begun to spread that Asman Kennedy, one of the senior architects and engineers of the project had arrived, nearly every interview had been cut short and a small migration of camera crews were making their way as quickly as possible along the edge of the canyon.

The nearest reporter began to ask questions while his vision broadcast crew was still setting up their equipment. "Mr. Kennedy, as one of the founders of this effort to create a new water supply for our City, how is work progressing and are you feeling any of the effects from the radiation from within the canyon?"

Asman graciously smiled for the cameras as he wistfully watched his co-workers rapidly retreat for a more hospitable climate. "I think we will make substantial progress with the dam in a relatively short amount of time. The important thing to remember is that we need to clear out as much of the contaminated soil as possible in order to ensure the safety of our people." Asman was a natural selection for the cameras. His clean, handsome features, slim sturdy frame and sun-browned skin would present well on the big screens back in the city. "We've cleared the span between the canyon walls and a great deal of land to the south of the dam-site. If you will direct your cameras over there", Asman pointed directly towards the activity whose focus seemed intent upon bridging the span between the canyon walls, "you will see that the foundation for several sections of the dam are already underway."

The cameramen adjusted their positions to follow where Asman had indicated, allowing the convoluted scene of activity on the canyon floor to be sent to their viewers. From the canyon's edge, the workers appeared quite small and the activity seemed to be moving at a near frantic pace. Many concrete and flex-stone forms had already been set up in a seemingly random format throughout the area where the dam was to be constructed while other forms were still being set in what appeared to be completely unrelated areas. Other distant workmen were busily mixing the chemicals and ingredients that would later become part of the dam's foundation. All the while still other remote people were walking around the work zones, pointing to their plans, people and who knows what else, creating quite a spectacle for the Vision crews and their viewers.

Asman continued to describe in what he would characterize as layman's terms what was trying to be accomplished, always referring to the bridging of the canyon and as tacitly as possible, ignoring all other references to any other area within the canyon. In the background, however, the microphones began to pick up the shouts and cries from the small group of demonstrators that apparently noted the migration of the Vision crews and were even now heading towards him and the reporters. Asman looked them over for a moment and shook his head in disgust. "I do not understand this", he said with a vague wave of his hand in the direction of the demonstrators. "We are providing jobs, we are making the land safer and more useable for everyone, we are providing a new source of water and energy, yet these people are STILL protesting."

The Vision crew immediately abandoned the scenes of distant activity for the up-close-and-personal and—with luck—confrontational view presented by the approaching intruders. Although there were not too many demonstrators, they appeared to be well equipped to advertise their thoughts and intentions. Every one of them was carrying a flamboyant banner with brightly lettered messages such as: "FIX OUR CITY", "DON'T CREATE NEW PROBLEMS", and "WE ARE BREATHING YOUR CONTAMINANTS." The written messages seemed appropriate enough, but the spoken—shouted actually—messages were much more aggressive. "DOWN WITH KENDAL ENTERPRISES", "STOP THE STUPIDITY", and "KILL THE CAPITALISTS—NOT US" were only a few of the quotes that were hurled towards Asman and the reporters.

The Vision station crew had split up. One team continued to interview Asman Kennedy while the other camera crew made its way back toward the protestors. While Asman continued to extol the virtues of the construction effort, the second camera crew attempted to block the progress of the demonstrators as they loudly continued to deride the wasted credits, effort and leadership of a once-proud and worthy company, Kendal Enterprises. The protestors slowly wormed their way through the station-crew blockade, around and through the small maze of cameras, cables and sound equipment. Despite their posing for the cameras, it was obvious that their goal was to make their way along the canyon's edge and get as close to Asman as possible.

An easily recognizable woman among the protestors had temporarily commandeered the attention of the cameras. Dressed for media exposure rather than the harsh elements, her bracelets made a dull, tinkling sound through her suit as she raised her arm and pointed towards the canyon floor and the new construction sites. "We do not need this wasteful spending of our credits", she announced. "We have plenty of water and we have no need for expansion. We need the York-City officials to concentrate on the existing woes of our city—not to create new ones!"

The small mob of people behind her lustily cheered their agreement. The camera crews were diligently working to get good shots of the demonstration. Wide-angled lenses were not being used here. The vision station director had made it clear; make the demonstration appear as large as possible in order to keep their audience interested. These cameramen knew that any footage that made these protesters look like they were few in number or not popularly supported would wind up on the cutting room floor.

Two cycles ago, the demonstrations were very well attended by a large variety of services. However, as the reasons for the new development became better known and more people found themselves gainfully employed, the amount of resistance had quite understandably continued to decline. Sometimes, to the dismay of the demonstrators, counter-protest groups would form on the canyon's edge in the attempt to discourage the naysayers. This particular group of demonstrators, with Jocelyn Kendal leading them, had persevered through all the adversity.

"This is York-City 17 reporting live at the canyon wall. Aren't you Ms. Jocelyn Kendal, the widow of Darren Kendal, and wasn't this construction the inspiration of your late husband's?"

"My late husband", began Jocelyn Kendal, "wanted the citizen's of York-City to have a better life. Darren Kendal wanted our city to be improved—not replaced. All this", Jocelyn vaguely waved towards the construction within the canyon, "is a complete waste of time and credits. I fail to see how this will help the citizens of our city."

The small mob of demonstrators began shouting at Asman, hurling insults and working themselves closer to the other camera crew. A small contingent of security personnel brought vehicles up to form a line to help divide the two groups. The interview microphones began to pick up the sounds of vehicles being struck as a few of the protestors threw objects towards Asman and the vision-station crew.

Several of the demonstrators suddenly rushed forward, running between the small line of vehicles and were stopped only when more security servicemen quickly emerged from their patrol transports. The small security force menacingly brandished their weapons in a convincing show of force to repel the demonstrators from Asman's interview. Although the advance was stopped, the demonstrators only shouted more loudly and somewhere close, the sound of shattered glass was picked up by the reporter's microphones.

Trish Vonner turned down the volume of her transport newsreel monitor with a sad shake of her head. Carol and Trish were reporting back to the Board of Directors while returning to York-City "The number of demonstrations is dwindling", she reported. I don't even know why she is keeping this up. She has made her point and York-City officials have certainly established that the construction effort will continue."

David shrugged his shoulders. "More people are being employed by the Construction Service than in any other time in recent history. Unemployment is down, the citizens seem content, and almost no one seems interested in fighting this project." David continued to no one in particular, "She isn't stupid . . . I wonder, what she is trying to accomplish."

Skip piped in from his side of the conference table, "This show of violence is a sure-fire way of making sure the City officials don't allow them anywhere near the canyon. You would almost think that she was actually TRYING to have her demonstrations stopped."

Max shook her head slightly and addressed Carol, "Could you show us the construction site again? I would like to see, despite Jocelyn's efforts, just how much further you and Asman have been able to progress."

Carol immediately began keying into her control panel and another monitor came to life. A slow, panoramic view of the canyon site became visible.

As Asman had indicated in his interview, a large tract of land had indeed been cleared of tainted soil. Already an immense amount of flex-stone had been poured to form the foundation of the lowest level. The foundation for the dam was also being poured with a small army of York-City officials looking on. Asman had a small, dedicated force of engineers at his disposal to assist him to keep the York-City personnel occupied. A forest of solar-disks was being erected on the opposite side of the canyon. As was expected, there were no officials from the City to be found on the still-undisturbed, radiated side of the canyon to oversee the deployment of the disks. A spider-web of cables was being deployed from the solar forest down the sheer side of the canyon wall to provide uninterrupted power to the construction site.

"The two lower levels should be completed soon", Max announced. "If anyone is curious about what is being built on the floor of the canyon, no one has spoken of it."

"That's the way we want it", David breathed slowly. "We want the opportunity to build for as long as we can with as little interruption as possible."

* *

The Honorable Posin Kourei leaned heavily on an exquisitely constructed desktop. Mr. Kourei looked very much like any mayor from any city anywhere in the world. He was of average height and a medium-to-large build, that is to say, he had the look of a man that did not miss his meals. He was always impeccably well dressed in whatever was the latest style. The green tie was always sported because, as he had been oft quoted, "It is a green-tie affair if I am in attendance." The bowler hat had come back into style and his was set deftly off to the side of the fingers of his right hand. The fingers of that hand were drumming slowly on his desktop. A tight smile below a precisely trimmed mustache usually showed even, white teeth. The mirth was missing from the smile but the teeth were still showing, "I do not want the demonstrations stopped", he announced. "I want the populous to be distracted by her idiocy for as long as possible. If the people decide to get angry, I want them angry with Jocelyn Kendal and her radicals. Is that something you can handle, Brose?"

There were six people seated on much-less expensively constructed chairs facing the York-City Mayor. One severe-looking woman wearing the uniform of the security service was also showing teeth. Again, there was no smile. "I cannot allow her people to continue to demonstrate if they break the law. Every Vision station in the city is broadcasting the demonstrations—as you ordered. How can I allow her to continue leading these riots if she cannot control her own people? You have certainly had people arrested and punished for lesser crimes." Captain Brose added with only a slight pause, "Your Honor."

There were sounds of uncomfortable shifting in the chairs but all eyes remained on the mayor. "I will speak with Ms. Kendal" the Mayor stated stiffly. "She knows the rules and she will abide by them. But, in the mean time, I don't care if you have to have an escort for each of the protestors, I don't want those demonstrations stopped", the mayor's words were clipped with finality. "I want the people to be on MY side until that city is built." Posin tapped his finger forcefully on his desktop, "If that means they hate Jocelyn Kendal and her ridiculous band of idiots, fine. But that means they have to be there, at the canyon, and they have to be protesting. Is that understood?"

"Yes sir", Captain Brose clipped back.

The Mayor eased back down into his plush executive chair. He folded his hands on his lap and nodded towards another uniformed official. "What information have *you* gathered?" he quietly asked.

Colonel Cushman was an intelligence officer within the protection service. He had been sent to brief the mayor concerning conditions outside York-City. The Colonel was, for the most part, quite unconcerned with the dynamics in the room. The Mayor could run his office any way he desired. Technically, he was not part of the Mayor's staff; he was here to report his findings and return to his office. That was all. "The rioting we have experienced since last year has been evident in every major city in this hemisphere. Since the time that you had accepted Kendal Enterprise's proposal and the beginning of construction for the Citadel, our rioting has," with a quick glace towards Captain Brose, "for the most part, stopped. It appears that the other major cities are attempting to enlarge their boundaries as they have concluded that is what you are doing. They don't seem to have the expertise to head the effort as you do. Their efforts have resulted in a release of radiation contaminates that is polluting both their air and water supply." The Colonel added, "As you would expect, radiation sickness has become a growing problem in many of the other cities and, again as you would expect, their rioting has escalated rather than diminished."

Many of the records from the past several hundred years had been destroyed or lost, and the latest round of politicians had done their share of 're-writing the past', no matter which city and no matter from which country that city used to belong. Regardless of the selective history that had been taught in the educational systems throughout the world, even the most ignorant person knew that the past democratic systems had, for various reasons, broken down.

Even though, in the past, an increasing number of leaders around the globe had begun to embrace 'democracy' as the best method to lead their countries, a democratic agenda meant that the people were supposed to have the control, not the leader. Too many leaders had difficulty releasing that control. Even the vaunted (although no longer in existence) U.S.A., the model of democracy, had begun to elect Presidents that had introduced socialism as a way of controlling the people and the economy. Riots had begun in some of the third world countries—ousting dictators, tyrants and presidents in an effort to gain (or regain) freedom. The riots continued to spread to other more powerful countries. These countries had leaders that refused to step aside and relinquish control. Tens of thousands of people were massacred. Inevitably, nuclear arsenals were put into use. Now, even though the land radiation levels have become somewhat reduced, entire sections of the globe are still entirely unusable.

The Colonel signaled for his presentation to begin and the central monitor came alive with segments of video depicting sickness and disease in sectors of many of the other, global cities. It seemed that every major city on the planet had problems with overcrowded hospitals, morgues and disposal units. There were also a great many scenes of riots and demonstrations that were made up of people hotly contesting the expansion and construction efforts.

The Honorable Mr. Kourie grimly smiled at the misfortune befalling his competition around the globe.

Colonel Cushman continued, "We have a unique situation here, Your Honor. Since the construction has been restricted to the canyon, away from the city and since it has its own power and water supply, we have experienced only a few of the problems that are already plaguing the other cities."

The Mayor appeared thoughtful for a moment before making eye contact with his Public Relations representative, Mary Robts. "See that Ms. Kendal no longer makes any more inferences to breathing containments." Posin then turned back to Captain Brose, "I want those demonstrations contained but not stopped."

Ms. Robts quickly bobbed her head in obedience. Captain Brose nodded also. But reluctance and distaste were written in her eyes.

CHAPTER SEVEN

With a now familiar pacing, David came to a sudden halt in what used to be his father's office. Photos of the various stages of the canyon construction were strewn across a large, plain desk with more photos tacked up on the wall directly behind the desk. David pulled out the worn executive chair and, after easing into its cushions, appeared to be ready to address his staff.

"Okay, let's get this started," David announced. "Asman, what's happening with the dam?"

Asman smiled before beginning his report, "The dam is coming along perfectly. The foundation has passed all inspections and the dam walls would be well ahead of schedule if we weren't purposefully delaying the construction. You know, this may be the first project I've ever managed that did *not* complete before the announced deadline. You are making me look bad."

"Oh my," David said with only a hint of sarcasm, "we all have our crosses to bear. We know all too well that we have the outer shell of five more levels to build before the dam can be completed. What about our City officials? Are we experiencing any problems with them?"

"I don't really know why, but the inspectors and bureaucrats seem to be happy with our progress and do not seem the least bit interested in our subterranean construction. They've seen the blueprints and are perfectly satisfied that a small ocean of purified water will be stored beneath the city", Asman explained. The few officials that bother to leave the cameras long enough to inspect the 'caverns' as they call them, are back to the surface as quickly as they can transport."

Asman continued his assessment, "The power distribution from the disks has been pretty impressive. It has been a relief that the inspectors have almost no interest in exactly how much energy we are creating. We've set up a fake power grid just in case they ever do get curious. By the way, there is every indication that we will be able to supply more than enough energy for the needs of both your cities."

"Actually, what has been impressive is that you have been able to get anything done at the dam site as well as get the power grid working while juggling all the supervisors with which York-City has inundated you!", David said with true admiration in his voice. "I have been fairly insulated from all the bureaucrats and I don't miss dealing with them at all!"

"All in all", David continued, "everything seems to be working according to our basic plan. I guess I really didn't think the plan would work this easily".

"It isn't", interjected Carol. "We have been aware of illegal personnel within the dam structure and we are beginning to receive reports of unauthorized personnel in the caverns." David smiled at the use of the new slang term for the levels of the city. "We are unsure whether they are people who are curious and have nothing better to do with their time, some of Posin's people, or maybe even some of Jocelyn's. It doesn't matter, though. It's time we got some of our own security down there. There is just too much at stake. The last thing we need is somebody's 'discovery' on the newsreels."

"We may have another problem" Trish Vonner interjected. "Jocelyn has been busy acquiring real estate around the canyon. For a person who seems dead set against anything being done to the canyon, she sure seems to be financially interested in the area. I have no idea what she is up to, but she apparently wanted and now *has* most of the property rights surrounding your city."

"Maybe she figures that she will be able to control what happens in the canyon if she can claim it affects the value of her property", Carol wondered out loud.

"Yeah, maybe", David did not look convinced. He pressed some controls on his console and Alican's monitor came to life. "Let's try to balance out the news", David mused. "Alican, tell us something positive."

Alican Sykes was patiently waiting for a chance to discuss something other than the new-City project. "Business is good, Mr. Kendal. All our maintenance projects are on schedule. So long as the people continue to ransack York-City from time-to-time, you will be able to keep paying our salaries."

"Interestingly enough", Alican continued, "York-City officials would like to open negotiations for discussions concerning possible building projects next to the dam within the new-City limits. I think they are initiating their take-over plan and they want to make sure we have it built just the way they want it before they take it away from us."

"That is a little sooner than we thought but at least it was expected. 'New-City' limits . . . Now that we are nearly at the point where we are actually BUILDING it, let's call it by its rightful name—The Citadel," David smiled. "Set up some meetings. We will be good little York-City employees and give them whatever they want so long as it doesn't interfere with access to the caverns. We've got our basic plans for our little guardian city and we have to make sure Posin and his crew go along with them.

"That's true," Carol mused, "it would be most difficult to relocate our freight elevators that supply equipment and personnel to the caverns, now."

"Speaking of the caverns," David gave a quick wave good-bye to Alican Sykes then swiveled his chair to face Skip White's monitor, "how are we doing?"

Skip White sat thoughtfully facing his monitor. His chin was resting on his fingers interlocked together, his elbows nestled into the soft armrests of his chair. Skip's office in the caverns was a make-shift trailer that was moved every couple of weeks to whichever area needed his undivided attention. Photographs similar to the ones David had been studying were tacked up on the walls and strewn across a battered desk. The large, executive chair was the only item in the room that Skip retained for his comfort. "We are certainly making progress", Skip intoned as he straightened up in his chair.

"As you already know, the lower three levels have been constructed and buried. We have crews working on the interior. The lifts are a god-send. We are getting all the materials we need, and we are stocking the levels as we go." Skip spread his hands out in front of him, "Take a look at the plans and we can check them off as we discuss them."

Skip disappeared from his monitor as the layout for the lowermost habitable level was displayed. "The lowest level is reserved for engineering. Remember, the plan was to subdivide each level into quadrants to allow for a variety of management. There are four, separate areas that will monitor the environment of all levels. Water, power, air and disposal will be controlled on each level but there will be the capability to override those controls from the master level, here, on the engineering level in case of problems or catastrophe." Small, red, markings appeared on the layout depicting the control stations on the different levels. "Monitoring and override control is being tested as each new level is connected to the grid. The management of any level can be transferred to any one of these four quadrants."

David breathed a sigh and then smiled while considering the proposed organization of the city. The small community that his father had put together for York-City to test and display the power of the solar disks had been organized in a similar manner as a managerial prototype. The ideology was to allow the city to manage itself without one central figure or party that could assume control. There would be an administrative area on every level with the responsibility to manage the level's operations but any one level would not be able to affect another level without the cooperation of the engineering level.

"The living quarters on our current level have been completed for quite some time", Skip continued. "We know we did a good job with them because we are experiencing some difficulty getting the construction crews to vacate their apartments as their responsibilities are completed." Skip displayed a video of small apartments bustling with activity as construction crews live their lives in the caverns.

"No *wonder* we have reports of unauthorized personnel in the caverns", Carol nearly shouted. "Skip, are you telling us that each and every one of those people in the caverns is accounted for?"

Skip looked a bit annoyed but his tone showed that he understood the concern, "Well, Carol, we have certainly tried to keep track of everyone and everything that has entered the level. After all, the only way in and out of here is through the lifts. However, it is quite possible that people have been smuggled into the caverns and we don't have the manpower to monitor every lift shipment. We definitely do not have the ability to stop it from happening."

David held his hand up to interrupt their repartee, "We understand, Skip. You are not there to babysit the shipments." David turned to face Carol, "We need that security you mentioned earlier and we need to put it together as quickly as possible."

Carol was already scribbling notes while nodding her head in agreement. "We'll need funding," Carol muttered out loud, "Skip, will you want a team on every level?"

"I don't want to have to worry about it", Skip answered. "Just get someone to handle it. We can run a sweep before each level is sealed. If there is anyone left on a level after it has been sealed, well, they will just have to stay there—if you know what I mean."

Carol raised her eyebrows and glanced over the table to her employer.

David was nodding his head but concern was written across his face. They knew exactly what Skip meant. Once a level passes the override control and environmental tests, all power and control are passed up to the next level. The now automatically controlled level was evacuated and sealed. Only David or Skip could authorize a lift to breach a sealed level. The sealed level is allowed absolute minimal power, heat, water and oxygen. If anyone decided to stay in a sealed level, they would most certainly remain there. Their burial would have to be performed once that level was reopened and their remains were discovered.

"We'll continue to use the level-seal as the absolute final sweep, Skip", David announced.

David caught Carol's eye for a moment, "We need to find a Head-of-Security and get a security force to work with Skip in the caverns. We will use the same Security Chief to work with you as the Citadel is built."

David powered up an empty monitor and called quietly, "Ms. Sykes? Could you join us for a moment?"

Mere seconds passed by before Alican Sykes joined the conference. "Yes, Mr. Kendal?"

"We need to find a Head-of-Security and get a security force to work with Carol in the Citadel. You will need to set up appointments with everyone in this committee with Skip being as close to last as possible."

Carol smiled to herself and nodded discreetly as she continued to write notes to herself.

Alican was busy typing into her computer but said, "Yes sir. No problem. Will there be anything else?"

David only smiled and said, "No, you've got enough on your plate as it is. Thank you."

Alican smiled back before severing the connection.

David turned back to Skip, "We'll keep you informed of our progress but you do realize that you will have to come up from the caverns long enough to help with the interviews, right?"

Skip frowned thoughtfully, "I will make myself available. Just get me somebody good!"

David and Carol glanced at one another for a moment before he answered the man charged with building a secret, underground city, "This security chief will be the best we can find."

Skip and Carol nodded their understanding.

The conference video interrupt lit up and, with a questioning look from David, Alican was reconnected to the room. "I have just received a call from the Kendal Estates", Alican spoke matter-of-factly. She locked eyes with Trish Vonner for only a moment but it was long enough to pass a message between the two ladies.

"Ladies and gentlemen", Trish suddenly announced, "this meeting is adjourned. I'll send out the minutes and the schedule for its continuation."

This time it was David's eyebrows that shot up. Skip merely announced a quick "good bye" before his monitor went blank. Carol and Trish stood up together and with a wave turned to join Alican outside the conference room. They were already comparing schedules for security interviews as they walked out of the conference room.

Max was patiently waiting on the conference audio. David looked around the very suddenly empty room. "Strange", he thought, "I thought I was in charge." With a rueful shake of his head, David switched Max to the monitor directly in front of him. "Hi Max. Is everything alright?"

* *

David reached across the linen covered table to gently grasp Maxine's hand, "I still cannot believe it", he said softly, "It's a girl?"

Max laughed softly. She thought to herself, *we're in one of the most expensive restaurants in York-City. This place is absolutely, unbelievably beautiful; I think we could walk for hours and enjoy the surroundings and yet he makes me feel like I am the only person here.* "Yes, the technician had gotten a clear view. *This child*", Max said pointedly, "is definitely a little girl."

Maxine and David had never been in the Chalet-Green before but the tabloids have always referred to it as 'the' place to be. When they entered into the restaurant and were shown to their floor, the sheer immensity of the restaurant was breathtaking. Several interior waterfalls flowed into small creek beds that networked across the floor that subtly divided the clientele from one another. A small, low stone wall further divided their table from the nearest patron, giving the impression of privacy even though there was well over several hundred other diners.

"So, where would you like to begin?" Maxine asked innocently.

"Let's start with the name. You go first", David said, letting go of her hand and leaning back in his chair.

"Okay . . . How about Marikayla?"

"That sounds like a few too many syllables. How about Vani?"

"No, I don't think that one will work, either. I knew a Vani once and she was a real . . . well, not a nice person. How about Elizaventurianna?" Maxine asked with a sly smile.

David very carefully began counting the syllables on his fingers. "Eight", David said with feigned exasperation. "How about we agree on a name that I can spell AND pronounce?"

"Okay", Max said with a wink. "How about . . . Dona?"

David was silent for a moment. "Well, yeah, I like that name. Are you kidding around or are you serious?"

This time Max reached over to take David's hand, "I have always liked that name and it *was* your mother's name. I think it would be perfect."

David took a few seconds to study his wife of less than five years. It was always so difficult to know what she was thinking. "If you are truly serious, then I am all for it."

"Of course I am serious. You are the one who is always joking around, remember?"

"ME?" David looked as offended as he could for a moment. Then, he smiled as he once again studied Max, "I think it is a perfect name!"

David's mother had died when he was very young. It was very likely one of the catalysts that helped to push his father's thinking towards the welfare of the common citizen. It was a simple traffic accident that had left him without a mother. There were just too many people traveling too far too quickly and yet it only took one person driving too fast to leave Mrs. Dona Kendal in critical condition at the local hospital.

Dona Avril Kendal had been the most selfless person you could have ever met, his father had told him on every occasion David brought up the topic of his mother. His father would describe his wife as beautiful but, to Robert more importantly, she was kind, considerate and compassionate. Perhaps she tended to think of others because she had worked in the service centers as soon as she was old enough to enter the work force. However, Mr. Kendal would argue that point claiming that she had always lived her life like that. She was just a very nice person, which is how Mr. Kendal would usually end the conversation; that is what the world needed—more nice people!

Max suddenly became very serious, "But what kind of world is she coming to?"

A concerned look crept over David's face as his brows knitted into a worried furrow. "I don't like where our city is heading", he said at last. "It seems that the corporate leadership is concerned only for their personal welfare and profit. Anyone who shows the least bit of compassion or concern for the common service-worker is believed to not understand the business world. And, then—"

"And then is quickly eliminated", Maxine completed the thought.

Max took another sip of her drink before adding to her husband's comments, "I know. Everyone thinks they have to make all the credits they can. The investors are demanding higher profits even if that means poorer products and working conditions. It's not like we are alone in the world. Every city with which we have been able to communicate is going through the same problem."

"Yeah, great, world-wide greed", David said morosely.

David had heard all of this before when his father tried to explain his motivation for helping people rather than just making a living. The elder Kendal had told his sons of the ridicule, even persecution, he had endured for not putting wealth and position above everything else. David had questioned his father, asking him why he bothered to put forth that kind of effort for someone else? What was wrong with being wealthy? Robert Kendal had merely gestured towards the estate and simply said, "We have all that we need—more than we need. The Lord has taken good care of us, don't you think?"

David shook his head ruefully as the memory faded, "It's no wonder the people are angry, disappointed and discouraged."

Max shrugged her shoulders, "It's no wonder they are rioting."

This expensive meal is quickly losing its savor, David thought to himself. Aloud he said, "It has happened in the past and the economy has always stabilized. What worries me is that it has not happened on this scale in a long time. There are still hundreds of thousands of people out of service and, even though the Vision Services have blocked nearly all news reports concerning the other cities, we know this problem is not isolated to our City."

"And yet, compared to what we know of the rest of the world, we are not doing too badly", David continued. "There are employment possibilities. Our new city is actually helping the economy and even the Honorable Mr. Kourei has not tried to levy new taxes or take away any more rights from his citizens." David smiled, but the smile appeared a bit uncertain, "I am sure everything will be all right."

"All right, huh?" Max repeated. "I don't know if that will be enough for our family, David. We have enough credits and we have the company with its patents—that's not the problem. Remember the accident, honey? Do you remember that the people had no idea who you were? You were just another hot shot executive being transported to some expensive destination while they can't even get food and medicine for their children. I don't want our children growing up like that. I know we think that Jocie is sometimes out of her mind but she does have a point. I want to know that we, our family, will be safe, too."

David's eyebrows raised a fraction, then asked, "I think everyone in the city would like to say the same thing; what do you have in mind?"

"How about we move into the Citadel just as soon as we have some of the living quarters built? I think that would get our family away from the big crowds and give us some sense of security."

David gave Max a quizzical look before replying, "You know that we expect the government to take over the Citadel before its construction is even finished. We may be trading one evil for another one. If the unrest in York-City is not solved, we may be less safe in the Citadel than if we stayed with the general populous." David interlaced his fingers and set his hands on the table, "Are you sure this is a good idea?"

It was plain from her expression that Maxine had already given this a lot of thought. Still, she appeared to mull it over for a moment before responding with a nod of her head, "Yes, I am sure that it will work. I believe it will be a lot harder for the crowds to get access to the Citadel. Less of a crowd will mean less of a problem", Max said with finality.

"Well", David said with a slow nod of his head, "I think your timing may be perfect." He reached across the cluttered table to gently take her hand, "I already have one security problem that has to be resolved—*in* the Caverns. I know this security person will also have to handle security for the Citadel as well. I am sure that I can take care of our problem and the security problems all at one time."

Maxine let a long, relieved sigh escape her lips. "I'm glad that's settled. You'll see, if nothing else, your commute time will be drastically cut back!"

David chuckled, "That's true enough." With a slight nod of his head he said, "I'll talk to Posin in the morning and get things going."

David smiled again—this time it was genuine, "A little girl . . . and she has such a beautiful mother!"

That little remark earned David a kiss; public display of attention be hanged!

CHAPTER EIGHT

David did not enjoy waiting, especially since he was fairly certain no one else had gotten in ahead of his first-available-time-in-the-morning appointment.

Just being allowed inside the Mayor's compound had proved to be a difficult task. The entire wrought-iron fenced perimeter of the governmental complex was patrolled by uniformed guards. There were two ways to get in and out; both required transport access, whether by a personal vehicle or by a government-provided shuttle. There were also two gated guard shacks whose personnel verified the identity and authorization of the person before further access was allowed. Further access included admittance to the specific building and floor by which the Mayor's suite was located.

"You may go in, now, sir", an attractive, young receptionist finally informed David.

"Thank-you", David replied and made his way around the Honorable Posin Kourei's youthful watchdog.

The Mayor was seated behind his elaborate desk, searching through a small stack of papers. The pretense, of course, was to show David that he was a very busy man and David was obviously interrupting important business. The bowler hat was neatly placed atop a hat rack just to the left of the immense window directly behind the Mayor which presented a grand view of the city. With only the briefest of eye contact, the Mayor said, "Please sit down Mr. Kendal."

A plain, wooden, straight-backed chair was David's only option. David moved it so he would not be sitting directly in front of the Mayor, then, took his seat with an almost patient expression on his face.

David and Max had spent most of the evening discussing how to present the relocation of his family to the Mayor. They knew that there really shouldn't be a problem. The move actually made too much sense to not approve. Really, the larger issue would be trying to keep Posin's entire cabinet from making the move at the same time. There could be some complications if too many officials were too close to the project. Who knows, thought David, the eminent hiring of a security chief may keep that particular issue at bay. He had already received news of a promising candidate.

Mr. Kourei looked up with feigned earnestness, spread his hands wide and asked, "How may I be of service to you, sir?"

Forty-five minutes later, David was hustled past the Mayor's watchdog on his way back to his own office. *That went well*, David mused while walking towards his waiting transport. *Posin was very accepting of the relocation plan. Sure, he made it clear that his people would need to be set up as well but, hey, we were expecting that.*

David's guider was waiting with the transport just a short way from the Mayor's heavily guarded building. "Mornin' Mr. Kendal. Where to?"

David nodded a quick greeting, "Let's head to the office." David hopped into the small, silver transport while the guider deftly entered the instructions into the console.

There had been no more incidents with mobs or rioters on the ways since the Kendal family tragedy. Security all along the transportation corridors had been increased tremendously since the incident. Individuals could still access the main thorough-fares but it would be extremely difficult to amass any kind of a crowd. The memory was still fresh in David's mind and the guider was well aware of it. Despite the City-added precautions, he wanted his employer to feel as comfortable and confident as possible. Although the additional effort was probably unnecessary, he took the extra precaution to keep the craft in the middle of the ways and made great efforts to have other transports close by.

David was once again focused on the newsreels. He scanned random areas of the city, listening for reported incidents of dissatisfaction from the citizens. *Odd*, he thought, *I know there are problems within the city but you wouldn't know it by checking the media.* David nestled into the plush seat and began ticking off items of interest from his short meeting with the mayor. *One, Posin was quick to agree to the relocation of his family. That was probably to make it easier for the mayor's staff to be relocated to the Citadel. Two, the Mayor was very quick to advocate that his people be moved as quickly as could be arranged.* David was gazing out the window of the transport without really noticing anything in particular when he suddenly exclaimed, "Will you look at all the security on the ways!"

Despite the guider's diligence to give David a feeling of comfort, the view from the transport view-ports presented an impressive number of armed personnel patrolling long sections of the corridors. There were members of the transportation security services at every access and entry point to the ways. It suddenly dawned on David that the other transports had personal guards along with the guiders and passengers. By all appearances, the city was being transformed into a police-state.

He had not noticed any changes but, then again, he knew that he tended to get focused on the task at hand and not notice a LOT of things. *I wonder what curfews have been put in place or any other loss of personal rights in order to keep order and protect the elite.* Thanks to the contributions of his father and brother, he was considered a City Executive, one of the elite. If the City has put forth *this* kind of cost and effort then it was no wonder that Max wanted to get out. It was an easy bet that the honorable Mr. Kourei had the same reasons to want his staff moved out of the city as soon as possible, too.

"Shall I wait for you sir?" the guider cut into David's thoughts.

David looked up in surprise, "No thanks. I'll be here for the rest of the day. Just be back by quittin' time."

The guider nodded in understanding and opened the passenger door. David scrambled out, blinking into the bright sunshine before entering into the Kendal office building.

"He's arrived," Carol quietly announced.

Boston Jeffries arose to his feet—again.

"He doesn't sit still very well, does he?" Carol said as she smiled towards Asman.

Asman shrugged his shoulders and smiled back, "Well, we could use someone around here who doesn't sit around all day."

Jeffries merely looked at them with a bland expression, "I work better when I am moving", he said with a wink.

Boston Jeffries was a middle-aged man of medium height and an average-to-heavy build. His fairly short, wavy blonde hair was parted on one side. He was clean-shaven with short, precisely-cut sideburns. His piercing blue eyes looked all the brighter under reddish-tinted eyebrows. Whereas the Mayor of York-City kept up with the latest fads and styles, Boston Jeffries did not appear to care about such things. He wore a dark fitted suit with a soft blue shirt and tie. The man looked . . . efficient.

The door to the conference room suddenly banged open. "Have you noticed the amount of security in the ways?" David asked as he quickly strode inside. He stopped abruptly as a well-built man walked past Carol and Asman towards him with his calloused hand outstretched.

"Boston Jeffries" he said as he grasped David's hand into his own.

David was surprised. Not that he expected a weak handshake from this man but that the grasp was firm without trying to overpower him. Intimidating and insecure people tended to demonstrate how strong they were by attempting to dominate another by using a crushing handshake. This man was here for the Chief-of-Security position—a position that is many times filled by arrogant bullies. Jeffries was obviously a powerful man yet he did not press the advantage. David smiled, *I like him already,* he thought. "I'm pleased to meet you, Mr. Jeffries. Please, sir, take a seat."

Boston Jeffries chose the seat next to the head of the conference table. Carol sat next to him while Asman sat directly across. David, of course, took his station at the head of the table.

"What do you know of us?" David asked as soon as everyone was comfortable.

Boston's eyebrows shot up at the unusual opening question to the interview. He clasped his hands in front of him on the table before replying, "You, your father and your brother have been instrumental in constructing tools for the benefit of the people of the City. You have strived to continue your family's legacy despite opposition from city officials. I had been appointed to manage the containment security of the community your father built while testing the solar disks." At this point in Mr. Jeffries' dialogue, Boston paused to lean back in his chair before continuing, "I am well aware of the amount of energy that was being created for that community but was NOT being shared with the general populous. Needless-to-say, I am very much intrigued with your new city."

Once again David was caught by surprise. Jeffries had been in charge of the security for the community that York-City officials had commandeered from his father. We know that the officials will, sooner or later, take away the Citadel. But we do NOT want them anywhere near the underground city. Yet, that is the very region this man would be safe-guarding! Surely Asman and Carol had known this information. Yet, those two members of his staff were sitting comfortably at the table, content in whatever knowledge they were waiting for David to discover.

David's lips formed a cautious smile and asked, "So, your idea of a security chief includes the understanding of power grids and energy distribution?" David glanced quickly over to his peers. It may have been a good question but he had apparently not found the right direction of questioning, yet.

"I like to know what is going on so I can ensure the correct people are allowed into the right areas", Boston explained. "I know what I was told concerning your power grids and consumption but, based on levels of comparison against other power sources, your community was only using a fraction of the energy that it was obtaining. I noticed that a considerable number of the disks had been removed prior to the City taking control of the community. I believe that the community is, now, using pretty much all the energy that it is acquiring. You have managed to conceal the power levels for now but, for what purpose?" He now locked his blue eyes directly onto David's brown, "I firmly believe that if I know the plan, I can deploy my security personnel adequately."

David shook his head slightly without breaking eye contact with Jeffries. *Does he already know too much?* he wondered. Aloud, David asked, "How much information did Posin share with you? Somehow I doubt that the Honorable Mr. Kourie told you much of *his* plan."

This time it was Boston Jeffries' eyebrows that raised a fraction. Boston glanced quickly across the table at Asman for a brief moment before answering, "I was not hired by nor did I work for Posin Kourie." The name was spat out with distaste.

"So, who DID you work for?" David asked.

"Captain Brose is the Head of Security for York-City. She hired me. I reported directly to her", Boston's reply was a bit more conciliatory.

David did not need to see the expressions on his colleague's faces to know he had 'scored'. Captain Susan Brose was not the Mayor's biggest fan. If Boston Jeffries had not reported to the Mayor, he may well be 'clean'. "So, why did you leave your position Mr. Jeffries? Why work for us?"

Boston glanced this time towards Carol before answering, "I did not 'leave'. The position was terminated the moment the Honorable Mr. Kourie confiscated your community. Kourie", he continued with disgust, "obtained a new security chief to watch over his new 'realm'. Let's be frank, here, Mr. Kendal. I am not a fan of the Mayor of York-City. I do not appreciate the way he performs the duties of his office. I do not like how he thinks about the people in *his* city."

Jeffries relaxed his now-clenched hands, and continued, "I would prefer to work for someone who actually cares about someone other than himself."

David nodded his head with understanding and approval. He looked first at Asman, then Carol. They had approved of this candidate before he had ever been brought in for the final interview. David stood up and extended his hand, "Welcome aboard, Mr. Jeffries. I think you will like your new job!"

CHAPTER NINE

"As you can see, ladies and gentlemen, the Citadel Dam is quite finished", Asman Kennedy intoned to the gathering of York-City officials. "And, as you can also see, our reservoir will need a number of years before we are even close to capacity."

The dam was monstrous—not so much because of the span from either side of the canyon walls, but from the height of the bridgework where the group was walking to the base of the canyon. The construction began nearly ten years ago to the day. From the beginning, the citizens of York-City were amazed as to how many metric tons of flex-stone was being fabricated and poured into the foundation and creation of the dam. Even so, that amount was significantly dwarfed compared to the volume utilized for the caverns.

There were the appropriate 'ooo's and 'ahh's from many of the officials but there were also tangible comments that Asman could tell that they were truly impressed, "We've seen video but we had not realized the immensity of this project" one official frankly remarked. "No wonder there were so many people employed. Just how many people had been assigned to this project?" another would ask.

There were a few of the officials that caused some concern, partially because of the amount of photos being snapped and notes being taken, and partly because of the questions they did *not* ask. Jocelyn Kendal and a thin, weasel of a man were among the 'officials' that had been sent by the city to tour the dam facilities and receive a first-hand look of the construction taking place within the boundaries of the Citadel. A second man accompanied them apparently for the single purpose of taking pictures of anything either of the first two people pointed to or talked about.

Jocelyn had curtly nodded a greeting to both Asman and Carol as each person had been introduced. Her two companions ignored the presence of everyone else as they waited on Mrs. Kendal and waited for her to select items for which they should be interested.

They spent a considerable amount of time discussing the power levels registering on the various monitors on each level of the dam structure. While many of the other officials appeared to be sight-seeing, this little band was taking note of the density of the walkways, security ingress and egress to the dam as well as the number of security guards assigned to each outpost. The 'weasel' seemed to have a lot to say about the readings and information gleaned from the various view-screens although all conversation terminated as soon as either Asman or Carol walked close enough to hear their discussion. All the while their third companion kept taking a continuous stream of pictures and video.

While most of the people in the tour seemed quite impressed with what they saw, Jocelyn and crew would mutter side comments of disappointment concerning the possibilities that had been, apparently, unrealized. The dam itself was too high—too many resources had been 'poured' into the project, the bridgework was too ornate—again, a waste of time and credits, and, depending upon whom was speaking, there was either too much security deployed or not enough manpower to protect such a costly venture. Despite their obviously preset opinions of the structure and their growing list of comments and complaints, the one item that was completely unarguable, even to them, was that the dam was working to perfection.

The design was fairly simple and straightforward. The smooth, concave curve of the dam wall stretched from the west side of the sheer canyon wall to the eastern side. The uppermost portion of the dam was unmarred by anything save the transport way and pedestrian walkway that the visitors were now traversing. Spillways had been constructed at either end of the dam to carry access water along the base of the canyon's granite walls. The overflow was directly in the center of the dam and as the group neared that point of the tour, the overflow walls were lowered to allow a much greater flow of water and a better demonstration of how the dam will function in the future.

The tremendous flow of water that was suddenly loosened from the growing reservoir cascaded into the canyon with a deafening crash. The turbines within the dam were absolutely undisturbed, continuing their function despite the sudden increase of volume. Some water was being allowed to spill down the overflow and, upon reaching the base of the dam, joined whatever water was already moving along the spillway to form a myriad of small rivers. The flows continued along the canyon floor only to join up with the original river bed many miles further south. The overall effect created a man-made island that had been built up to a tremendous height.

As impressive as the dam appeared to the onlookers, the view *from* the dam was even more spectacular. No matter which direction the visitor decided to gaze upon, the landscape was uniquely different. To the north was the slowly rising reservoir, with the waterfall still emitting its charge, albeit not from as great a height as before, into the new-forming basin. Already the radiation levels were being lowered as the water covered the canyon floor and climbed the sheer rock walls. As a result, some vegetation was already struggling to grow and spread around the valley. Birds that had not been seen in quite some time were beginning to establish nesting areas. And, if the scent of clean water can be counted as part of the 'view', then, instead of the stench of broken, radiated earth, the aroma of clear water was swept to the passersby as a crowning touch of a sweet vision.

Many of the visiting officials merely stood at the guardrail staring over the reservoir-in-the-making. They would slowly breathe in great droughts of clear air, and sigh. The fresh, unsullied backdrop seemed to bring forth lost memories of independence and hope. These people could sense the opportunity for a new start and a chance to live a better life.

While facing north gave a feeling of peace and tranquility, the southern view displayed a scene from the history books depicting the creation of a bustling new town. New homes were being built as far south as the eye could see. Not the apartment-building-like homes characteristic of the residences within York-City but actual *houses*. Already children were playing in fenced-in yards where the grass was only just beginning to take hold in the freshly plowed earth. New ways were being established; dirt roads until the paving process could be completed, networked across the land. These ways connected the homes and the properties and led inevitably towards the new buildings being constructed for the administration and commerce in this 'new land'. Searching deeper into the canyon could be seen, far below, a flurry of streams of water combined together to form two small rivers that surrounded the 'island'. These two streams combined once more to create a small river that continued its journey south and away from civilization.

While the construction of the dam with its power and water interconnections to the 'caverns' and the Citadel was Asman's responsibility, the layout and functionality of the cavern's guardian city was Carol Brunson's. Carol noticed with pride that most of the York-City executives stared unabashedly at the Citadel. She pointed out the new living quarters and housing projects, so different from the cramped areas within the City. There was a hunger in their eyes as they evaluated the new sky-line being constructed just a short distance away. Here was opportunity, just across the short gulf of the dam, for a different life. By all indications, in the Citadel, a person could have ease and comfort that those left behind in York-City would most likely never have a chance to obtain. Carol also noted with sadness how these executives yearned to take possession of the fledgling city. Like long-caged prisoners sensing the opportunity for escape was near at hand, they would talk in hush whispers among themselves about the freedom that seemed so near at hand.

It was interesting to note that few, if any, gazed back the way they had come. Nor did their eyes stray east, towards the opposite side of the canyon. Although looking to the east and west also presented two very different landscapes, these visitors expressed absolutely no interest. To the west could be seen the sprawling expanse of York-City. The immense sky scrapers jutted into the skyline and the teeming population scurried across of the face of the city at what seemed to be a frantic pace. Great clouds of industrial progress spewed filth into the afternoon skies. Millions of people were crammed into the finite boundaries of the over-built city and the stark contrast of the city limits to the unlivable, radiated areas seemingly just outside of the city's boundaries made the metropolis appear that much more cramped, dirty and over-used. With only a quick scrutiny of the long-standing once-international-capital city, the observer was left with a shortness of breath, a sick feeling of growing anxiety and the pervasive feeling of being . . . trapped.

A quick study in the opposite direction offered no better a perception. The eastern landscape was empty. That is to say, empty of visible life. The eastern rim of the canyon and the land beyond appeared to not have been touched by humans since the radiation wars. Contrary to bedtime stories told to the children, the land did not 'glow' like the old science fiction stories would have you believe. Yet, almost nothing grew there. The wind blasted across the desolate terrain with little save the tumbled boulders, rocks and whatever was still standing from past generations of civilization to slow it—which was not much.

Asman and Carol continued to point out various landmarks as they came into view, the evidence of the several coves just beginning to form within the reservoir and the Citadel's new Governance buildings that, from the outside, were nearly completed. For the most part, Asman and Carol were willing to let the obviously impressed officials point out their own discoveries so that they only had to offer comments and information to satisfy queries from the visitors.

This is working out even better than I thought it would, Asman considered. *I suppose I have grown used to the scenery and the construction so that I am not affected like they are. I would have thought that all the newsreel coverage would have prepared them for all of this.* Asman paused to gaze about the area trying to imagine seeing the dam, reservoir and the Citadel in person for the first time. The sheer beauty and industriousness of the city and the dam was breath-taking—even inspiring. *Still,* he thought as his gaze went to the depths of the water below the dam, *I wonder how well it is going 'downstairs'?*

* *

To say that Boston Jeffries was surprised at the enormity of the enterprise that his new employers had undertaken would have been a gross understatement. Staggered and stunned may be a bit closer to the reaction that the new security chief was feeling as he was once again escorted into the security lift that would take him to the next level of David Kendal's city.

Earlier that day, Mr. Jeffries was transported to the new office building of Kendal Enterprises within the Citadel. Boston had kept up with the construction process of the dam and the new city by way of the newsreels and, although he was impressed with the progress, he was not as overwhelmed as many of the city officials and inspectors had been. Sure, the city planners had done a magnificent job with the structures, roads and ways, the parks and residences and the utilities that offered power and services. The dam itself was an immense structure but, he half shrugged to himself, it was still just another reservoir and just one more city.

"Excellent, Boston, right on time of course", Skip White rose from where he had been leaning casually on a desktop. He slapped the security chief on the back instead of shaking his hand and immediately began guiding him down a long corridor towards an office labeled appropriately enough, "SECURITY."

"What do you think of our little construction effort so far? C'mon, be honest, are you impressed?" Skip asked with a keen look in his eyes.

"Well, to be quite frank, Mr. White, I've seen all of this before. It's a city. It's new and it IS impressive but it is not really THAT large. It's bigger than the community that Robert Kendal constructed, of course, but", Boston spread his hands out in front of him, "nothing that can't be dealt with", he continued with a slight shrug of his broad shoulders.

"Oh, I see. You are impressed, but not *that* impressed", Skip stated with an innocent smile. "That's fine. You only have a few more places to visit. Then, we can sit down and you can tell me what kind of resources you will need."

Boston watched his peer through slightly narrowed eyes. His training and previous experience in both the city police and security forces was loudly proclaiming that something was amiss. *He's hiding something*, he thought with a small frown.

"Let's start in here", Skip led the security chief through the receptionist's workplace and into Boston's inner office.

Jeffries looked about with some interest. There were the usual administrative accruements, executive desk, office chairs and tables. There were books, awards and papers properly displayed within bookcases as well as on a large desktop already crowded with phones, a computer, sensory monitors, papers and pens. Just inside the doorway immediately to his left were two comfortable-looking visitor chairs with a small table placed between them. Directly across from the desk was a large, sturdy bookcase that would need a small work crew to move should he want to rearrange his office.

The absence of windows didn't bother Boston one bit. The title of 'Security' usually meant that he would be dealing with classified documents and communications. The only other wall in the room, where a window would have been a nice feature, was set up for pictures, diplomas and other displayable documents.

Skip sat casually in one of the chairs and left the new security chief to walk slowly around the room. Everything seemed to be in place. Care had been taken to help him feel right at home, complete with a freshly made name plate placed respectfully towards the front edge of his desk. Even the pencils were freshly sharpened.

Something, however, was just not right.

Boston turned to study Skip White for a moment. Skip was quietly watching him with an expectant air. *I don't suppose that I am expected to find something out of place because everything certainly appears normal.* Boston turned back to his desk and looked around the room once more. *Actually, it almost looks as though someone has gone through an awful lot of trouble to make this office look 'normal'. Maybe I should be looking for something that should be here, but is missing.* Boston walked the room once more, stopped briefly to study the items in the bookcase. *Hmm, there was no dust, no rubbish so either the house-keeping service had just been here or,* "This is just for show", Boston said as he turned to face Skip. "Was this a test?"

Skip looked somewhat disappointed, "Actually, I had hoped it would take you longer to figure it out. One of the first items you will have to do is make sure this room looks and feels real." Skip rose from his chair and pointed towards the bookcase. "Please forgive the melodrama" he continued as he reached over the desk and pressed an obscure button beneath the desktop. "I've always loved this sort of thing in the old videos", Skip said with a half-smile as the bookcase swung into another room.

Skip gestured for Boston to enter first and, mimicking the half-smile of his colleague, the security chief walked slowly into the dimly lit area. Actually, it was dimly lit only until he stepped inside. The overhead lights suddenly glowed and quickly lit up what appeared to be a very small, almost completely unadorned room. The wall directly opposite the doorway displayed a control board that contained a small bank of numbers. As he stepped forward to study the controls, the bookcase door silently closed behind them; revealing a large monitor that very clearly displayed the office they had just vacated.

Boston was amused, "A private viewing area of my office?" he said aloud to Skip. He glanced over to his companion for clues to this latest bit of entertainment but Skip smiled back at him. Boston turned back to the control panel and after only a moment of study slowly shook his head before he smirked, "A hidden elevator?"

Skip merely gestured towards the panel, "Why don't you have a go?"

The security chief was intrigued despite himself. With a thoughtful expression on his face, he studied the few controls and the series of switches that seemed to control the feed to the bank of monitors inside the elevator. After he played with the different camera angles that displayed the room they had just left, he pressed one of the few buttons on the panel.

An interior door slid across the doorway, sealing off the bookcase entryway, then, a soft, movement could be felt as the lift carried them downward. Boston involuntarily glanced up as some hydraulic movement could be briefly heard overhead. He gave Skip an inquisitive look.

"A solid wall has been slid into place behind the bookcase while we are gone", Skip said as he smiled. Then he nodded towards the monitors. The inner office was no longer being displayed. Instead, a fair-sized section of the landing area was being displayed, presumably to allow the travelers an opportunity to be prepared for whatever was awaiting their arrival.

A soft chime was heard as the lift came to a halt. After a brief pause, the door slid open revealing a cavernous room, somewhat dimly lit but with the appearance of a ceiling easily fifty feet high. Without exiting from the lift, Boston could see the opposite wall of the room but it was too far off to accurately measure the distance.

Skip gestured for Boston to step out but not until he had locked the position of the lift. Skip caught Boston's eye before saying, "As you can imagine, there are not too many ways in and out of here. You will want to make sure you remember where you parked."

Boston nodded as he turned about, trying to get a grasp as to what he was looking. Skip only smiled before walking around to the other side of the lift and into a much larger control room than the one they had just left.

Boston followed him into the room but paused at the doorway, lifted his hand to vaguely encompass the area they had just left before asking, "This is a storage area?"

This time Skip was impressed. Most people would be stunned at the sheer size of this particular area, surprised that it even exists, probably amazed that there was any kind of a structure beneath the city above. Boston was surprised, of that there was no doubt. But the revelation did not deter him from continuously, and correctly, analyzing his surroundings.

"Again, I apologize. I was looking forward to seeing the expression on your face. But, I could have shown you this on the monitors while we were upstairs", Skip absent-mindedly gestured 'up'. Then, he gestured towards the many controls and security monitors.

Boston appeared relieved for a moment as he instantly recognized a typical security monitoring board. He quickly crossed the room and sat down in front of the control panel. Slowly at first, then with growing confidence, Boston began to manipulate the cameras and displays on the monitors. He leaned back in the chair and sighed with a growing understanding. "This is really no more than a very, very large room, with a lift and a control room." He looked up at Skip, "Why all the secrecy?"

Skip drew a deep breath. The expression on his face changed from being inquisitive to instructive and his voice became matter-of-fact, "This is the staging area for the rest of the city. Nothing, and I do mean nothing, goes any further until it gets cleared at this level." He sat down next to Boston and brought another screen to life. "By further, I mean that nothing can enter David's City except through this staging area."

The controls at Skip's fingertips displayed, one by one, each level of the underground city on separate monitors. The architect of the 'canyons' finally received the facial expressions from Boston that he had been waiting for all afternoon. The smirk on the security chief's face slowly faded to a thoughtful frown, then, mild shock as the color slowly drained from his face.

CHAPTER TEN

Several hours later, Boston was still seated at the security panel manipulating the controls that allowed for viewing various sections of each level of the underground city. Skip had long since retired to a recliner across the room to watch the various portions of the city as they were displayed on the monitors. Boston would pause from time to time during his viewing and leave a particular scene on the screens. This was Skip's cue to explain what was being monitored in more detail than what the readouts and statistics below the displays had already revealed.

"Those generators, like the ones you glimpsed on the last level, provide air replacement and circulation. We use pretty much the same technology to cleanse the air that we use to purify the water", Skip quietly explained. "You can see on your left display that there is a redundancy of generator capacity that has been built into the process. I suppose it would be possible to have a problem with the air supply on any one level but oxygen could be supplied from the neighboring levels if a true emergency situation arose."

Skip White was in his element. The team had exhausted every scenario they could think of trying to anticipate every catastrophe imaginable and have a viable, practical solution available. He had spent the last decade of his life implementing those solutions and to have a captive audience, someone who was truly interested enough to ask questions and then to attentively listen as he expounded upon the accomplishments, well, this was like heaven to him!

"Oh, you've dropped down to level five. That is the only level with an actual events stadium." Skip smiled, stretched and struggled to his feet. "The other levels have civic centers, auditoriums and smaller sports arenas but if a city-wide event was needed, there would (and should) be only one place that supports it." Skip began to wander around the control room while talking, "You will notice that there is ample space for restaurants, pubs, and whatever amenities the populous would like to have available to the event patrons."

Skip glanced absent-mindedly at his watch, then, took notice again as to how comfortable the security chief appeared. "Haven't you picked out a place to visit, yet? We don't have that much time left, today, and it would help your perspective if you could actually see some of the places you've been visiting via those security monitors."

Boston looked away from the monitors and, rubbing his eyes, said, "Sure, I found a spot a couple of hours ago." With a straight face he added, "I've just been waiting for you to stop talking."

With exaggerated sputtering and complaining about the abuse for which he was being subjected, Skip motioned for Boston to follow him to the other end of the room.

Jeffries shook his head, "another hidden elevator" he groaned. "Don't you people trust ANYBODY?"

Despite his words to the contrary, the security chief actually very much approved that no one could access the levels below the staging area without first being forced to stop here on his floor. "My floor", he mused to himself. "Man, they sure have me hooked!"

Skip entered the same lift as the one they originally rode to the staging level, only this time, since they entered from the inside of the security control room, a control panel was accessible that was not visible on their previous trip.

"Where to?" Skip asked as the control panel door slid open.

"I would like to see the treatment level, 'Ground floor' if you please."

Skip eyed his companion for a moment. Sure, it was an innocent enough request but that was one way that, as the lift passed through the city, the new security chief could 'see' the landing area of every level as each level was reached and bypassed. Skip was just a little annoyed with himself that he may have underestimated, perhaps seriously, the abilities of Mr. Boston Jeffries. "Sure thing", Skip cheerfully complied, "smelliest level in the city!"

Boston kept his eyes glued to the monitors, making mental notes as each level was reached, then left behind as the duo continued towards the canyon floor. He marveled that care had been taken so that each level seemed to have a different layout. The landing areas showed a variety of designs and intricacies that fairly screamed of an attention to detail unheard of in York-City. An architectural schematic would appear for every approaching level denoting the infamous "you are here" arrows to assist the visitor in acclimating to the new environment.

Finally, the lowest level was reached and the lift came to a soft halt. The rear door to the lift opened revealing a control room very similar to the one they had just vacated. With a lift of his eyebrows, Boston followed Skip out of the elevator and entered the sparsely lit room.

"This level has been sealed for quite some time", Skip explained as he powered up the security board. "I can show you around a couple of the sections of the plant but I do not want to nor can I release the seal of the entire level without direct approval from David."

Boston smiled. He had been briefed concerning the 'sealing of each level' but he had not been totally convinced that the 'seal' was no more than a well orchestrated bluff in order to exert some control over the people already living in the caverns. He watched as Skip disarmed several, small sections and queried the readouts being displayed below the monitors noting the oxygen levels had already nearly reached life-sustainable levels.

Skip pointed to a couple of coats hanging next to the exit door, "We're going to need those. The heat will not be at a comfortable level for several hours and, since we won't be down here long enough for that, I didn't bother to turn it on", he explained.

Boston nodded both understanding and approval as he walked over to the door and selected a jacket that would fit his broad shoulders. He tossed another one to Skip before putting his hand on the door, "ready?"

Skip zipped up his coat, "whenever you are."

Boston opened the door with a grunt. The pressure outside the room had not yet equalized with the livable environment inside the control room. It was definitely colder in the 'outside' area of the treatment plant and he quickly stuck his hands into the lined pockets. After only a dozen steps or so he also realized that Skip was still joking with him because there was no 'smell' on this level as he had alluded to earlier.

The treatment plant on the engineering level was built to be able to process sewage from all the levels. Yet, this was a redundant feature, too. Every level had this capability so that the engineering level could be, should be used only as necessary. Most of the processing machinery was contained within sound-deadening areas such that only a soft hum was discernable while walking from one building to another. *One item of note*, Boston thought, *is that everything was actually larger than how it appeared on the monitors.*

Skip escorted Boston through the partially unsealed areas within the facility. Monitors were everywhere displaying the various contents being processed with multiple readouts describing the statistics and thresholds of the machinery in use throughout the plant. "You should be able to obtain the same readouts in your security control rooms, on every level, as well as on your staging level, that are available down here", Skip explained in his instructive tone of voice. "The idea is to have a surveillance team on each level to monitor the various activities so that, if anything begins to go wrong, besides the alarms that would sound out here", Skip gestured towards the next set of display screens, "they could be proactive to get the right people to the right place to make whatever repairs are needed."

"Are all the levels like", he paused for a moment and waved vaguely at his surroundings "this? You know, do they all have this quantity of sensory equipment, display screens and technical readouts? That would be an awful lot of information, maybe too much for practical research and application."

Skip nodded appreciably, "All the technical levels are nearly saturated with sensors so that, if anything should go wrong, help could be summoned as quickly as possible. The living areas do not have anywhere near the number of sensory receptors. We wanted to be able to safeguard the city without sacrificing the privacy of its citizens."

"Of course, that intent could be modified according to whoever had control over your city, right?" asked Boston innocently. They had completely traversed the small section that had been earlier unsealed and were now headed back to the security control room.

"Yes, that could happen", mused Skip aloud. "Yet, we have attempted to install power checks, overrides and redundancy in all areas of control so that no one person could or should be able to exert control over the entire city." Skip quickly added, "A well-led organization may be able to assume control over key elements of the city but how long could it last? Each level has the capability to monitor and, if necessary, mimic almost every possible function that has been assigned to the technical levels."

Skip stopped outside the control room and shook his head in derision. In a quiet, reflective voice he repeated, "Yes, it could happen. It would be a shame if all the people in this city allowed themselves to be subject to a dictator, a tyrant or even just a well-meaning leader that only wants the best for everyone."

Boston opened the door to the control room, and as the warmth flowed past them into the corridor, he gestured for Skip to enter the room. He quickly followed his companion inside and shut the door securely behind him. Once their body temperature had begun to resemble something normal, the coats were shed and re-hung next to the door. Skip ambled over to the control panel, "You may as well take some notes, I would be very surprised if you were not doing this fairly soon."

Indeed, Boston took copious notes while Skip explained the instructions to once again shut down the oxygen levels and re-seal the level. "It sure doesn't take a lot of time" Boston muttered as he watched the gauges and readouts show the continuous drop in the atmosphere outside of the control room. It was a little unnerving as to how quickly the oxygen was bled from the now-vacant level.

Skip looked at the security chief for a brief moment and gave him a quick 'thumbs-up' sign before straightening up to perform an examination of the control room as a quick 'once-over' check before they departed. "Looks good", he said, "We didn't spend a lot of time down here so there isn't a whole lot for us to shut down. Just make sure the coffee pot is turned off before you leave. You ready?"

Boston had also walked the room, looking for items of interest that may lend to questions in the future. "Sure, are we going to hit any of the upper levels on the way out?"

Skip shook his head after checking his watch, "Not a chance. One, the top three levels are in various stages of construction. Two, I need to get you back to the citadel to complete your orientation and most importantly, three, I don't want to miss dinner!"

* *

Boston Jeffries spent the next three days in his pseudo 'upstairs' inner office laboriously pouring through the data that had been collected from each of the eight levels. The amount of information being absorbed via the sensors, then, processed, condensed and sent to the security chief's console was astounding. At first, the sheer volume of data was so daunting that he spent most of his time merely organizing and storing the information for later use. As he slowly became used to the type of information and the repetition of data, especially from the sealed levels, Boston began to get a better understanding as how to utilize the data for his particular needs.

The next three weeks were spent in the staging level security office studying the data and making short forays into the caverns. Most of the trips were to assist him in becoming more familiar with each accessible level and the work crews deployed throughout them. There were two trips in particular that he made into the caverns; once to plant specific items on various unsealed levels and once more to retrieve them. He wanted to test the sensor readings and their ability to pick up organic, metallic and biological data. Satisfied with his results, he glanced at his wrist watch before drawing a deep breath and once again pulling the manifests of the materials being delivered into the caverns back in front of him. "It seems", he muttered to himself, "that it may be almost impossible to find any illegal personnel that have already been accepted into the workforce. But I am pretty sure I can keep any more from getting in."

A small light momentarily lit up on his desk top. *Right on time*, Boston thought to himself. He quickly re-checked his outer-office security monitors. Satisfied, he pressed the button that released the bookcase door to the cavern lift. The bookcase slid quietly open and Skip White strolled into the room. He stepped aside to watch the bookcase silently close behind him, then stepped up to the now-standing Boston Jeffries, "Hello Boston" he stuck out his hand.

Jeffries quickly grasped it and motioned Skip towards an easy chair that he had purchased to mimic the one his friend had in his cavern office.

Skip smiled and promptly plopped into his chair before he asked, "What do you have for me, today?"

Boston quietly outlined the new sensors and software requirements that he wanted added to his staging area. He explained how he could use the data gathered from his new sensors to identify anyone and anything that was not on the manifest list.

Skip nodded with appreciation and said, "No problem. I can have those sensors installed and ready for your use within the week. But, you do realize that you may become unpopular pretty quickly, don't you?" Skip laughed as he saw the look of surprise and puzzlement that appeared on the security officer's face. "C'mon, surely you know that some of the 'illegal' personnel have been smuggled in for, ah, entertainment purposes, just as some of the smuggled materials are used to make good old fashioned moonshine. You may well put some people out of business."

Boston just shook his head ruefully for a moment, "It's always the same. If I do the job right; I get criticized."

Skip just laughed, "I'm not being critical, I am just informing you. Once you've compiled your list, run it by me. If there are any materials that you haven't already identified their use, I'll see if I can shed some light on them for you."

Boston nodded appreciably, but before he could say anything else, Skip added, "That goes for any personnel you find. By the way, how are you at taking bribes?"

The security Chief's eyebrows rose perceptively before he answered, "Not good. I never have been. Why do you ask?"

"That's fine. Just be aware that you will no doubt be approached. Those people that you may be putting out of business will very likely not go without some sort of a struggle. I will need to know their names, naturally."

Boston watched Skip carefully, "Naturally." It was very likely that Skip already knew which persons would approach him with a 'business proposal'. Not much happens on Skip's watch that he doesn't already know about. Skip was merely reminding him that the security chief had the power to arrest and hold people but Skip had the final authority over the personnel within the caverns.

At that moment, the outer office monitor came alive. The face of a serious young man appeared briefly on the screen, "Ms. Brunson and Mr. Kennedy are here to see you, sir."

"Excellent. Send them in."

Carol Brunson quietly entered the room. She stopped only long enough to look over the room to identify any changes the security chief may have made to make the room appear more 'real'. With a short nod of her head and a wink to Skip, she casually slid into a small lounger close to the door.

Asman strolled into the office stopping just long enough to shake hands with both Boston and Skip before settling into the only other chair that was not in use. "Did we miss anything?"

Boston quickly caught them up on the latest sensory additions that would have to be installed in both the Citadel and the caverns.

Carol nodded appreciably as Boston explained that the improvements would no doubt affect how the shipments from the Citadel would be packaged and received.

Asman merely shrugged. He had been expecting this or something like it almost from the moment Boston Jeffries was hired. "As more and more people arrive and the city government makes a greater presence in the Citadel, we will have to be more careful. In the 'old days', Skip and I were practically the only ones who even knew there WERE lifts to the caverns."

"The 'old days' . . . you mean three or four cycles ago?", Skip chuckled. "But, yes, you are right. There are just too many people that could notice. Still," he sighed, "since levels four through eight are completed and sealed, they won't require any other shipments. And levels . . ."

Skip interrupted himself and looked towards Boston, "This IS what you wanted us here to talk about, right Boston?"

Boston had asked for the Citadel and the 'caverns' key players to meet with him and generally discuss what was happening in their prospective environments. He was hoping to acquire a basic knowledge of the activities and problems that existed so he could do his best to have solutions and manpower available should the occasion arise.

The security chief briefly nodded and Skip continued, "Levels four and five are both in various stages of being sealed. As each sealing stage is completed, the levels are thoroughly inspected to insure all the people and pets are gone. Oh yes, there are plenty of pets down there", he added when he saw the surprised expressions on their faces. "The inspectors are also supposed to ensure that any and all necessary materials have been replenished. It is surprising how some of what we call 'necessary' materials are also considered necessary by the construction crews. A lot of that stuff just disappears."

Boston and Carol were looking at Skip in amazement. Skip merely laughed, "The workers take things because they think they will need them on the next level and don't have enough belief in the management" as he pointed to himself, "to ensure that they have those same items on the next level. It all works out. We find the materials and store them away for when we are ready to seal the next level and they do it all over again. Besides", he said with a short shrug of his shoulders, "if all the items are not found, usually, only a small, replacement shipment is all that is needed to make sure that the level has everything that it needs."

Skip leaned back in his chair and stared at the ceiling while he recalled information concerning the last three levels. "Let's see . . . Level three is almost completed. The living areas will have to be inspected carefully because the work crews from levels two and three were combined awhile back which means they have lived there for quite some time. They will be pretty reluctant to leave."

Asman and Carol squirreled a little deeper into their chairs. They had heard all of this before. Boston was the one who needed to pay attention and he was busy taking notes and checking off items on his notepad.

"Every level has a small sea of purified water", Skip continued. "Boston, what do your sensor readings have to say about the status of the water?"

"The water is perfect and there is going to be a lot of it." Boston looked up from his notes, "With all the water from the dam you would think that eight levels of underground lakes would be somewhat unnecessary."

"I suppose that depends on what kind of usage is expected and the long term availability of the water from the reservoir."

Boston had become familiar with the redundancy of materials, power, water, toilet paper . . . It seemed that nearly EVERYTHING was duplicated.

Skip glanced at Asman, "Are the trees ready?" he asked.

The 'trees' which Skip was referring to were actually a wide variety of trees, shrubs, plants, flowers, and vegetables that had to be obtained, transported and stored until the levels could support their growth. Every level had a small hydroponics garden area and those areas had to be carefully protected when the levels were sealed in order to ensure their survival. Level three, however, had the largest of the hydroponic farms. The underground vegetation was being grown using simulated sunlight and the water being drawn from the dam and the underground reservoirs. Water has always been a precious commodity and the designers of David's City have ensured that each level would always have a sufficient store of it.

Boston nodded his understanding; he had forgotten about the hydroponic farms and gardens. For as much time as he had spent reviewing the video and sensory readings from the growing areas, he knew better than to forget about them. A fair number of workers had built shelters, some even homes, in the gardens since the bio-sensor readings had not shown that there were humans 'growing' with the plants. His sensory enhancements to the farming sectors readily displayed the illegal activity and he had the workers (and the pets) promptly removed.

"Yes, they are ready. You'll be receiving your 'trees' starting next week. Boston, you should already have the manifests." Asman rolled his eyes, "remember, the shipment may be delayed if we get too many questions." He has always had difficulty removing the quantity of plants from the Citadel and delivering them to the cavern lifts with secrecy. As he has said at this time in the events calendar for each level, "People don't care if you are moving a bunch of boxes. People ALWAYS seem to notice when fruits, vegetables and trees suddenly disappear."

Skip and Asman continued to discuss the shipments expected for each level. All the flex stone had long since been installed but level one still needed building material for the internal structures while the work crews on level two were still trying to complete the last of the plumbing and electrical work.

Boston continued to take notes. He needed to be very much aware as to who and what might be on which shipments to keep any contraband from appearing in the caverns. He had a hunch that, as the last levels were being completed, people would be making their greatest effort to secret themselves and whatever materials they ordained necessary for their survival in the caverns.

The security chief finished writing down the last comments from the two engineers when Skip asked, "Does that give you enough information about the shipments to the caverns for now?"

"It does, thank you. I'll be watching the shipments a little differently by the end of the week and, don't you worry, I'll let you know who complains or asks questions about the heightened security checks." Boston closed his notes, stood up and stretched.

Skip grunted his understanding then turned back to Carol, "So, how's it going in your world? Did Max and David move in yet?"

"Oh yes," Carol began. "They've moved in a week or so ago. She really likes it there. Tensions had been running pretty high in the city again so, as you can imagine, she was really looking forward to getting out of there. She was just telling me . . ." Asman gave Skip a quick wink as Boston let out a soft groan and slowly sat back down.

He softly cracked his knuckles before he pulled open his notes and reached for his pen. With a quiet sigh he prepared to write down whatever tidbits of information Carol might give him that would help him with his 'upstairs' security responsibilities, within the Citadel.

CHAPTER ELEVEN

"There has been a what?!" David exclaimed loudly over the audio. "Where? How bad is it?" David had leapt to his feet when he heard Boston's brief description of the most recent citizen rampage. His security chief began to fill him in concerning the details and David began his characteristic pacing in front of his cluttered desk.

Over the past several months, the city had suffered through more riots and demonstrations. A small number of the demonstrators had gotten quite violent, and were quickly arrested for general destruction of property, harassment, and assault. However, for the most part, these acts of frustration from the private citizens had been merely an annoyance to the governmental officials of York-City. The Mayor's answer to the problem of unrest among his citizens had been to beef up the security, erect monitored walls and barricades around the buildings and facilities considered 'critical' to the city and issue warnings to the populous that violence in his city would not be tolerated.

For the past few weeks, life in the city had appeared to have returned to a fairly calm state, as if the Mayor's tactics had done their job. But, as Max had put it, tensions were definitely running high. Despite the employment opportunities provided by the construction of the dam and the creation of the Citadel, there were just not enough jobs for the number of people that needed them. And, now that most of the construction had been completed or was rapidly nearing completion, much of the Kendal Enterprises-employed work force had been returned to the already bloated non-servicing pool. It should not have been a surprise to anyone that a growing number of the populous had become increasingly dissatisfied with the lack of progress towards their welfare. That prevailing attitude from the common people, coupled with the Mayor's 'don't EVEN get angry in MY city' policy, had provided the opportunity for violence to once again erupt within the Honorable Posin Kourie's troubled metropolis.

"Let me get this straight, there have been three explosions in the city and they were all the result of the detonation of private transports?" David was incredulous. He could recall from history that, previous to the radiation wars, fanatics, called terrorists, used to blow up cars and trucks at strategic points within a city to cause destruction and widespread panic. Lately, there had been violence in the city, sure, but that kind of wanton destruction, oblivious to who was caught in the maelstrom, had not been seen since the reformation of the city.

Jeffries continued to monitor the newsreels as he spoke with his boss, "The city's power distribution center has been crippled and the barricades in front of the Mayor's mansion have been wiped out. As expected, a small army of city guards had been immediately substituted for the barricades until the steel and concrete barriers can be replaced." Boston was attempting to provide David with enough information as quickly as possible so that David would be prepared to handle the requests for energy, sanctuary and who knows what else that would no doubt come his way.

David switched on the newsreels in his office to find that nearly every station was showing the same scenes of destruction and chaos. The location most often displayed on the view screens was the mayhem being enacted in front of the Mayor's mansion. The Mayor's estate and surrounding property were in flames and not just from the explosion of the government transport. A small army of hostile people had sought protection from behind various sections of the vehicle's wreckage; the bodies of their former comrades were strewn about the once-manicured lawn after their latest foray to overwhelm the guards protecting the mansion. The immense home had not been touched by the fires and explosions but there were plenty of furious people trying to get close enough to correct that oversight. The city guards were performing an excellent job holding their positions against a numerically superior force, probably because the guards were well-armed whereas the irate mob being kept at bay were not. His father's words from long ago came unbidden to his mind, "When the right to bear arms is taken from the people, no matter the reason provided by the political party responsible, the people's ability to defend themselves from tyranny is also taken away."

From time to time, the bedlam at the Mayor's mansion would be interrupted in order to show live video from what used to be one of the primary power stations in York-City. The stunning scene of human carnage was sickening. Since this facility had been strengthened into a veritable fortress, many citizens had been massacred as they assaulted the well-defended stronghold. Yet, this attack must have been well contrived because the frontal assault had been a diversion while a secondary attack of the walls of the energy station were breached away from what had been considered the primary point of attack. "They used the frontal assault as a distraction", David mused aloud, "in order to pull away enough of the station's resources to break into the facility from the east side. That must have been where the other transport explosion took place."

The stations were continuously updating the viewer with scenes and dialogue of progress being made by the governmental officials as they swapped back and forth between the two chaotic scenarios when a thought occurred to David that he immediately voiced. "You said there were three explosions but I am only finding information on two. Where was the third one?" David asked Boston.

There was only a short pause before Boston Jeffries replied to his employer, "The third one was at the entrance to the Citadel." Boston paused briefly, then, continued, "It is possible that he detonated that one himself in order to keep the crush of people out of our city and to preserve the integrity of the dam." Boston's voice was carefully neutral but David was already sensing that something other than the explosions was wrong.

David quietly asked, "And what does Asman have to say?"

"Asman Kennedy is dead, sir." Boston took the time that his boss was using to process the shocking news to take a deep breath of his own. "A huge crush of people had rushed the Citadel using the entranceway from the dam. Asman had the construction cranes place huge sections of flex-stone across the dam to block their path. That divided the force of people and stopped any more of them from getting closer to the city. However, the smaller mass that had already gotten past the blockade not only continued towards the Citadel but, it turns out, were armed with some explosive devices, a lot like the one that killed your father and brother. They torched the cranes and touched off a series of fires while they made their way towards the city."

David had halted his pacing and was, instead, breathing heavily and leaning against the wall of his office. He was doing his best to stave off the memories of the night that the rest of his family was killed. "Concentrate." He kept telling himself.

"Mr. Kendal?" Boston asked.

"Yes, I am still here, but you will have to repeat that last part", David said slowly.

Jeffries spoke slowly but clearly, he did not want to have to repeat this a third time, "Mr. Kennedy took his private transport and flew out of the city, straight up the entranceway toward the mob. The transport exploded just as it reached them. They may have thrown something like when . . . , um . . . , before . . . , or Asman, himself, may have exploded it." The security chief sounded distant but his words were still quite clear. "I had him on audio", he continued. "I had finally made it up from the caverns and had the lifts closed when he told me that they were not going to get any closer." Boston took another breath, "that's when his transport blew up."

David thought he was stunned after watching the newsreels and the videos of the city-wide destruction. But now, as he staggered back towards the director's chair pausing again to lean on his desk, he felt again the horror and shock that he had felt when his father and brother had been killed.

Boston sensed David's shock over the audio and kept talking, hoping that his words would help distract him, "I have it all on video and I have a copy of our transmission. I cannot determine how his transport was destroyed, yet. But, I CAN tell you that the debris from its destruction killed a fair number of people in the crowd and managed to block the only other way into the city." Boston felt exhausted, "We have rounded up both crowds and have the mob that had confronted the transport in custody. We'll keep them until the city guards come and get them."

The security chief was grasping for something to say to ease the pain, and after another short pause said, "He very likely kept the new city from being ransacked by that mob of people and I am SURE he saved the dam from being severely damaged."

At first, David could not manage to say much of anything. With a ragged breath he tried to continue the conversation, "It may be awhile before anyone will come for them."

Boston waited. He may have to repeat himself after all.

Another breath and David's voice began to steady somewhat, "York-City is in a State of emergency, I doubt the Mayor will spare anyone to come out here; he no doubt believes that he has enough problems of his own."

Finally, he was finding some stability, "Yes, there is no doubt that Asman protected his last project, the Citadel and its people with his life. He has always been one of my heroes. Now, he is a hero to many more."

Boston continued to be silent.

David was working through the haze of confusion and doubt, "Would you find Skip and ask him to join you up here with me? We are going to have to be prepared to lose the city sooner than we had hoped."

David broke the connection and dropped unceremoniously into his father's chair. "Why?" he thought. "Why does it have to be this way? Why did it have to be Asman?" He looked up at a picture of his father and brother, "Why did it have to be anybody?"

* *

The Mayor certainly had plenty of his own problems. One third of his staff had been killed in this last attack. Power, transportation and communications throughout the city had been disrupted. There was roving bands of people, armed with make-shift weapons, ready to set upon anyone that had the appearance of a government official. He had set up a COMM link from his mansion and was even now broadcasting to what was left of his leadership corps, "No, I will not allow a single guard to leave here." Mr. Kourie paused for a moment while his security force pleaded in vain for more troops, "No, you will just have to figure something else out. What you CAN do is put every residential area into a complete blackout. I only want our facilities to have access to the power and water supplies. Kill the power to every other sector. Then sweep each area with whatever the troops that you have left. Shoot anyone that resists. Arrest anyone that you have any reason to believe was involved."

Mayor Kourie turned to the communications controller and angrily spat, "Where the hell is David Kendal?"

"We've got him, sir. We were waiting for you to finish before we cut you over", the technician looked distinctly uncomfortable trying to explain the delay to the Mayor.

David's image suddenly appeared on the Mayor's main view screen. A metallic voice announced David's arrival on the COMM link.

"Mr. Kendal", the Mayor began without preamble. "I want your discs installed in my headquarters and any other facility that has had its energy disrupted. How soon can that be completed?"

Posin Kourie was an accomplished politician. He had the capability to stir the minds of thousands whether he addressed them from the podium, broadcasting studio or from a simple fireside setting. He also had the ability to show his arrogance and desire for control at a moment's notice. In his current state of mind, he was exuding an air of absolute control and dominance. He expected everyone to do exactly as they were told as soon as they were told and he wanted the results from his orders to happen NOW.

"Power restoration is already in progress, sir. We've already dispatched—", David began.

The mayor had motioned to switch over to another view screen. He had given his command. He fully expected the youngest Kendal to jump at the order and have power restored to his command centers before the end of the day.

"Brose?" the Mayor snapped. Captain Brose had been waiting to serve him long enough. "How long before we are in the Citadel?" Posin had found the name of David's little creation quite amusing. He had sent his 'requests' for buildings, facilities and power needs from the time the fledgling city was first erected knowing full well that he would acquire it when the need suited him. 'The Citadel' was exactly what he desired right now. It would give him the space needed to adequately control the city populous while ensuring that he and his people were not impacted by energy needs or lose any of their acquainted comforts.

Captain Brose answered carefully, "I have our people in the Citadel on standby, sir. The computer switchover will be initiated as soon as the power distribution levels have stabilized. We can be in your new headquarters within the week." Susan Brose may not respect the Mayor, actually, she despised him but she WAS the Head of City Security Services and she was the absolute best person available for her job.

"Good." the Mayor clipped. "See that your time-table is accurate." He signaled the COMM controller to end his outgoing transmissions and replace the display with the news of his city. Now that his commands had been given, Posin wanted to relax in his immense easy chair and watch his orders being meticulously carried out.

The media stations had been 'his' for quite some time now and they had their orders as to which sections of the city were to be publically broadcasted. Since only his administration's facilities now had the capability to view the broadcasts, they were free to report on details within any sector of the city. It was quite satisfying to watch the crews falling all over each other to give him the best and latest details of his city-wide cleanup effort.

One of the attacks was very well covered on his third monitor. With morbid curiosity he watched as his small bands of heavily armed security forces attacked sparsely armed citizens. It did not seem to make a difference to his troops whether the citizens were armed or not as they fired into the crowds. At first, more people simply replaced those that had been gunned down. It didn't take long, however, before the crowd began to split up; some merely ran for whatever cover they could find, others took strategic positions to further the standoff while still others just ran away.

Other monitors showing the conflicts from within other sections of the city were displaying much the same scenarios. Many brave but foolish people were efficiently countered while whichever people did not escape in time were arrested and stuffed into military transports. It was with grave satisfaction that the Mayor witnessed the end of many of the riots in his city. Posin shrugged his shoulders, as he mentally calculated the cost of overtime that would have to be paid. The disposal units will be very busy for the next week or so.

He only had one more item of business to attend to. "Is she still waiting?" Posin called out to his communications officer.

"She is, sir."

"Put her on audio, only."

The COMM controller signaled to the mayor that his contact was available on his audio and, after a moment or so, Posin picked it up and said, "Meet me in my office in the morning. You need to sign some papers." Without waiting for an answer, he severed the connection and went back to watching his city being cleansed.

CHAPTER TWELVE

The new Kendal Engineering Enterprises building erected within the boundaries of the Citadel was not an overly large edifice, nor was it ornately adorned with sculptures, shrubbery or ornamental facial-work. The rectangular-blocked building *was* completely self-sufficient, however, and the entire facility utilized every bit of the most modern technology available to the builders. Moving walkways had been employed from the multiple subway terminals and transport parking areas powered by the discreet usage of the solar disks. Within a short walk, be it via the mobile walkways, or the walk/bicycle paths, were the athletic facilities, cafeterias and nearby restaurants and bars. The foyer within the entryway to the first floor was spacious and open, with several information stations to assist the visitors and businessmen to their proper destinations. Every floor employed solar-shielded windows that harnessed the energy from the abundant sunlight yet allowed maximum viewing potential from inside the building. Horizontal transportation was available from the glass-walled elevators, down the halls, to every conference room on each of the ten floors.

Every conference room was equipped with liquid, plasma view-screens and monitors both mounted on the walls and available for individual use on the large conference tables. All along the hallways and between the rooms, holographic images displayed various examples of the latest inventions and technologies and how they were put to use within the Citadel.

The members of the Citadel and Cavern project teams were not interested in any of the modern marvels or refreshment conveniences. David Kendal, Skip White and Boston Jeffries had already arrived and had staked out their respective places within the executive conference room. David was pacing behind his chair at the head of the heavy, maple conference table, while Boston was already seated at the table opposite David but nearest the door to the room. Skip sat uncomfortably in a stark, efficient chair nearly dead-center between the other two men absently fumbling with the view-screen controls that operated the abundant monitors spread liberally throughout the room.

A muffled disturbance just outside the conference room door was an indication that more of the team members had arrived. A soft click of the security lock being disengaged was quickly followed by the entry of Carol Brunson and Trish Vonner. They both smiled their greetings as they headed for opposite sides of the table, sitting down close to Skip but leaving David to himself at the far end of the conference room.

David gave everyone a chance to get settled before starting the meeting, "Alican Sykes will not be present today since this meeting has everything to do with areas outside her interests." Without further preamble, David looked at his chief engineer, "Skip, please bring up the Citadel."

Skip entered commands into his console and obediently produced a holographic image of the new city on the table directly in front of David. Skip looked up at David with an inquiring look and, at a nod from his employer, included the dam and the immediately surrounding area.

The reservoir looked stunning. The level of water had continued to rise, giving life and beauty to an area that had, for decades, been decimated by radiation and ignored by its closest human inhabitants. The railings bordering the walkways that traversed the dam glistened in the holographic-provided artificial morning light. A wide entranceway on the east side of the crevice edge clearly marked the beginning of the transport path along the dam that was bisected exactly in the middle of the dam with a roadway that led directly across the chasm of rushing water and into the city that Carol and Asman had designed.

The stark contrast between the austere efficiency of the dam and the splendor that was exhibited along the entranceway to the Citadel was clearly defined and displayed for Board members. The structure of the dam and the transportation ways to and from the facility were efficient, clean and open while the pathway to and from the Citadel, beginning at the center of the dam was landscaped to give the impression of preparing to enter a carefully prepared garden. The conduit over the water freed from the spillways was lined with railings and borders to guide visitors safely across the frothing water. The dull roar and light mist created from the man-made waterfall added to the illusion of entering into a lush, new land. Nor was the visitor disappointed! The protective railings gave way to shrubbery and trees—continuously watered by the ever-present mists. Flowers, grasses and decorative flora had been planted, tended with meticulous care, to become increasingly visible as people approached the gateway to the new city.

The water beneath the entranceway gave way to mounded earth that had been heaped up to create the immense man-made island between the steep canyon walls. Groves of deciduous and evergreen trees had been planted within each terraced wall of the Citadel to give beauty to the entranceway as well as retard erosion from the foundation of the new city. Just outside of the outstretched reach of the branches of the closest trees to the Citadel's gateway stood two guards, planted boldly on either side of the broad entranceway. These minutely detailed statues, easily twice the size of an average-sized man, were carefully carved from stone to resemble historical colonial soldiers from the former U.S.A.

Skip, Carol and Trish were excitedly discussing the myriad of details, both of thought and design that had been incorporated into the construction of the entranceway when David nodded to Boston Jeffries to begin the next portion of the presentation.

Slowly, the vision presented by the holograph began to change. Boston carefully overlaid the holograph's image with video, then, added audio captured from the tragic event that led to Asman's death.

A huge crowd of shouting, angry people had suddenly appeared at the entranceway of the dam, easily overpowering the small security group that had been placed there to handle the normal operation of the dam. Another security force had been sent from the Citadel to bolster the garrison already stationed at the canyon's edge but, despite the haste made by the second force, the infused crowd had already overran the gateway guards and were advancing unhindered towards the broad, connecting tarmac that connected the bridgework of the dam to the corridor to the Citadel.

Asman and Boston's voices could suddenly be heard over the roar of the demonstrators directing three huge cranes to block the corridor with sections of flex-stone that had been discarded as rubble. Howls of protest erupted from the crowd as the huge barricade was painstakingly placed in their midst. The operators tried diligently not to crush anyone as the crowd continued to swarm between the stones and debris until, finally, the flow of human madness had been cut off.

A small group of people in the forefront of the mob had managed to get ahead of the mass of stone that had been carefully placed on the walk and transport ways. Perhaps these people were encouraged and inspired by the ones stranded behind the barricade. Maybe it had been the plan all along as fires were set and small explosions began to erupt just at the point where the corridor from the Citadel bisected the dam ways.

Amid gasps and groans of dismay from the conference room spectators, the additional security force had arrived and instantly charged into the dense crush of people. Although the defense of the city was valiant, once again the smaller security force could not stop the press of the larger mass. After an all-too-brief skirmish, Asman and Boston's backup troops were pushed aside and the emboldened mob continued to march steadily towards the Citadel.

Railings and borders were torn from their holdings and thrown into the foaming abyss. Trees and shrubs that were planted as inspirational banners along the entranceway of the new city were set ablaze as explosions continued to rock the passageway to the city. Small craters pock-mocked the once-smooth corridor as the crowd pressed ever closer to the two stationary colonial guardians.

Boston cautiously worked his controls to bring the spectator's focus to the entranceway of the Citadel. It was towards this gateway that Asman drove his small, personal transport from the haven of the Citadel and halted, for the moment, just behind the protection of the immobile guards. The security Chief's face grew hard as his own words echoed within the small conference room, "I am out of the cavern's, Asman. Wait for me. We still have time!"

The holograph suddenly switched to the inside of Asman's craft. The pilot, Asman himself, sat at the controls alternating between seething with rage and extreme disappointment and sadness as the oaths shouted from the approaching people grew louder in the background. His hands twitched on the controls as he tried to convince himself to wait for the security chief.

"One minute." Jeffries cried desperately over the audio. "Just give me one minute!" Boston had another security force already en route to the Citadel's entranceway. This force was much more seriously armed such that, while it made them less mobile, they would easily halt and repel the advancing mob.

Asman continued to watch the mass of angry people approach the Citadel's entrance with the smoke and ruin of his dam in the background and the destruction of his new city their obvious next goal. He knew that if Boston's troops arrived in time, his city would be spared much of the devastation that had been inflicted to his dam. He also knew that Boston's arrival to the gateway without the armed troops would not, could not stop the crowd.

"They will not get any closer", Asman spoke quietly but clearly into his audio. With that simple declaration, Asman switched off the power to his communications console and, moments later, the sleek craft pulled swiftly from behind the stone guardians and propelled itself towards the mob.

With Asman's video stream cut off, Boston immediately reshaped the holograph image to revert to a wide-angle, aerial view of the section of corridor just outside of the Citadel. The conference room spectators quickly identified the colonial guards and the dark craft picking up speed as it shot from the beleaguered city. The crowd did not hesitate but continued advancing menacingly forward. An explosion rocked the conference room holographic image the moment the small transport entered into the approaching crowd.

The black, heavy smoke slowly cleared away from the scene. The small craft was utterly destroyed. At first, there was no sign that anyone was moving. Gradually, from the outskirts of the ring of fire and debris, small, jerky movements could be seen from some of the bodies that had been blasted by the explosion. Much further from the detonation, some people were cautiously trying to get to their feet. The wild mob of people that had been halved by the placement of the stone barricade had been nearly decimated when Asman's craft exploded. Shock, dismay and fear had replaced the anger and determination that had been so prominent among the marching mob.

The crowd was no longer interested in causing havoc and destruction. In what seemed like a long time but was in reality only a few more minutes, Boston's heavily armed troops finally arrived. The people began to waver and back away from the advancing troops. Boston's voice could once again be heard through the melee, "Stay where you are." The baritone voice was calm, in control and resigned, "Put your weapons down. You are under arrest."

A small number of armed troops surrounded what little was left of Asman's cruiser. The moment the leader of the force signaled to his small company that the area was secured, Boston had the 3-dimensional image frozen. A heavy silence hung in the air within the small conference room.

David gently broke the stillness, "He would not let them damage his city." Simple words, he knew, but Asman's actions could be simply explained. The time-table portrayed by the holographic display had made it clear that the heavily armed cavalry would not have arrived at the entranceway to the Citadel until after the destructive mob would have already entered into the city. "That mob would have disbursed and caused untold destruction to his city and his people before they could have been stopped and rounded up."

The talk around the table slowly began to revive as each person related experiences of Asman's dedication to his work. All conversation was centered on Asman and the city, his death, his work, and how he died by the hands of the same people that had killed his friend and David's father. It was obvious that he had been completely dedicated to his latest creations since he gave his life for their protection.

Finally, Skip pushed away from the table and leaned back in his stiff, office chair and said, "Boston, you need to be commended, as well. The Citadel didn't even receive a scratch, there was no structural damage to the dam and what damage *was* done is already being repaired."

Boston merely shrugged and shook his head, "I didn't do enough." He studied his hands on the table before he continued, "It took me too long to get up from the caverns. By the time I had all the locks in place and I had gotten to my transport, he had already left the Citadel gates."

Carol's face was still puffy from crying as she came to his rescue, "You saw the holograph. You know very well that he had already made up his mind. There was nothing you could have done."

"She's right", piped in David. "There was nothing any of us could have done. And," David hesitated for a moment, licked his lips uncertainly before continuing, "I am no longer certain that our efforts to 'Save the City' even make sense anymore."

Carol Brunson sat immobile with her mouth open in surprise. Trish wasn't much better off. "Wh . . . what are you saying . . . ?" Trish finally was able to ask.

David glanced towards Skip before he tried to explain. "My father and brother were killed by the citizens we have been working our whole lives to help. Now, Asman is dead. We have done everything we could think of to help these people", David said slowly, "and yet some of our best blood has been spilt by them!" This time David took a moment to lock eyes with Skip, then Boston, "I don't know if we can make sure it won't happen again."

"So", Skip leaned forward onto the tabletop, "we just quit? We just abandon the caverns?" Skip's voice fairly dripped with sarcasm, "THAT certainly makes sense!!"

"No", David countered, "We have to finish the caverns", he pointed to the holographic image of the destruction, "but we have to ensure our own safety within the Citadel or the caverns will never be completed."

Carol Brunson unexpectedly cut into the conversation, "That may be harder to do than you think." Trish nodded grimly to her left as Carol continued, "The political situation in the Citadel will make it more difficult, sometimes impossible, to gather and transport material below. Mr. Kourie has control of the Citadel now, remember? His officials are crawling all over the place. They are looking for anything for which they do not already have absolute control and immediately confiscating it. Equipment, property, people, it doesn't matter. The second we attempt to collect anything at the lift sites, the caverns will very likely be discovered."

Carol tilted her head towards Boston but kept her eyes on David. "Sure, we have some pretty slick ways of hiding the lifts but it won't take a dedicated team from the Investigative Services long to find them. And, when they do, you will lose your underground city", she said with finality.

The frown on Boston's face was not encouraging, thought David. Then, looking around the table said, "We will just have to be even more vigilant sending our teams and equipment downstairs."

"It shouldn't be THAT difficult-", Boston began but was interrupted by Trish Vonner.

"It may be harder than you think, Boston", she began. She looked around the table for a moment and observed looks of expectance, confusion and even dread from her peers. "Are you aware that Ms. Jocelyn Kendal has just been added to Posin Kourie's staff?" Surprise replaced all the expressions only to be quickly replaced with dismay and concern. "Her official title is the Chairperson of the Department of the Interior—that is what he is naming the Citadel, his 'Interior Capital' of York-City."

Trish paused for a moment while she listened to something on her audio. "Actually, it will be a LOT more difficult than we thought. Jocelyn is just finishing up her portion of the State-of-the-City address", Trish continued. Looking directly at David she asked, "Would you like to have me re-broadcast it into our conference room or just give you the high-lights?"

Something in Trish's demeanor gave David a sinking feeling. He let out a long sigh before answering, "As much as I hate to put everyone through what will most likely be a terrible ordeal, we should probably see it. Would you, please, display her address on the main conference screen"?

Trish was already entering the commands to replay the video-feed back through the conference room monitor while her peers mentally prepared themselves.

David had reconvened the meeting after Trish announced Jocelyn's appointment to Posin's staff. After all, the primary reason for the previous meeting was to help everyone understand what events had transpired that led up to the death of their friend and peer. Boston's presentation had perfectly captured the tragedy. Unfortunately, the broadcast of Jocelyn's sudden promotion had ruined an already melancholy meeting.

"I've gratefully accepted the position within Mayor Kourie's staff to reorganize and staff the personnel within the Internal Capital. Much of my task will be to monitor the inner workings of the city to ensure there are no more abuses of power like what has been done by the previous administration."

David and Carol sat bolt upright in their chairs while the look of surprise was immediately replaced with absolute outrage. "What is she talking about?! What abuses?! Almost everything we did was at THEIR request! How could she have even suggested such a thing?"

Trish had been ready for an outburst so she was prepared to interrupt the broadcast while her boss and friend vented for a few moments.

Almost simultaneously, David and Carol realized that the video had been paused. With only another comment or two of justification for their anger, just a little red-faced, they re-took their seats. David signaled for the broadcast to continue.

"Mayor Kourie had noticed that the managers of his internal city had been taking liberties with some of the big businesses that had been enticed to relocate to what Kendal Enterprises called 'The Citadel'. It seems that costly land and space allocations had been given to some companies at a substantially lower rate than many other businesses were able to negotiate. It also appears that the previous administration have handed out some unjustified tax breaks and building incentives to friends and colleagues. Mayor Kourie has requested an inquiry of investigation be conducted to identify any other special treatment that had been awarded for possible future favors." At this remark, Jocelyn Kendal gave a small, disappointed smile for the cameras before continuing, "Not too long ago, Kendal Enterprises was a well respected business completely devoted to the welfare of the people of our city. With the untimely demise of Darren Kendal-", she paused momentarily at this point of the broadcast to wipe a tear from the corner of her eye. After another brief moment to compose herself, she continued, "and Robert Kendal, the two engineers most responsible for the company's success, this company has spent most of its time and energy acquiring the patents and inventions that should have been applied in our city, using the new technologies, to provide relief from escalating costs and provide desperately needed employment."

Carol had hunkered down into her chair with a scowl on his face, muttering to herself and trying hard not to make eye contact with anyone in the room.

David had gotten back on his feet and was pacing back and forth behind his chair. "This is so wrong on so many levels" he muttered. He looked up at Skip, wishing he could direct his questions to Asman, "Obviously, she is trying to discredit the company, but, isn't there too much proof to the contrary?" Skip was sitting impassively in his chair waiting for David to work his way through his thoughts. David started to pace again, "We have employed more people in the last ten to fifteen years than any other company has employed in the last five to ten decades! The people KNOW this. Surely they won't actually listen to this trash!" He stopped pacing long enough to search the faces of the members of his board of directors. Plaintively he asked, "The people DO know better, don't they?"

Blank and concerned expressions were all that he received. With a frown and short shake of his head, he signaled once again to Trish.

Grim faced, Trish pressed the controls to, once again, continue Jocelyn's address.

"As you can see, some of the biggest business owners are the ones that now actually 'own' these properties", Jocelyn stated matter-of-factly while pictures of beautiful homes on spacious lands within the Citadel's boundaries were portrayed for the viewers—the same viewership that lived in the old, cramped, apartment-style, York-City housing. Many of the estates being paraded on the view screens were absolutely magnificent to behold. The well-manicured properties contained sculpted fountains in stucco-walled courtyards with private transport entryways and beautiful, well-tended gardens. The homes were almost obscenely large with multiple fireplaces—FIREPLACES—something that has not been seen (except in the Mayor's mansion) in decades!

"It might not make a difference whether the people know better or not, David. This kind of propaganda is not going to help us at all!"

The four executives continued to watch as the city they tried so hard to design and construct to be clean, attractive, productive and efficient was being harshly criticized for being exactly those things, but, only for special, hand-picked big business executives. Most annoying for David and his board was that nearly every home, property and building that was being portrayed as belonging to some private sector 'fat-cat' actually belonged to the Honorable Mayor Kourie and his governmental staff!

A sweeping video of lush farmlands was now being shown to the Mayor's captive audience. Pictures of fields, ripe with fresh vegetables being efficiently harvested, were displayed with captions at the bottom of the screen depicting the high prices of the same produce being sold within the York-City shops.

Carol had been advertizing to the populous for the last few years that the cost of purchasing fresh produce should drop dramatically; although the prices never did decrease. The implication of Jocelyn's words was that something or someone has been artificially manipulating the prices. Another insinuation was that at least one 'someone' was making a fortune pocketing the difference in prices. The malicious advertising was not just implying nor suggesting that corruption was wide-spread throughout the new city, but was downright accusing her and David, the manager and financier of the Citadel, of downright robbery of the cash-strapped under-employed people of York-City!

The scenery changed once again during Jocelyn's broadcast although the message that was being preached by David's sister-in-law remained the same. Pictures of small forests of fruit and nut trees that had been planted on the edges of each terraced level of the Citadel were now being displayed to the hungry masses. The forests appeared clean and quite prosperous; the fruit trees in particular were heavy-laden with near-ripe produce. Identical forests existed, of course without the knowledge of the general public, in many of the underground hydroponic farms. The pictures dramatically changed to show those same orchards in a dreadful, untended state. Vivid pictures rolled across the view-screens depicting a wasted harvest lying spoilt on the ground, unreachable by the hungry populous of the 'old' city. Jocelyn continued her dialogue of chastisement as she bemoaned the waste, "had the city been properly managed, this produce would have been distributed to our city to feed the poor and hungry. This, this monstrous squandering of our resources must stop!"

With another sad, disillusioned shake of her head she continued, "It is hard to believe that in this day of renewed technology and media coverage, corruption of this magnitude could exist this long and cause such damage to our environment and our people!" A grim smile slowly crept across her face, replacing the furrowed brow of disappointment, "However, we have discovered the fraud and abuse. We will pronounce a righteous punishment upon the perpetrators! We will appoint good, honest people to manage our interior Capital and we will enact laws that will permanently discourage this type of activity from ever happening again!"

David watched Carol carefully. This was a woman that had always been devoted to her 'projects'. She and Asman had labored long, hard, days and nights to incorporate the best designs and technology into their creation. Now that the fruits of their labor were finally in evidence for everyone to see, instead of being justly praised, she was being brutally destroyed. Her face was ashen, whether because of anger or shame, David could not tell. Her hands, clasped in front of her on the conference table, were shaking. Rage, probably. David was caught as flat-footed as everyone else and no words were coming to mind that might sooth Carol's spirit. Actually, that was not true. There *were* words but his upbringing kept him from uttering them in this present company!

Jocelyn's next presentation included colorful charts and diagrams that depicted the amount of energy that was being created from the dam and converted from the solar disks deployed about the new city. Mirthless chuckles escaped from several of the board members as the wildly fictitious data was analyzed by energy experts (hired by Ms. Kendal) to portray Kendal Enterprises as, perhaps, the most corrupt business since before the radiation wars.

David wearily waved to Trish, signaling her to stop the offending broadcast. "Do we have any legal recourse?" he asked no one in particular.

There was a short pause while Skip, Carol and Trish looked at one another to see who would take the lead. With a small shrug of her shoulders, Trish piped up, "I'll speak with our lawyers to see what can be done." Her slumped shoulders and resigned expression probably spoke louder than her next words, "But, since that last series of riots by the public, Posin has kept a leash on all vision and audio services. We won't have an effective way to get a rebuttal to the people. Anything that we try to send across the airways will need the City's approval and, although I am sure the broadcast we just watched had it, I sincerely doubt WE will get it."

The intercom light suddenly began blinking an ominous red. David took a deep breath before he touched the button, Yes, Alican?"

"We have a problem", she began.

The room erupted with laughter. After a moment David, with a lopsided grin, continued the conversation, "I am sorry Alican. Things had gotten a little out of control in here. What seems to be the matter?"

"Our security personnel are being told to leave their posts", Alican was struggling to stay calm which was more than what could be said of Boston Jeffries.

"What?" Boston thundered!

"We have been notified that they will be escorted to this facility", with that latest statement, Alican's view screen suddenly began to show video from the Citadel's gateway station. Boston's security garrison was being systematically loaded into governmental personnel carriers while the carved colonial soldiers looked on with indifference. Alican switched to the station cameras that scanned the entranceway to the dam to allow the stunned executives to watch the near-same scenario being repeated.

Boston stood directly in front of Alican's view screen seething with anger. "They have no right . . ." he began in a menacing tone.

David stood and walked over to stand beside his distraught security chief. He nudged Boston's shoulder before he quietly said, "It may be that none of us have rights, any longer."

CHAPTER THIRTEEN

Both children are off to school, Max thought as she leaned back into the cushions of her living room easy chair. *When I went to school . . .* , she paused now to laugh at herself. She had never thought she would ever sound like her parents but, 'With age comes wisdom'—something else her mother used to always say. Max smiled and let her mind drift back to some of the information she had learned while in school.

Maxine had attended the same schools that her parents and grandparents had attended. She knew that at some point in time the well-used buildings and dilapidated sports fields had been new but that was a very long time ago. Her Upper-Level school (they used to be called 'high' schools, she believed) had more than 500 students in attendance at any given time for the past several decades. The government had long ago decided that refurbishing the old schools from time to time was much more efficient than building new ones. Besides, once the general population had become stable in both number and location, it only made more sense to keep the educational systems in the same geographical area.

The stability of the city's population had been an issue as the people in and around the city strived to survive the initial blast and subsequent waves of radiation that drifted across the face of the planet. New York City was no longer inhabitable. The amount of structural damage sustained from the atomic explosion was much too high to consider attempting to rebuild. Not only was the city destroyed, the entire eastern coastal region of the former U.S.A. was iridescent with radiation. Not too far west of what used to be New York City there were a series of lakes and wildlife protected areas where a community of survivors began to gather. Many of the people that had endured the initial blast and the later radiation clouds succumbed to the illnesses they had sustained from exposure. Yet, despite the harshness of the elements, more people continued to straggle into the growing colony.

At first, the possibility of the survivors to be prepared for retaliation from the attack had caused the fledgling colony to become extremely protective as defensive barriers were erected and carefully guarded. Anyone that approached their primitive barricades was thoroughly scrutinized to ensure the safety of their surviving civilization. Yet, the conflict (it used to be called 'war') that was expected never materialized. As each surviving community eventually came to the realization that the calamity that had befallen the U.S. must have transpired throughout the world, the colonies began to focus on rebuilding their cities.

During the first half century, there was an initial growth spurt within the populous of the growing city. The increase of the city's population began to level off as it became more evident that each city had a much smaller piece of un-radiated world with which to sustain. As technology and medical cures were both discovered and rediscovered within each individual city, the population finally began to stabilize.

There was no such thing as a 'cap' or maximum number of children allowed to a family, although legislation to that effect had been bantered around since before the radiation wars. A 'large' family was defined according to whoever was in power at the time. Suffice to say, however, that over the years, a 'normal-sized' family was considered to have two parents and two children. There were plenty of incidental negative side-effects inflicted upon the people for whom the city considered to have large or 'unusual' families. These parents always seemed to have difficulty obtaining good and steady employment even though this was precisely what they needed to support their family. Every child from every family could obtain an education, but children from those larger families were almost never assigned to the more advanced positions that required a higher education. It did not take too many years before the people policed themselves and kept the population growth to a minimal level.

"Funny", Maxine muttered to herself, "David and I had never considered having more than two children. Even though a new city was being created and we knew that there would be more room, food and opportunities, we automatically stopped our family size at the accepted, magic number."

She was very proud of her children and also extremely grateful that they had the means to raise them outside the boundaries of York-City. Dona was an energetic child with bright eyes and what looked to have a bright future. She had soft, golden hair for which her mother wanted cut short so as to be more easily managed while the young girl preferred it long with the opportunity to entertain different styles. Her eyes looked so much like Maxine's that her father commented on them almost every night when he returned home. Although Dona was still very young, only twelve years old on her next birthday (which was rapidly approaching), she had a strong, lean athletic body that would serve her well for nearly any service for which she may decide to enter.

David and Maxine thoroughly enjoyed her quick wit and charismatic antics. David would arrive home from work 'just in time' to join Max as spectators to an energetic performance that had probably been painstakingly rehearsed for most of the day. Then, on their weekly family night together, Dona may spontaneously embark into an acting fantasy or comedy show that could entertain her parents for hours.

There seemed to be some kind of proverb that suggested that children that came from wealthy parents, people who had worked hard for their possessions and status in the world, would most likely turn out to be lazy, insolent and self-centered. Dona was not one of those children. Maxine and David's first-born had a natural gift for compassion; to truly care for those people who seemed to struggle and strive for the basic needs in life. Perhaps the genetic makeup just happened to line up correctly in order to allow the creation of a person that was sincerely grateful for her opportunities and wanted to help others have the same.

There were many well-meaning psychologists that would have remarked that their son, Trevan, could have some serious problems dealing with such an outgoing and extraordinary sibling but, instead, the dark-headed youngster looked forward to planning and participating, acting and singing, or just being the devoted fan of his older and gregarious sister.

Trevan appeared to have inherited the physique of his grandfather. Even at a young age he had a sturdy, clean build, strong legs that consistently placed him in the winner's circle of a number of sporting events and the promise of a thick, powerful upper body that had already earned him the respect from many of his older rivals. Even though Trevan had the athleticism that was characteristic from his father's side of the family, he actually excelled in comprehension and interpretation; Trevan liked to read. His sister could pick up information just from watching others perform the task. Trevan could learn to do ANYTHING from reading the manual or a self-help book.

Both sister and brother had quick, easy smiles. Their competitive natures almost never won out over their desire to work with other people or participate in 'service projects' organized by their mother in the new neighborhoods of the Citadel. Maxine used to take them with her to her workplace and show them examples of the various employment services that existed in York-City and the new opportunities that were being created in their new city. The children would use their mother's work-audios to call each other, pretending to help someone into a service that was 'just right for them'. For all the positive teaching from the environment Max provided for her children, perhaps the most powerful concept the children learned was that no matter how badly someone wanted to be placed into a career path, it would not, could not be possible without the successful completion of the necessary education.

Dona and Trevan rightly considered their educational opportunities as the one, best path to whatever dream they decided would be their future. So, even though they had not yet set themselves apart within any particular school subject, they threw themselves into their studies certain that 'something' would spark their interest; 'something' would stir a hidden desire and their destiny would come into focus. David and Max had always tried to be on hand to further those interests and explain the many possibilities available to those who were willing to work for their future.

That was all before the 'cleansing'. That was before Maxine was forced away from her chosen profession and before David had to be escorted to his office building by city officials. The sleek, personal transport and the assigned guider had been taken away and reassigned to a more trustworthy individual. One whose thinking and goals were more closely aligned to the goals and objectives set forth by the Mayor of York-City.

On her way to work, Maxine used to join the neighborhood throng on the moving sidewalks while escorting her children to school. New friends and even newer acquaintances would point out the latest additions to the growing Citadel skyline as seen from their homes. The children's sudden laughter would drown out the latest member of the community's words of praise and expression of sheer joy of now living within the Citadel and away from the congested and dirty streets of York-City.

It was a short jaunt to the children's educational facility and an only slightly longer journey to the waiting subways that would take the working parents to their places of employment. The high-speed transportation services provided by the city management made it convenient to access any section of the Citadel. Shopping, entertainment, and businesses were within fast, easy reach while riding in the comfortable and secure subway cars.

Now, anyone attempting to board any of the forms of mass-transit available in the new city needed to show authentication papers that allowed them to be transported. A verifiable work visa, your assigned shopping day or an approved document that allowed for 'other' reasons for transportation was necessary or access was, sometimes not very discreetly, denied. This was the same technique that the Mayor had put into effect for York-City after the last series of riots had damaged the power grids and threatened the lives of his staff. Marshall law had been instituted in order to bring order to the streets of the city under his strict control. Those disturbances in York-City were also the catalyst that prompted the expeditious move of his Honor the Mayor and his minions to his new city.

A new land manager had been appointed by the Chairperson of the Department of the Interior and he relished his duties and performed them to the best of his ability. There were a few people that had voiced displeasure that Jocelyn Kendal had exerted her influence to get her son placed into such a 'high-visibility' position. However, Sunis Kendal had majored in land development and real estate in a world that had little vision of land expansion. As the new city had begun to become a reality, Sunis was already well on his way to being considered a new authority in land and property usage.

Sunis Kendal had made some immediate changes to the city's infrastructure in order to align the new city with many of the practices long-since employed within the old city. These changes were, of course, heartily approved by the Mayor and his staff but were quite difficult for many citizens of the Citadel to accept and conform. Some of these changes included the adaption of curfew restrictions applicable to non-governmental employees and restraints limiting the utilization of the mass-transit system.

Jocelyn's son had developed into a tall, nicely-formed young man. Sunis was as tall as his father but with a slighter build that favored his uncle David. He had the same light hair color of his father but wore it according to the most recent fashion styles; including the 'business beard' that was the latest rage. He kept the beard fairly close-cropped with the edges cleanly shaved but wore it thick enough to show that the facial hair was clearly not 'stubble'. He exuded the air of a clean-cut and experienced entrepreneur, not a young man fresh from college.

The executive suite that had been set aside for the new land manager of the Citadel overlooked the same gardens that the Honorable Mr. Kourie's did in one of the most modern buildings within the city that he now managed. He always wore a dark suit as it gave him a more serious businessman's appearance and, like the mayor, he would from time to time carry a green-tipped cane. He did not need it; he was in fine physical shape from spending plenty of time in his family's activity rooms and spas. However, he enjoyed the dignified look it gave him when his photos appeared on the city's view-screens and publications.

Maxine had been denied all use of the mass-transit systems except for shopping trips on her designated days and certified medical emergencies. She still walked with her children to their small neighborhood school, but she envisioned that benefit was probably not going to last much longer. Soon, another educational facility will be completed that will join quite a few neighborhoods together and Dona and Trevan will be transported there.

Maxine sighed. Individual education along with the student's opportunity to challenge the status quo of the teaching institutes was, already, rapidly coming to an end. It was so frustrating to have had such a brief few years of freedom in the Citadel, only to watch it be so quickly stripped away.

She had been given a fragile, crystal trinket as a memorial of her fine service as one of the best York-City Resources Services representatives before her career came to a sudden and apparently permanent halt. The city had offered to keep her on 'retainer' should the need of her excellent services be once again required but, except for some very minor access capability to the city computer systems, she was quite unexpectedly left without employment.

David fared little better. He no longer had use of his personal transport and guider; those non-essential items were appropriated by the government and re-distributed to someone who, by their determination, had better reason for their use. David either rode the public subway to work or was retrieved from his home by a governmental transport and escorted to his office. The official reason, as told by the media, for the close supervision was his gross misuse of power while executing his duties as the Manager of his self-proclaimed city, the Citadel.

Being escorted to and from any destination was, at best, an inconvenience. Having someone watch his every move, monitor his every communication and give approval for his every decision was downright irritating. After all, Kendal Enterprises was his company. He felt that he should have the authority to run his own business how he thought it should be run. He knew better than to question the status quo; no one had those rights except the elitists that ran the city.

For a brief period of time (in its infancy), the Citadel had been a model of both beauty and efficiency. Even though the new city was still far from being completed, the direction the new owners were taking the Citadel was almost a complete reversal from the dreams and desires of its creators. The various neighborhoods that had been purposefully spread throughout the boundaries of the city were being consolidated—like within York-City. The many school systems, created to allow diverse and easy-to-access education, were being shut down while large, new educational facilities were being constructed as the smaller schools were merged together. It was so much easier to ensure only approved subjects were being taught when the students were being instructed by approved professors—like within York-City. Even the various shopping areas and the smaller, often considered 'quaint' shops and markets had been eliminated so that the curfews and controls could be more easily administered to the still fledgling population.

The results were predictable. There were entire sectors within the Citadel that were completely deserted while the inhabitants of other areas struggled to find and maintain housing. Since all the populated areas of the Citadel were being over-used, contrary to the design for which it was built, filth and refuse was not being removed as quickly and efficiently. In a matter of a very short period of time, crowded and dirty conditions suddenly existed. Was it any great of a surprise that, now, evidence of mice, vermin and insects that had not been seen in that area for generations were quickly infesting many sections of the city?

Naturally, the people were not pleased with the changes in their environment. The government, however, was already enacting laws to fix the perceived or reported problems by curtailing the use of disposable items, power, transportation and water. The media was assisting the city officials by spreading the government gospel that using less and wanting less was better for everyone. Now that the population was being consolidated, and everyone was being informed of the laws and regulations, the controls being enacted by the government were becoming easier to enforce—just like within York-City.

* *

Life within the 'old' city had been changing as more emphasis was being placed on the 'new' city. The riots and demonstrations had quite suddenly stopped as the Mayor had placed harsher controls on the citizens of his city. Strict city-wide curfews had been enacted and the citizens knew that being caught for being disobedient was not a pleasant experience. The prison units were packed to over-flowing but, as the Mayor had said, "There can always be made more room for those who cannot abide my laws."

The power grids had been cut off for designated sectors of York-City in order to discourage the citizens from forming alliances and banding together to create another coordinated attack against the city government. Although the city officials had been pleased with the results, they had not considered how the citizens were faring with limited or no government-controlled power and water sources. Fortunately for the citizens of York-city, the governmental officials assigned the task of keeping a tight rein on the populous had decided that their methods of control were working and their attention was increasingly more focused on life within their Internal Capital.

The officials had become less intrusive into the affairs of the people so long as they continued to follow the restraints as outlined within the curfews, transportation and power usage. A closer inspection into the ruined areas that had borne the wrath of retaliation from the city government would have revealed that civilization still existed, even thrived.

Slowly, small groups of citizens banded together to provide food, shelter and protection for themselves and their families. The people were desperately impoverished but they still wanted to live. They figured out how to use the Solar Disks to capture and utilize energy and were careful to ensure the power usage could not be traced by the York-City officials. The disks were used whenever and wherever possible to provide the energy for the basic necessities of life as well as to communicate with other surviving communities. Pockets of resistance continued to grow in number as more of the destitute were found and rescued throughout the city.

They had also worked out how to use the water purification technology they stole from Robert Kendal's 'Community'. Even though many private buildings, offices and residential apartments had been reduced to rubble, some facilities still existed that could be used to store water and provisions. With just a little ingenuity and labor, many of life's necessities were being setup and protected.

An underground network was developed that supplied banned materials, commodities and medicines. Food was being cultivated in abandoned greenhouses and distributed throughout the communities. The people continued to seek for ways to circumvent the stranglehold on the city. Even ammunition, phased out weapons, grenades and home-made bombs were being discreetly stored away for possible future need.

The people were learning to adapt to life without the constant meddling of its government and they were preparing to ensure that their lives would not be interfered with again.

CHAPTER FOURTEEN

"The information you've given me, thus far, has been quite useful", Jocelyn was speaking to a darkened monitor inside her private office.

The private office assigned to the Chairperson of the Department of the Interior was located on the 43rd floor, building four on the Presidential Boulevard of the Interior Capital City. The secure complex encompassed six, massive buildings and surrounding courtyards which included, of course, the offices belonging to the fairly new Department of the Interior.

The terrain bordering the complex was heavily fortified with wrought iron fencing, reinforced with steel cables and concrete barricades. The ground outside of the fortifications had been completely cleared of all obstacles to ensure that anyone approaching the complex was easily detected and, if necessary, targeted. Uniformed troops continuously patrolled the perimeter of the governmental center with an unfailing changing of the guard every six hours.

Inside the fortifications, completely surrounding the complex was a beautifully landscaped environment that had the appearance of an extensive flower garden, complete with fountains, sculptures and neatly trimmed hedges and bushes. Scattered throughout the fragrant setting were small statues and busts that depicted celebrated officials from the city's grand past. Small, man-made waterways crisscrossed the gardens replete with small waterfalls and miniature pools and ponds.

The visitor center was an imposing structure; although still dwarfed by the nearby edifices, it was the first building in the complex; positioned as a guardian to the governmental compound. The visitor's center was a massive administrative center that acted as a traffic cop to the entire complex. Without the proper authorization, correctly signed forms or approved security, entry into the next ring of the inner circle was irrevocably denied. Receptionists were literally housed in this building to ensure the most privileged personnel could be ushered inside, no doubt with their appropriate entourage, at a moment's notice.

"You have provided us with amazingly precise plans and designs with the most minute details of the city—including lists of the citizens that live within each of their quaint, little neighborhoods", Jocelyn continued speaking to the blank screen.

Jocelyn had tersely ordered her security team to crack the encryption code that was being used in order to at least have a visual of the person on the other side of the off-site connection. So far, however, her informant had been able to remain invisible and unknown. The payment transactions that had been made were completed in such a manner as to be completely untraceable. The voice that rarely spoke across the secure channel was so distorted that Jocelyn was only vaguely convinced that it belonged to a female. Even the audio recognition software deployed by her security team continually gave conflicting results.

She had decided more than once that it really did not matter if she ever found out who this person was, just so long as she got the results that she wanted. Still, she hated not having complete control of her assignment.

"Our contract is nearly fulfilled. Just get me those reports that show the power distribution levels and the schematics that authenticate them and you will receive your last payment." Jocelyn had no idea how the information was being gathered but everything had been incredibly accurate to this point. "Do you anticipate any problems obtaining this information?"

There was an annoyingly long pause before a false, static-charged reply was heard, "No problems."

The connection had immediately gone dead quiet once again. She was always annoyed when her contact did that . . . Jocelyn was never really sure if she was still on the line or not. She very much disliked the feeling of stupidity that she may be speaking to empty air. She glanced to the monitor that displayed her communications officer but, as if he had anticipated her query, he could only shrug a response. *Whoever this is, he is GOOD.*

Finally, just as she reached for the button that would terminate the outside connection, a sharp crackle was heard from the informant's line, "There is more."

Again there was a long pause across the connection. Jocelyn refused to say anything, *Let him wonder if I am still here for a change*, she mused to herself.

The voice changed pitch and the speech pattern became absurdly slow but it was still clearly distinguishable, "Double payment."

Jocelyn's neatly groomed eyebrows arched above her flashing green eyes for a brief, startled moment. A small sneer crept across her face but, before she could reply, the voice, in a lower tone and spoken even more slowly was clearly heard without any static whatsoever, "Worth it."

The sneer that had distorted her fine features began to melt away as she considered the proposal. The power usage data was the last piece of information she had required. What could possibly be more important—worth it, according to her spy—that she would need to pay double the price? Yet, everything provided so far, the data, pictures, plans and personnel files had been absolutely 'worth it'. And, what had turned out to be critical information a few years ago, the security assignments and movements, had been essential to her promotion within Kourie's empire.

Now, with a thoughtful look on her face, she spoke just as slowly and clearly into her audio, "It had better be. If you waste my time, I'll have you hunted down and crucified."

Jocelyn was quite certain that her informer had never heard the threat. She was fairly confident the line connection had been severed before she had even decided to answer the question. Still, even though there was no one to heed it, the words needed to be said; making threats had always made her feel better.

* *

The announcement was being broadcast once again. The baritone voice and the uninterested tone always remained the same. The announced time, however, was different each time it was broadcasted, "Twenty-two minutes, Thirty seconds until this level is sealed. Please report immediately to an exit lift."

The small crowd of people gathered in the Security Chief's staging level largely ignored the annoying message. There were still a few anxious women waiting for their boyfriends or husbands to arrive from the final level to be sealed. Every time the message announced the lessened amount of time to report, the ladies would look up at the large, digital display as if to confirm the content of the declaration.

Boston Jeffries carefully watched the security screens that continuously monitored the landing and immediately surrounding areas around each of the lift sites. He was pretty certain that his surveillance was a waste of his time. He had personally supervised the sealing of every level since he had been hired several years ago. He had upgraded the sensory equipment and software before each level had been sealed, but, despite his efforts, there had always been someone left waiting at the lift's doors when the clock had run down to zero. Somehow, a few people had always been able to elude his careful inspection and remain behind.

The sealing process entailed the depletion of oxygen to the point that human survival was impossible without some type of device that could manufacture or store air until the level was once again revived. Boston's sensory examinations included scanning for power usage, since, once the power to the level was cut back to less than two percent, it was fairly easy to discover any illegal machinery that the vacating workers (or workers attempting to stay behind) had left running for their survival. The security chief had sent teams into the identified areas and, although the devices were always discovered and incapacitated by Boston's men, it was a rare occasion that the persons hoping to benefit from the mechanisms were found and brought to safety.

"Nineteen minutes until this level is sealed. Please report immediately to an exit lift."

Boston glanced at his watch and shook his head ruefully. He knew the remaining time broadcasted within the message was exactly accurate but he found himself verifying the countdown just like those still waiting on the lift dock. Every sensory reading that he had available was registering an absolute lack of life on the first floor to David's City. Every monitor and readout was displaying concrete evidence that the final level was ready to be sealed. If it wasn't for the ladies waiting on the dock, he could have already begun the process that would shut down the final level as well as end any remaining human life within the underground city.

He glanced at his watch again. It was only twenty minutes ago that he had brought the waiting women into his security sanctuary to show them a detailed layout of the entire first level. He watched their expressions carefully as he scanned through each sector hoping some stray emotion would betray where the hidden men may be concealed. There was an indication or two that one particular area seemed to attract their attention but no matter how many agents had been sent to the area or what equipment was painstakingly utilized, no one was ever found. All he received for his vigilance was short sentences that indicated where they had worked, entertained and lived during their underground stay. The ladies had said nothing about for whom they were waiting.

Just a few months ago, as Boston toured the final level within the underground city, the scenery he had observed of the last stages of completion was absolutely stunning. A thriving, vibrant community had developed from what had only been the empty shells of buildings, store-fronts and apartments. The many parks and streets that only a scant few months earlier were vacant and barren were filled with men, women and families laughing and enjoying themselves in their self-made community.

The rules formulated by the Board of Directors had been modified, scrapped, re-written and finally ratified as laws to control the behavior within the city. Each level was created and populated then, emptied and sealed in favor of the birth of next level. With the creation of each level, the laws that had governed the previous levels were once again scrutinized until, finally, a system of regulations was agreed upon that would ensure the best chance of survival in their underground world. These people had the opportunity to build something from nothing; had the privilege of testing the viability of living, not just surviving, in their new world.

Of the many people that had been pressed into service to clear the canyon floor and pour the trillions of tons of flex-stone, only a fraction of those people had been chosen to work within the city. Most of those same people were still in attendance now that the final level was prepared to be sealed. These people had built their apartments and made them their homes only to move out and up to the next level and do it all over again. This would be the last time that they would have to leave their subterranean homes. This was a city that had been truly built by the people. Each closing of a level and the creation of the next level was like witnessing the growth of a child progressing through each phase of its life. The hearts and souls of thousands of good men, women and children had been tried and tested during the birth, and death of each level.

Naming the city that stood as the guardian to the caverns below was easy. "The Citadel" seemed to be a natural choice. Finding a name for the subterranean city was hard. Ideas had been submitted by every member of the board. Every name was seriously considered, but despite the effort put into this administrative detail, a fitting name had not been found. Interestingly enough, it was the people who, as they were vacating their homes from one level for the next, kept referring to the caverns as "David's City." This name also was a natural selection; after all, it was through David's direction, persistence and his reverence towards the vision of his mother, father and brother that the dream was actually becoming a reality, not to mention almost all of the financing.

The only real problem was that David didn't like it. "There *had* to be a better name than THAT!" he exclaimed when he had heard the name.

Boston had only grinned and shrugged his shoulders and tried to explain "You can call it what you want, but, if that is what the people who live there are calling it, that is what it will be."

"Fourteen minutes and thirty seconds until this level is sealed. Please report immediately to an exit lift."

Only one week ago, the level was (still) a bustling, frantic hub of activity as the final touches were placed into every section of the level. Each sensor was being checked and re-checked to ensure readings monitored from up above would be diagnosed accurately and correctly acted upon in the event of a problem, difficulty or crisis. Emergency back-up systems and water containment areas were being evaluated, again. These systems not only meant the survival of this level but could have an impact upon the entire city. Water and power back-up and distribution systems were connected throughout the entire complex just in case either of these systems failed on any level. All communications, power stations and sub-stations were being run through the final, rigorous trials that the sealing of the previous levels had proven to be more than adequate to not only close a level; but close a city.

The only remaining restaurants were closing down; perishable foods were being boxed and transported into the storage areas within the staging level. Pharmacies had pulled their drugs, stores had cleared their shelves and all manner of paraphernalia had been gathered into the rapidly filling bunkers within the security of Boston's staging level.

An incredible amount of personal effects was still being hauled out of the housing quarters and the lifts to the staging floor were in continuous operation as the final level was, piece by piece, being evacuated. The children exited the lifts with tear-streaked faces, their hands desperately clutching their most prized possessions. Boston always heard the same question from the mouths of the people both young and old, "Why do we have to leave?"

"Eight minutes until this level is sealed. Please report immediately to an exit lift."

The entire Board probably had more discussions on this topic than almost any other phase of the underground city. Why, indeed, empty the last level if the very next step for the city was to be its population? It had made sense to clear each previous level to ensure that there was no one and nothing left behind that could cause harm or injury to the eco-systems put in place that was needed for the survival of the level—perhaps the entire city.

Once the final level had been built and had reached a functioning state of existence, was it really necessary to displace the thousands of people who had helped create the city in the first place? Was it really crucial to force the removal of the very people that were to eventually return and call it home, a haven from the political forces that were systematically stripping each freedom and individual right from its citizens?

David had made it clear that he had absolutely no intention making the final decision concerning the re-population of the city. The methodology that must be utilized to end the construction phase and begin the colonization of the city needed to have everyone's full support. There was no doubt that completely emptying the final level would be very painful to its inhabitants; however, an even more critical decision would be to choose the people who would have the opportunity to start new lives. This particular god-like proclamation was one that David and his friends and peers wanted very little part.

One line of reasoning that had made the most sense and at the same time relieved the board of the responsibility of that dreaded decision was to allow the current residents to choose their own neighbors. But, first, the city must be emptied. It had been unanimously agreed that the overall security of David's city had to take precedence over the feelings of the people that would be displaced. As Carol had stated, "Why go through the trouble of securing every other level and then allow something or someone to remain in the last level that could cause the entire city to collapse?"

Boston, of course, immediately gave his support to Carol's line of reasoning, "We know within a 98% certainty that all other levels are set to proceed with the best chance of not just survival, but success. Why would we want to jeopardize the entire city? We don't want to stumble at the finish line. We must make sure the entire complex is safe and secure or, instead of giving people a new chance at life, we could be sending people to a very large (and expensive) tomb."

"Five minutes and thirty seconds until this level is sealed. Please report immediately to an exit lift."

"As difficult as it may be to get our people to leave their homes", began Skip, "they would understand that they will have the chance to not only return but bring back others with them as friends and neighbors."

"And if they tell too many people", David asked out loud to the entire group. "The entire city would be compromised. I would consider imploding the entire structure before I would allow Posin and Jocelyn get their hooks into it."

"That's the key to the project, right?" Trish's brows were knit into a tight frown. "Either we bring people in ourselves so that the security of the city is guaranteed, or, we trust the very people who will live there to police themselves."

"It is not a novel concept to give the power to the people. But, it could be a devastating choice." David was, obviously, struggling with the idea of losing control of his city. "Everything we have worked for could be gone, ruined within hours. Is it worthwhile to risk throwing it all away on an ideal?"

Throughout the history of the earth, many of the different religions and faiths have taught that one of God's greatest gifts to mankind was the gift of agency. The gift was given to His creations to choose good or evil, right or wrong. Whether His children would decide to do the things in their lives that would be best for them or to elect a path that would take them to their own eventual destruction.

"Two minutes until this level is sealed. Please report immediately to an exit lift."

History is replete with the descriptions of heroes who had chosen the right course for themselves and for humanity. Unfortunately, there were also many villains who had painted the history books with stories of corruption, greed, and the blood of the innocent all for the purpose of self-gain, egotism, and power.

"Do we truly think this will work?" David wondered aloud. He felt that he could almost understand more of Mr. Posin Kourie's decisions now that he was in a position to lose something very precious, something that had been his to control, to the will of the people. Intellectually, the answer was quite simple; the people should have the power. Emotionally however, the same decision was so much more difficult to make.

The board members patiently waited for David to work through his line of reasoning. Of course the decision was, ultimately, David's to make. Distress was plain to see on his face, his usually peaceful features were distorted with anxiety as the fear of losing their city seemed to be inevitable. The seemingly tangible concern slowly began to fade away as a calm reassurance replaced the fear and doubt.

There was another plan. There was a need to be able to deal with anyone who had worked within the caverns that had shown a reason to be dissatisfied or distrusted. Since these were the people that would not be invited back when the time came to colonize David's City, they had to be convinced that the caverns either no longer existed or were completely uninhabitable. The plan was simple; explain to them that the city must be sealed for at least a generation in order to store the necessary power and water. Then, after everyone had been evacuated from David's City, simulated explosions within the canyon would be discharged. A carefully worded press release would make it clear that the underground city had suffered a catastrophic end.

One of the two plans would be in effect for everyone who had been inside the caverns; however, no matter which plan was chosen, everyone had to leave the caverns. Boston and Skip diligently selected and interviewed each exiting family. Slowly and cautiously, specific work crews and their families were extracted from the caverns and discretely reinserted back into York-City society after they were thoroughly indoctrinated with 'The Plan'.

David suddenly smiled as he remembered a line from an ancient movie, "So let it be written. So let it be done."

There was a quiet exhale of air as if the members of the board had been collectively holding their breath. Skip and Boston nodded as if they had known David's decision all along. Trish had not bothered to hide her relief. *Now they could make the final preparations for the last stage of events.*

The people had to be made to understand the vulnerable state the city would find itself if they spoke too freely or explained the possibilities within the City of David to the wrong people. The hope that fueled the strategy was that the people who had worked so hard to create the levels, structures, communities and homes would not willingly invite undesirable or destructive elements into it. After all, these people had spent the last several years of their lives in neighborhoods unmolested by city officials. They also spent time with their families enjoying personal freedoms and beautiful surroundings that they had only dreamed about before they had become employed by Kendal Enterprises to work in the caverns. They were very aware of the many opportunities that existed and could be destroyed by their own words and actions.

The mechanical crews that had built the oxygenators that would keep everyone alive in their underground homes had formed a pact that they would find other, worthy mechanics who would keep the apparatuses functioning properly. Hydroponic experts covenanted with each other that even if every person in the city perished, their farms and forests would survive; they would only invite the best horticulturists to guard their gardens. Families huddled together, alone or with their closest friends, and together they agreed that they would only talk to members of their families that truly deserved their love and respect and the opportunity to live in the underground city.

"Thirty seconds until this level is sealed. Please report immediately to an exit lift."

No one wanted to be written into what might be a very short history book as the one who had jeopardized their new sanctuary. The people had been armed with a criteria list of their own making and they knew that if they made a significant miscalculation, it could ultimately be the mistake that caused the demise of the entire city. The caverns had survived many growing pains from its infancy during the pouring of the lowest level through the adolescence of the growth of each subsequent level. If it was to survive its adolescent years, its inhabitants needed to choose the best of friends and adopt the best habits.

"Ten", an obnoxious klaxon horn fairly vibrated with short, sharp bursts of sound.

Boston glanced at his watch and, again, shook his head ruefully. He had the level sealing process literally 'down to a science' and, even though he would continue to monitor the landing at the exit lifts for anyone who had suddenly lost their nerve and wanted out, but he didn't expect to see anyone. This phase of the City of David was nearly complete.

CHAPTER FIFTEEN

Paranoid, that's what I've become, thought David as he checked the foyer of his office once more before attempting to contact his wife. "Hi Max", he smiled into the audio link, "is everything okay?"

"Give me a second", Maxine spoke quietly into her audio. She performed a quick scan of the monitors that gave a near complete view of their entire home then activated the audio scrambler Boston had installed for them. "Yes, for the moment everything is fine." When David and Max first began using code words in order to ensure their conversations would be private, Maxine felt very foolish. However, in the last three weeks, three families that lived fairly close by had been unceremoniously packed up and transported back to York-City. She knew that she had several conversations with members of those families where criticisms of the current administration had been expressed. It could be a coincidence . . .

"How's the list coming?" David kept his sentences and questions as short as possible. He was never sure how much time he had before his assigned jailers would be back at their monitoring stations in the other room. Boston had installed a similar scrambling device in his office, but, he knew if he used it too often, it would be discovered and removed.

"We are up to just over fifty percent", Maxine, too, was answering with short sentences. "So far, our people are being very cautious."

Max was diligently compiling the records of each person that had been selected to move into David's City. It turned out to be very helpful that she had worked within the City's resource services for such a long time. Her main computer systems access had been deactivated almost before she left her office for the last time. However, anybody who has ever entered data into a computer would have learned to make alias access IDs, just in case. Now, those aliases were coming in handy!

David nodded and just a hint of relief was reflected over the audio, "That's all we can hope for." After a brief pause he continued, "We don't have a lot of time to get this accomplished."

He's worried and I don't blame him, Maxine thought to herself. *We are hoping that nearly four hundred people can keep their mouths shut when talking to the wrong people and get the word out correctly when speaking to the right ones. Still, almost one half of the expected new population had been identified.* "Everyone is well aware of the time limit, honey", Max wanted to be conciliatory but sometimes a comment like that could come across as patronizing and that would only fuel whatever was bothering him.

"Yes, you are right, of course", David knew he sounded terse but he had a bad feeling and just didn't like having no control at the moment. "What about the dead people?"

David felt badly as soon as he asked the question. Sure, he had to keep the questions brief, but, there had to be a better way to ask that one!

Maxine didn't like the way he phrased that question, either, but she resisted the temptation to scold him.

An interesting development had occurred that, had she not had access to the city's computers, she would not have known . . . nearly every person that had been assigned to work on the dam and cavern project and had stayed on the project until the last level was sealed, had been declared missing, then deceased. This was quite the fortuitous discovery! The city officials had noted that there had been quite a few Missing Person reports and, despite the best efforts of the Investigative Services, these people just could not be found. With all the violence that had been evident during the many riots and demonstrations, it was easier to merely pronounce them deceased and close the files.

The Board had been more than a little worried that nearly their entire canyon-designated work force had not been releasing back into York-City. Instead, hundreds of service workers and their families had been retained within the caverns to continue building each level of the city. Now those people had, only a few days ago, been sent back to York-City. Their stay in the old city recruiting their future neighbors should only be for a very short period of time. The hope was that few, if anyone, would notice them. Then, they would return to the caverns as part of the colonization effort. The last thing David needed was the further complication of governmental officials searching for the long missing workers!

Now, however, with the city records declaring the Cavern workers either missing or dead and no one even looking for them, they had effectively become invisible to the above-ground civilization. Every one of the released workers could come back to the caverns with very little worry that city officials would even notice, let alone try to find them. If the newly invited people could conveniently disappear the same way, why, that would be PERFECT!

Maxine had been assigned the task to compile the registration information for the new recruits and feed the data into the Cavern's computers. Now, she was also assigned the morbid job of updating the data in the City's files that would proclaim those new colonists as missing or deceased.

"Everyone that has been cleared to proceed to Boston's level has had their files updated with a life status as *deceased*", Maxine answered neutrally. "Has anyone noticed the activity?"

The movement of people from York-City to the staging level lifts had also been a concern to everyone involved. The migration of the colonists had turned into quite the covert affair. Smuggling people past the sentries that guarded the entryway across the dam continued to be the most worrisome. No one could come up with a plan that walked the recruits across the wide-open tarmac along the dam bridgework and into the Citadel had even a reasonable chance for success. One method that *did* seem possible was utilizing the governmental transports that routinely gained access through the checkpoints. Typically, one or two families were packed into the transports that delivered goods to the Citadel. A number of quick-stop sites had been set up to off-load the people then get them moved to one of the very few lifts still in operation that had access to the caverns.

I am continuously amazed as to how closely they monitor me and my actions, but do not bother overseeing the commerce traffic to and from the Citadel, David thought to himself. "No, as of yet, no one has noticed or reported anything", David replied. A small, dim indicator suddenly lit up his desk. David quickly switched it off before continuing. The stress had quickly returned to his voice, "I've got a meeting soon so I will talk to you later, okay?"

Code words, Maxine thought to herself. "I love you, too. Bye", she said aloud before she ended the connection.

David's two watchdogs had returned to his outer-office foyer. The moment they had signed into their systems to monitor his communications, his desk indicator had dimly lit up with an orange tint. Had someone already been monitoring his communications, whether from his outer-office or from another location, that indicator would have been a stark red color.

If we can just get through the next seven days without this blowing up in our faces, David thought.

* *

Boston checked the results from his facial recognition software—again. His staging level was quickly reaching the point where he could begin the unsealing process, a level at a time, and allow the colonists to start their lives anew. Face after face had been identified and matched to the data Max was still loading into his security files. Most of the people milled around excitedly in the spacious storage areas that were designated as authorized for departure. The colonists had been further segregated into groups that were delegated for specific levels. The assignment was not a surprise to anyone; most everyone had selected their specific location and anxiously waited to get started.

Boston had one third of his security force scattered throughout his level on alert and poised to apprehend anyone that had not been identified against Max's registration files. Most of these people took their capture with a shrug of their shoulders and were brought peaceably to one of Boston's holding areas. These were the unidentified persons that were honestly surprised when captured and led away. Usually, though, after only a few hours, they would be released as more of Maxine's registration data was accepted into the Cavern's computers.

A few, however, caused quite a stir. The moment it appeared that agents from within the crowd were closing in or circling a little too close for comfort, they would instigate some kind of disruption that would give them a chance to escape the fast closing trap. Although they may temporarily escape capture, Boston was unconcerned. The recognition software would eventually pick them out from the crowd and another ambush would once again be set in motion.

One man, as the security officers reached out to grab him, had opened a briefcase to display an impressive amount of explosives, claiming he would detonate the device if he were not allowed into the caverns. Boston had personally escorted him to a private lift and, after ensuring the man had gathered all of his personal effects, was sent via the lift to a maximum security cell. The entire episode was captured on video and often replayed to the captive audience within the staging level to discourage any more radical behavior.

The security chief spent most of his time devouring the data that was issued to his command console from each awakening level. The rest of his security force was testing the operation of the mechanics, sensors, water and power supplies on each level as it was unsealed. So far, every system had checked out beautifully. Boston smiled as he received another audio report from a member of his team, "Excellent, Thomas. Yes, that is exactly what we had expected." The security officer had reported the power levels from the station that serviced the north-west quadrant of level one. The levels were only low because the plant was still in the early phases of being powered up. "Check it again in about ten minutes and report in." *It would sure be nice*, thought Boston, *if every level would wake up like this.*

Odd, thought Boston, *I know I've been down here a long while and I know that I've gotten to know a lot of people . . . '* He hesitated. He had been watching the faces as they were continuously being displayed and re-checked against his software. *And, I'll bet I know half of this lot by name. Still, I thought I saw something that wasn't right.* He squared his chair to the video recorder and started the process of playing back the last ten minutes or so. "Something", he muttered "is not right . . ."

There was a small bank of monitors that had remained dark and unused since the Boston began the process of unsealing of David's city. The first monitor, the one that was designated for problems or situations on level one, suddenly came alive. With a soft groan Boston rolled his chair over to that monitor and switched his audio over to the matching circuit, "How many?"

There were two agents zipping up the last of several morgue bags. "Four, sir" was the reply. "We found two adults, both male." There was a short pause before the agent finished the report, "And two children. They will be sent up for identification in a few minutes."

This situation, although not unexpected, was still dreaded by Boston and his crew. Boston signaled to a couple of his agents and, with pursed lips, they made their way into the crowd to find the women that had only days before steadfastly denied that anyone had been left behind. The sudden moment of silence, quickly followed by tears, wails of disbelief, and words of consolation from the crowd followed the women as they were respectfully escorted to another small security lift. Boston sighed and shook his head. *It didn't have to be this way*, he thought. *I suppose, though, if you believe the people in charge are truly not looking out for your best interest, then you would have to protect yourself the best you know how.*

A monitor that had been displaying the people as they milled around sectors of the staging level suddenly showed the face of one of his crowd control agents. "Sir? We got them. These are the last ones."

Boston selected the control that gave him a wider view of the area and two well-built men with their hands bound securely behind their backs came into view. The security chief studied them for a moment. They were fairly comfortably dressed; the clothing was the type used for hiking or walking. They had no luggage, or at least none that could be found. They had no papers of identification on them whatsoever, which was not that uncommon for the new colonists. But, for someone who did NOT belong here, it was VERY unusual.

"Lock 'em up. Make certain they cannot communicate with anyone or each other. We'll have to interrogate them later." Boston was not pleased. Oh, he was glad they were caught but the timing was troublesome.

The left-most monitor from the first level security control room blinked once again, then, revealed another one of Boston's young lieutenants. Boston switched his audio to that circuit, "This is Jeffries."

"All systems are up and active, sir. No, um, other unauthorized personnel were found." The agent was attempting to display his best at decorum. This was, after all, a historic day so far as the City of David was concerned. Soon—quite likely *very* soon—people would begin to be transported to their respective levels.

Boston's thoughts were on the same page as his reporting agent, *So many more things could have gone wrong,* he thought. *But, now, we are on the brink of launching a new civilization.*

There had been plenty of milestones that had been systematically checked off: the creation of the dam while many of the levels of the caverns were created, the painstaking use of the most modern technology to give the underground city its best chance at survival, even the design and architecture for each level were ground-breaking in so much that the land and the products from the land needed to be as recyclable as possible. A 'Green environment' had been very popular just prior to the radiation wars, but civilization had historically only cared about the environment when it was convenient. David's city needed a clean and recyclable ecology, not for convenience sake, but in order to assure their continued existence.

The beginning of the actual colonization of the City of David was truly a momentous occasion. Never had a city been built in its entirety before people were allowed to inhabit it. Boston had the video cameras recording the proceedings both on his level and at each landing for every level that would be populated during this wave of colonization. Under typical circumstances, an event of this magnitude would be inundated with dignitaries, vision stars and a crew from every vision station in existence. Instead, with Mayor Kourie's police force dutifully engaged watching David and every member of his Board of Directors, it was impossible for David, Maxine or anyone else on the board to actually attend this significant event.

"We can begin the colonization whenever you are ready, sir", the agent continued with practiced dignity.

"Thank you, Mr. Simons", Boston responded with the same formality. Boston switched his audio to the staging area loud speakers, "Ladies and gentlemen, will you please gather to the large screen opposite the personnel lift? Concluding instructions have been prepared to assist you with your final transition. We will start the presentation once everything is in readiness."

The timing was VERY troublesome; the thought came to Boston once more. It was just too close. Had Mr. Simons' announcement come before the capture of the last two unidentified men, he would have had to postpone the presentation while the crowd was put through an exhaustive, methodical search. Instead, just moments before the hunt would have begun, those two were suddenly caught.

The excitement among the colonists was already at an intense state. Yet, the air fairly vibrated with an increased charge of electricity as the people surged together and made their way to the large view-screen. A celebratory spirit was strong among the colonists. The fresh, positive attitude of determination and optimism by the recruits was easily reconciled with the spirit of the authors of the city, David's father and brother, who had perished in the riots long ago. Hundreds of excited men, women and children moved impatiently to stand or sit in front of a large auditorium-style screen. The noise level rose appreciably while mothers called to their children, children called to their friends and men jostled their way into prized positions.

The immense screen was still displaying the various checklists for each level. A cheer was generated by the crowd as each remaining item was unhurriedly checked off.

The facial-recognition software was still operating but Boston turned off the recorder for now. "Overcome by events", he muttered aloud. "I'll have to check this out the next time I have a chance." He made a notation on his clipboard then, after taking a deep breath, he turned his attention to the anxiously waiting crowd. Boston had already received a confirmation from his crowd-control agents and his security monitors showed that everyone was in place. Now that every unsealed level was lit up on the large screen, meaning the levels are ready to receive its inhabitants, the captive natives were growing restless.

The lighting in the vicinity of the auditorium screen was dimmed. David and the Board of Directors had recorded a message to be played before each wave of colonists was allowed to enter the lifts. The screen itself was now dark, music reminiscent to an ancient film, 2001: A Space Odyssey, floated from the loud speakers, gaining strength as the screen began to shimmer with light. Images of the Citadel in its various stages of development appeared, then faded away only to be replaced with others.

Carol Vonner's voice narrated the progress of the guardian city's development, spending considerable time describing the formation of the dam and the powerful energy source the channeled waters had become. Many large, terraced farms, fields and orchards were displayed during their peak time of production. The smell of oranges, apples and fresh cut wheat and alfalfa pervaded the entire staging level, teasing the colonists with scenes of above-ground opportunities that would not ever be theirs.

The pictures of farm and rural areas were systematically replaced with graphic displays of new industrial sectors. The stark skylines of new business office buildings, storefronts, malls, and governmental complexes stood as sentinels to the fledgling city. Pictures of comfortable homes and apartments were displayed as Carol continued to unfold the vision that its designer and creator had for the Citadel before his untimely death. She continued to hail the accomplishments of Kendal Enterprises and its elite engineers until a final, glorious, scene of the Citadel and its inhabitants slowly faded from view.

Suddenly, the expectant colonists appeared to have been transported into what seemed to be a dimly lit elevator. The doors had only just closed and the stark, little room seemingly began to move downward. A small chime was heard, over and over again, as the entire audience was lowered beneath its guardian city. The elevator slowed, almost to a halt, as it approached each level. Through the view-port constructed into the elevator, every colonist could glimpse a view of each level. The voice of Skip White quietly explained the phases of its construction, the unique design and purpose for the level and, finally, an account of each life that was lost during its construction.

A bright, glowing orb that gave the illusion of mid-day warmth at its zenith in a clear blue sky was prominently displayed when they arrived at level four. Cloudy skies partially obscured the soft glow of a three-quarter moon that silhouetted the down-town skyline on level Six. The twin sports arenas and civic centers on levels two and five appeared almost majestic, gloriously lit up for upcoming events and surrounded by spacious and meticulously landscaped parks.

The underground seas with their man-made beaches inspired gasps of awe as the invisible voice described the engineering feat necessary to create such an incredibly vast, column less chamber. The children giggled with joy when visions of people and pets were superimposed onto the vast beach area. Small, gentle waves caressed the imported white sand and, once again, a blazing sun was shining overhead.

Less dramatic but just as impressive were the engineering sectors that housed the massive installations of water purification machinery, the back-up power plants and power conversion equipment that would become the life blood to the entire city. The members of the board were adamant that, this more industrial of levels, would have its share of aesthetics. So, pools, hot tubs and recreation facilities were liberally spread throughout the level up to and including an enclosed, man-made mountain that allowed climbing, biking and even skiing.

The quick peek into the new land very much excited the colonists. The noise level had once again erupted into an overwhelming cacophony of sound as families and would-be neighbors spontaneously discussed their hopes and dreams of their future within the City of David.

As the last views of the underground city from the elevator view-port finally faded away to darkness, low, ominous notes fairly grated from the staging area sound system. Pictures of selected areas of York-City were displayed with ragged, darkened edges on the auditorium screen; people appeared to be working unceasingly and children wore cast-off clothing and attempted to amuse themselves in decrepit, dilapidated schoolyards. Whatever joy and freedom the expected colonists had experienced while glimpsing the land that would soon be theirs; had suddenly been replaced with feelings of horror and sadness. Boston's staging level grew quickly quiet as memories from a not-so-long ago past were momentarily revived.

David Kendal's voice spoke clearly through the portrayals of the ghetto-like life, "Ladies and gentlemen, boys and girls; you are ready to embark upon a journey that has never been attempted in all of our history within the human race. Your actions, the actions of your children, your friends and neighbors will be the deciding factor as to whether this city becomes a garden and a haven for your families, or another wasteland that begs for disease and destruction."

Maxine had counseled her husband to keep his remarks as positive and upbeat as possible. David, however, wanted these people to understand the sacrifices that had been made by so many people in order to give them their chance for a new life—unfettered by the oppression that has been the trademark of their government for so long a time. In the end, he had agreed to present a challenge to the future citizens of the City of David.

Scenes from the underground city began to be displayed once more on the auditorium screen. The pictures showed the construction crews and their families as they lived their lives within the levels of the city. Every image demonstrated someone or some family assisting another accomplish a task. "You must remember", David continued, "to help your friends and neighbors; treat everyone as you would wish to be treated."

The screen came alive with scenes where accidents had happened and an entire neighborhood turned out to assist. There was even video of neighbors who had visited people in the hospital, the small, exuberant crowds whom attended the children's sports events and solemn people, dressed in black, who were present at a funeral service for one of the fallen construction workers.

"Please", now there was sincere pleading in David's voice, "know that it was through the mercies and blessings of God that we were able to build this city." The people were aware that the Kendals were a God-fearing family. They were probably even expecting some kind of a lecture but believing that it was coming and now having to listen to it were two different things.

"God has never given us a lot of commandments", David continued. "Yet, as each of you has lived through the creation of one level to the next, you were aware that we continuously refined the rules and regulations that you lived by until, at the final level, we had instituted our 'Laws to Live By'. Everyone here had to abide those laws or leave the city." There were many heads nodding and a quiet murmur of agreement. "You all know the laws and have, each of you, agreed to follow them. But, there is more; you must teach your children and your children's children if you are to survive."

The crowd grew quiet as David slowly and distinctly listed the laws that many of them had long-since committed to memory. "We are all of different faiths", David began, "therefore, pray to your God and keep His commandments." As David spoke, the large screen came alive, displaying the different church buildings already constructed on the various levels. People, dressed in all manner of religious clothing, were attending their services unmolested by people not of their faith. "Do not blaspheme the name of your God nor anyone else's; be true to your faith!"

The people began to relax a little; David was not trying to convert them to his faith, he was entreating them to be faithful to theirs. "Treat your neighbor as you would want to be treated", David continued. The screen displayed a scene where the family-next-door was heading over to their neighbor's yard with rakes, shovels and bags to assist them with their leaves. The owner of the yard full of leaves stopped the neighbor and told him that they did not need to help. After all, he said, they didn't even have trees. The neighbor only laughed and with a wave of his hand, he and his family descended upon the leaves and in a short amount of time, the yard was neat and clean. A small voice from somewhere in the crowd suddenly shouted out, "Hey, that's ME!" Laughter filled the level as the feelings of goodwill began to spread throughout the crowd.

Boston paused the presentation until the crowd was once more ready to listen. The people grew quiet once more as David's voice sang out from the massive speakers, "This city has never had much use for prisons—I hope we never do. So, remember the commandments from the scriptures; do not kill, do not lie, do not covet and do not steal." The screen had darkened to show historical pictures of prisons that had long ago been torn down and replaced with economical and space-saving chambers.

"If you see something that you want or believe you should own it, then WORK for it until you have earned the means to procure it by your honest labor." Once again a short video was displayed for all to see. Many people were working long and hard hours and a city was slowly being built. Short interviews were held with a few of the workers and every one of them explained that the fruits of their labor had secured for them everything they had ever wished for.

"Again, do not cause one another harm. You MUST always consider the needs of the next generation. No matter how much you may want gain for yourselves, you must be responsible for the sake of your children and the welfare of the entire city."

The people were, once again, nodding their heads in complete agreement with David. Again, cheers and applause spontaneously broke out from the crowd.

The presentation was suspended for a shorter period of time before David continued. "Finally, when you select a leader, choose wisely. Please, please remember the commandments of our God that has allowed us to build this city. Please have faith in yourselves and treat your neighbors with love and respect."

There was, once again, a pause in the instruction. This time the silence stretched out long enough that some voices in the crowd were just beginning to murmur their impatience when David's voice was heard once more. "I . . . We want you to live. Live free. Live happy. Live your lives the best that you can." The sheer emotion in David's voice caught them off guard. Scattered, at first, then from everyone in the debarkation area, the people began to clap and cheer.

This was, beyond any doubt, a new beginning, a fresh start for the people and the true beginning for the City of David.

CHAPTER SIXTEEN

"This place is so amazing", she spoke softly to no one in particular. Actually, no one was paying any special attention to her anyway. Nearly everyone had at least visited each of the levels at one time or another. She didn't want to stick out by gawking every time she turned a corner, but, "wow", she again uttered aloud.

This time a family walking together not too far away turned and smiled at her. They waved cheerfully as they continued on their way to the amusement park that had seemed to so impress the visitor.

She had been assigned to level three and had set up residence there. She had found a cute, little two-bedroom apartment that overlooked a winding (carefully controlled) stream that she had fallen in love with the moment she saw it. She had roamed most of her level for the past several weeks and, she had to admit, she was absolutely astounded with what she had seen. The technology and household conveniences in use seemed to be wholly devoted to the comfort and welfare of the residents. Of course, the availability of oxygen, water and energy was the first priority but, everything else, the gardens, amusement parks, housing, and office buildings seemed to have been constructed to allow the most freedom and ease as possible to its inhabitants. Even the household conveniences that were freely supplied to the new residents were there for the free use of its citizens. Now that she had branched out and had begun to tour the other levels, the immensity of the project, the sheer cost and use of man-power was finally beginning to sink in.

Her first thought was how much this endeavor must have cost the people through taxes or, perhaps more likely, the misappropriation of city funds. She remembered that David and Kendal Enterprises had been removed as the caretakers of the Citadel for their misconduct and possible fraud. She fairly bristled at the very thought of the many hundreds of thousands of people that had unknowingly contributed to a paradise that they would never see. Then, she remembered; no one in York-City is even aware of its existence. City credits could not have been used and, therefore, the citizens could not have contributed even one cent to this place. *Then, how . . . ?*

Not able to grasp concepts had never been a problem for her. However, this undertaking was so enormous, that the thought of the existence of a city capable of supporting thousands of people without anyone's knowledge was just preposterous. Yet, here she was, walking the streets of what appeared to be a newly created paradise. There were no crushing crowds, no venders hawking their wares and apparently not enough people (yet) to have to worry about crime.

She took pictures of everything. Even though she spent a lot of time in what would have to be considered tourist attractions, she took just as many shots of the power plants, power conversion facilities and the subterranean seas. She remembered how the seas were depicted during the colonist's final instructions and how the people were enthralled with the idea of 'going to the beach' once again. She remembered how she had inwardly scoffed at the very idea that they existed, let alone actually even coming close to the propaganda shown to the colonists. In spite of her skepticism, she had probably taken just as many pictures of the beaches, waves and the few boats that were being piloted on the relatively calm waters, as she took of anything else.

She eventually worked her way back to her one-bedroom apartment. The whirl-wind tour had been fast and extremely productive. She had been gathering information for years now and had been handsomely paid for her efforts. From time to time she had second thoughts—Asman's death had bothered her a lot more than she wanted to admit. She looked out over the landscape that was visible from her apartment and could only wonder again, *How?* How had David been able to accomplish this? No one had paid a fee to enter into this city. There were no taxes to pay; no payments of any kind. Still perplexed, she turned from the window with a slow shake of her head.

It would be nice to stay awhile longer, she sighed. *But, I need to get back.* She slowly (and to her surprise quite reluctantly) packed her personal things into a fairly small carry-all. It was certainly not her intent to call any more attention to herself by making it obvious to the passers-by that she was leaving. The furniture, dishes and most of her clothing would be left behind. The information with which she was armed was going to bring her the largest paycheck she had ever received in her life. Besides, almost everything that she was abandoning here in the 'caverns' had been bought with the allowance funds that her employer had provided. 'Caverns', she smiled. That was such a quaint name for something that was so much more. She wandered back to her second story window and gazed out at the small stream that meandered past her complex. Small birds, *ducks, I think they are called*, were bathing in the clear, clean water.

I've got to get to the personnel lift and hope I can get out of here before it's too late. Actually, she wondered, *was she trying to leave before she was caught, or maybe before she changed her mind to leave at all?* When she had first contrived the idea of giving information to Mayor Kourie, she had envisioned little more than caves etched out of the soil used to fill the canyon. Now, after seeing with her own eyes this underground miracle, those second thoughts kept returning to haunt her.

It's a good thing I was able to free my bodyguards from Boston's cells, she thought. *I will very likely need them to get me out of here.*

She had never really been sure if her small effort of subterfuge had ever truly convinced the security chief or not. Boston's security crew kept setting traps for her and her guards. She could see that the security net was becoming ever tighter around them. The two men she had brought with her had already employed a number of diversions that had enabled her to discreetly move to other sections of the staging level, just barely one step ahead of Boston.

The final ruse had been to let her men be apprehended in the hope that the timing of their capture would allow her the opportunity to descend into the caverns. The diversion had worked insomuch that she had entered into, well, paradise! But her men needed to be set free and have time to once more get past the staging level security team before there was even a prayer that she would be able to escape the subterranean city.

* *

Boston Jeffries was NOT amused and he was not about to be put off. "What do you mean, 'release them'?" he shouted as he entered into his clerk's office.

Boston's administrative clerk was started by his boss's sudden and loud entrance. "That's what it says, sir, release them. There's something about how they got there by accident and we have to let them go." He was nervously standing now and wanted nothing more than to deflect his boss's anger to another direction.

"Give me that", Boston reached out and snatched the paper from the clerk's shaking hands. *I am NOT storming*, he thought. *I am just feeling slighted. That's all.*

The letterhead on the memo clearly defined that the correspondence had come from Mr. Kendal's private office. "They believed they were joining a number of other people being sent into the storage rooms beneath the governmental complex. They had no idea where they were. Don't worry. The city is not planning to press charges." PRESS CHARGES!?

It looked as though the security chief was going to ball up the message and hurl it across the room. Instead he took a deep breath and tersely told his clerk, "Get Kendal on audio."

There was a short pause while the clerk attempted to contact David Kendal. Boston used that time to re-read the memo and compose himself. *Why would these men be released after such a serious breach of our security? They had managed to make it all the way into the staging areas!*

Jeffries did not like the looks of those two men. Both were powerfully built without the over-musculature physique found in bouncers at bars or recreational body builders. They carried themselves with an attitude of almost careless confidence. He had watched the video of their arrests over and over again. Each time he reviewed the videotape of their capture, he noted with a stronger conviction how they had handled their arrests with ease and expectancy. One of them had even turned and crossed his wrists just a split second before he had been ordered to do so by his security crew.

Sputtering sounds across the small office caused him to look towards his clerk. The young man was obviously having difficulties locating Mr. Kendal.

"Sure, I get it. Mr. Kendal is not available. Who CAN I talk to?" The exasperation in his voice was easy to discern and quite understandable. Ever since the York-City government had ordered a team of agents to dog their director's every move, he was more often than not, impossible to reach.

"What about Sykes?" Boston asked. "She would know where to find David."

The clerk covered the audio before replying, "She hasn't been seen in days." An impish look appeared on the clerk's face, "Maybe she and Mr. Kendal . . ." The clerk did not pursue that line of talk any further than that. Boston's eyes had turned to hot coals and the imagined flames made the clerk jump as far away from the security chief as the audio extension would allow.

Boston's clerk suddenly turned back to the audio, "Under-secretary WHO?" The now completely flustered clerk babbled over the audio. "Look I need to speak to . . ."

Boston was attempting to distract his clerk, hoping the young man would just hang up, by running his index finger across his throat. The color drained from the clerk's face as he absolutely misunderstood his boss's sign language. This was NOT what he had thought was meant when a person was allowed a 'last phone call'.

Boston shook his head and rolled his eyes, then, reached over and cut the connection. "I was trying to tell you to forget about making the call", he explained. When the clerk did not look as relieved as Boston thought he should, Boston sighed and said, "Don't worry about it. It was only a joke. I get it."

The clerk only smiled weakly back at his boss. He glanced nervously towards the doorway which, he figured that if he got there quickly enough, he might just be able to escape.

Boston nodded towards the exit. "Go ahead. Take the rest of the day off. I'll probably be out for the rest of the day anyway." He turned and walked toward his inner-office. Almost the moment eye contact between them had been broken, the clerk scampered for the door and freedom; leaving the door wide open.

Boston merely shook his head, turned back around, and walked over to shut and lock the inner-office door. Then, he turned back and entered into his personal office, securing that door as well. "It's just as well, I suppose", he muttered to himself. He sat down at his desk and tried to activate some of his staging level data but to no avail. The data he wanted to review would not, because of his own security controls, transfer out of the caverns.

"Figures", he muttered as he activated the small, private lift that would bring him down to his security staging level. "Something is not right." The bookcase silently slid away from the elevator door and the doors opened with a soft whoosh. With a practiced touch, he pressed the buttons that would cause the elevator to bring him down to his staging level sanctuary. *I have a bad feeling that I know where I can find the answers, though*, he thought as the lift doors closed silently in front of him.

As was his habit, he set the control to pause the lift at the landing, keeping the doors closed, in order to check out the monitor that scanned the immediately area outside of the lift doors. As usual, there was no one in view of his cameras. The doors slid open and Boston walked around to his internal security office. Absentmindedly, he thumbed in the combinations and heard the soft click as the automated locks released the door.

Boston smiled as he entered into his near-private sanctum. It really wasn't that long ago that Skip White brought him down here for the first time. He had not been overly impressed back then; he had known next to nothing as to how this staging level was the final defense of the city below his feet. Now, however, he was totally devoted to the protection and secrecy of David's city. He turned the coffee maker to brew then walked around the room switching on the banks of monitors and printers.

He spied his clipboard, picked it up, and flipped through his pages of notes. *That's it*, he thought. *I was studying the video scans of the colonists.* Boston walked up to his desk, leaned over, and activated the computer system before re-engaging the video replay. He gingerly set down his hot cup of coffee, allowed himself one more stretch, and cracked his knuckles before dropping into his chair.

Jeffries had been searching the facial recognition videos for whatever anomaly his subconscious had flagged as a problem just before the colonization had begun. He began to search the tapes once again. The coffee grew cold and stale as he stared bleary-eyed at his monitor. Face after face was displayed for a few seconds along with the identification data that Maxine had entered into the Cavern's records. Hours passed and Boston was slowly getting the message that he was going about this task the wrong way.

There was just too much tape to process. The faces had begun to blur together. At any given moment, everyone that was displayed on his monitor appeared to be a suspect. Hours later, however, while attempting to verify his suspicions, no one any longer appeared suspicious and he was at a loss to explain what had made them distrustful to him in the first place.

Boston got up and paced the short walk across the floor of his sanctuary. He suddenly snatched up his cold mug, dumped its contents into the sink, and refilled it with a fresh brew. He muttered out loud, "This time, I'll track our captives. There has got to be connection between those two men and whoever I am looking for."

He sat back down at his console and, once again, played the video that showed the capture of the illegal colonists. This time, he searched among the colonists that had been standing close by his captives. One by one, Boston would select someone else in the nearby crowd and run programs that would search the recognition tapes for a match.

This process of elimination, he decided, was going to take awhile. He set the computer parameters to continue searching and selecting people, then walked over to an uncomfortable looking cot, stretched out on it and fell into an exhausted sleep.

It wasn't too long, however, before his console chimed, signaling the processing had completed. With a grunt, Boston rolled off the cot and stumbled back to his console. *That's more like it*, he thought. *Only about a half dozen people seemed to have hung around his captives the entire time they were in the staging level.*

He brought up the first of the identified colonists and studied the candidate carefully. There didn't seem to be anything remarkable about him. He was of an average height and weight and his profile listed him as a food vendor assigned to level three. Leaving his profile on one monitor, Boston brought up the man's family and neighbors. "Nothing", he muttered. With a slow shake of his head, he brought up the data on the next candidate.

A fairly attractive woman stared back at him from his monitor. Again, Boston scrutinized the woman carefully. Again, there was nothing remarkable about her. She was a software engineer who specialized in gaming and gambling. It was not a great surprise to note that she had been assigned to level six where more casinos had been built than on any other level. Leaving her profile on one monitor, Boston brought up her family and neighbors. Again, he slowly shook his head and selected the next person from his program-generated list.

Boston gaped at the screen. Of the many times this woman had been photographed by the security cameras, there was only one time that her full face had been captured. The identification information displayed below her picture meant nothing to Boston. But the face on the screen he knew very well. For all his devotion to his security programs, it never occurred to him to match the identities of the colonists to other possible identities.

"I've got to get this to David", he said aloud and immediately began to gather the incriminating pile of information into a semblance of order.

At first, Boston found himself muttering words like, "I just can't believe it." But, as he began to match her schedule over the past few years with major events within the Citadel, the evidence continued to mount to the point that anger had begun to replace disbelief. Disturbing patterns began to appear. Usually days before a particularly destructive riot had broken out, she had taken a brief vacation, only one or two days, but she had been back in her office before the crisis had evolved.

Boston sat back to compare his notes, *She had always come back in time to accompany David and access the damage, supply comfort, and even perform volunteer work that had earned her no shortage of accolades from her peers,* thought angrily! Here was a video clip where she had accepted an award for outstanding service from Mayor Kourie that corresponded, almost to the hour, when a huge sum of credits had been transferred into one of a growing list of bank accounts.

He sat back in his chair, fuming. Suddenly he grew cold. Hoping there was no correlation, but knowing there was, he pulled up the informant's schedule within a few weeks of the riot that took place at the gateway of the Citadel. She was away for four days—FOUR DAYS—then, one week later, the Dam and Citadel had been attacked. He remembered that he had wondered at the coincidence that on that particular day most of his security force had been drawn off from the dam to handle a problem on the far side of the Citadel. Portions of the dam had been destroyed before he could get anyone back there to confront the rioters. Asman's untimely death had been the result from that attack. He clearly remembered the tears that she had shed that day. *Now*, he thought, *now I want to see REAL tears!*

He heard the security lift park and lock into place behind him and with a raise of his eyebrows checked his watch. *Shift change*, he thought, as he stretched in his chair. He pressed 'send' on his computer and swiveled his chair around to look into the face of one of the two men that had only recently been released from his cells.

CHAPTER SEVENTEEN

The man had left the elevator and was calmly standing just a few feet away from the rapidly closing lift doors. His arms were folded casually across his chest as he leaned lightly against a table. A sidearm, almost hidden by the crossed arms, was strapped to his side just above his left elbow; his right hand lay nonchalantly across the butt of a small caliber pistol. He did not appear to be the least bit concerned of the security chief's discomfort, but Boston was quite sure that if he made a sudden movement, this man would kill him without a second thought.

Boston glanced quickly around the room, *where was his security? Why was this man here?* He had a weapon but it was in the holster of his gun belt hanging on a peg just above the table the man was leaning on. All the security cameras and monitors were outside the room, in the staging area, with alarms that would notify the various security teams. But, there was absolutely no way to contact anyone that there was a problem inside the security office!

Boston looked as disarming as possible and started to rise from his chair. Before he could even begin to stand, the man pulled the revolver and moved quickly across the room, his arm outstretched, "Don't move", he said quietly. Boston froze for a moment, then settled slowly back into his chair while the man continued more slowly forward to stand behind him.

Several minutes ticked by and Boston, a little perplexed by the behavior, slowly leaned back in his chair and casually placed his elbow on his desk before asking, "Are we waiting for someone?"

The first man grinned and nodded even though Boston could not see him, "An acquaintance of yours." He snapped a quick glance at his watch, "It shouldn't be much longer."

Just moments later, there was a brief knock on the door that opened to the staging level. The gunman quietly asked, "Let him in, won't you?"

Boston's eyes flickered briefly to the security cam outside the door. *The other one naturally,* he thought. He didn't move but casually stated, "I'll have to unlock the door from the console."

The gunman frowned for a moment, "Fine, do what you need to do. Just do it slowly."

Boston glanced back at the gunman for a second as he eased forward in his chair. *I will only get one chance at this, he thought*. He cleared his screen and slowly brought up his security protocols. He selected several different screens, quickly entering data before he stared at the question left unanswered in front of him, "DISENGAGE? (YES/NO)".

The intruder poked Boston in the back with the barrel of the revolver and said with a sarcastic sneer, "The answer, in case you do not remember, is 'YES'."

With only a few, brief keystrokes, a distinct click of a door lock being disengaged was heard from behind the gunman. The man half-turned in surprise and, without hesitation, Boston twisted in his chair and cracked down hard on the hand that held the gun at his back. The pistol careened wildly off of the armrest of the chair to bounce then slide across the floor.

The man howled angrily and swung his fist at the side of Boston's head but it was too late. Boston had already moved out of the chair and was lunging for his gun belt hanging not ten feet away.

The intruder leapt for his own fire arm, reaching it nearly at the same instant that Boston had pulled his revolver from the holster. Jeffries again did not hesitate. In one quick motion, he turned and fired at the man lying on the floor only a few feet away, then suddenly moved to the right, in front of the closed elevator doors and fired again.

The gunman had reached for his weapon and rolled away from Boston so that Jeffries' first shot hit the floor right next to him. As he completed his roll, he came up on one knee and fired at Boston—where the security chief had stood just moments before.

Boston's second shot had found its mark. The gunman, hit with a bullet from point-blank range in the chest, was thrown nearly half-way across the room. Boston fired again, an insurance shot, then, stood stock still. His gun remained trained on his adversary while he watched for any sign of life. The gunman remained crumpled on the floor, his blood splayed across the wall and chairs. The only movement came from the twitching of the man's dying nerves.

Boston took a deep breath and looked down at his own trembling hand. *It has been a long time since I have had to do that*, he thought.

He glanced back towards the slain gunman one last time before he looked up at the monitor that showed where the other gunman had been but was now no longer in sight. Boston walked over and sat back down at his security terminal and began to shift the angles of the cameras outside his office. *There was no place to hide out there*, he thought. *He has to be out there somewhere.*

A grim smile grew slowly on his face as he checked the readouts that registered the living conditions within the staging level. He had initiated the sealing process on his own level while bringing up disarming protocols for the security doors. Outside of this room, the oxygen, power, and heating levels were already nearing their lowest levels. *Had this fellow*, he thought, meaning the dead assailant lying behind him, *had been successful in killing me, there would have been a good chance that both of them would be nearing an unconscious state by now.*

The smile faded away as he realized that he was still unable to locate the other gunman on his monitors. He frowned, "Where-"

A blinding explosion rocked the room. The wall behind the computer console that Boston was using was suddenly blown inside, carrying flex-stone, twisted metal and shards of glass into Boston. The force of the explosion sent him sprawling across the room and slammed him into the wall next to the dead gunman. The other gunman walked slowly into the dust-filled room amid the squall of security sirens and popping glass from other monitors being exposed to both the heat from the explosion and the blast of frigid air from the staging level.

The man kept his weapon pointed at the security chief while he made his way to his companion. He briefly checked for a pulse and, finding none, continued over to Boston. A substantial section of the wall was lying across the big man's legs and, although Boston was still alive, he would not be able to leave his sanctum under his own power. The gunman took the weapon that was lying in the rubble next to Boston before backing away from the unconscious security chief. The frost on his breath was clearly visible as he walked through the damaged room.

He ransacked the lockers and cabinets and quickly donned a coat with SECURITY emblazoned in bold letters across the back of it. A workman's hat covered his head but left his ears exposed to the deepening cold. It took longer to put on the gloves; his fingers had become increasingly numb while he was setting the explosives and the brief amount of heat that had emanated from the detonation had done very little to provide enough warmth to help his dexterity.

His breathing had become more labored. He knew that he needed to get oxygen soon or it won't make any difference that he had found some semblance of warmth. The man staggered towards what appeared to be a maintenance door and pried it open to find a small store of oxygen tanks. On a shelf beside the tanks were unopened boxes containing masks and hoses. His vision had blurred again and the frost from his breath was further clouding his sight but he managed to tear open the boxes and assemble a mask and its hose to one of the oxygen tanks.

He knew that he was blacking out from oxygen deprivation but he was content, believing that he would live to see another day. *I still have to make sure that Sykes gets out of the caverns alive or I won't get paid*, he thought as the exhaustion firmly took hold of him. With a weary sigh, he sank down to the floor with the mask firmly in place. He closed his eyes and leaned against the wall beside the tanks that were conspicuously labeled 'EMPTY—Do NOT USE'.

CHAPTER EIGHTEEN

Maxine tried again to contact her husband. David wasn't answering his audio nor was he picking up the messages she had been leaving him since this morning. "I wish Alican would hurry up and get back", she muttered to herself. "She has always been able to find him."

She looked at the images on the monitor that scanned the street in front of their home. *There are even more people out there*, she thought. She glanced nervously at her children who were sitting at their work stations attentively processing their school work. Dona and Trevan appeared to be totally engrossed in their studies but Maxine knew they had been listening intently to every cautious message Maxine had left for their father.

Max checked the outside monitor once more before, with a decisive nod of her head, she turned to her children and said, "Okay gang, I need you to put away all your school work and meet me in the den."

Dona looked up with almost genuine surprise, "Really, momma? Are we done for the day?"

Trevan was not anywhere near as diplomatic as his sister, "Good", he said with finality. "I was getting tired of pretending. I've been done for hours!"

Dona rolled her eyes at her younger brother, "Shush", she scolded him quietly as she stacked up her books and pens and prepared to trudge off to her room and put them away. She hesitated long enough to look uneasily at the monitor, "There are even more people out there now, momma." She met her mother's gaze for a moment before she turned to back to the hallway and walked silently past her brother towards her room.

Trevan obediently followed behind her but kept up his side of the conversation, "So, now we get our stuff, right?" he said nervously. "Should we get our stuff, now, or wait until she tells us to bring it?" Trevan's voice grew muffled as he continued to walk down the hallway to his room.

I hope I haven't waited too long, she thought. The crowd outside had been steadily growing since the children had come home from school. This reminded her of the time, not too long ago, when several of her neighbors were unceremoniously packed up and sent away. A mob had been hired to make sure that no one else interfered and the vision stations made it look like it was the supposedly angry rabble that had done the dirty work. But within the past half hour, Maxine recognized several of the people that had recently joined the crowd. Each one of the newest members worked within the Mayor's office. She knew it was time, maybe past time, to leave her home.

Dona was standing outside the den's double doors, "Momma? Are you ready?" she asked quietly.

Trevan, dragging a neatly trussed back-pack behind him, was working his way towards the den.

Maxine smiled in spite of herself, "Yes, sweetheart. Go get your 'stuff'." She should have known that her children would have already figured out what needed to be done.

Maxine walked down the hall to her bedroom. Lying on her bed were two bags. One of the bags she had very much hoped she would not be the one to carry. Now she hoped she wouldn't have to carry it very far before her husband would join them.

She pulled the smaller bag off the bed and slung the strap over her shoulder. She surprised herself with a small smile, *I suppose if I have forgotten anything, Donna or Trevan will have packed it*, she thought.

With a grimace, she dragged the larger bag off of the bed and it thumped loudly to the floor. The sound reminded Max that she had probably brought too many unnecessary items and may soon rue the day that she had packed the few extra things for the children. Fortunately, for at least part of their journey, the bags could be dragged on the small wheels attached to the base of the bags that work so well at the subway and parking lots.

Maxine was hardly surprised to find her children patiently waiting for her to arrive. They were nervously pacing among their bags and each had a light weight jacket tied by the sleeves around their waists. Their stuff (as Trevan phrased it) had been sorted and packed for weeks. They had all their own necessities, some spare clothes, credits, and papers that should get them through most any checkpoint should they become separated. Max carried paperwork for herself and for David with the hope that he would soon meet them on their journey.

The children had wanted to 'ride in the closet' since the day that the family held a special meeting in the den to discuss emergency procedures. Remembering back to that day, Dona was a little put out since she already knew all about how to use the windows as emergency exits and how to contact the rescue units. So her surprise quickly turned to intense interest as her parents discussed the possibility of having to leave their home in a quick and discreet manner. Trevan had become so excited about the very idea of secretly escaping bad guys and sneaking off into the unknown that he had run back to his room for his secret decoder ring!

David and Maxine had taken turns explaining and demonstrating how to unlock and open what had turned out to be a false front to the massive fireplace in the den. Dona and Trevan had watched in wonderment as a simple dumb-waiter system took the items they placed inside a tiny room out of sight, then, at a touch of a button, their possessions were brought back up to them. To the wonderment of the children, Max had pulled the items out of the small space and climbed inside, taking their place. She shuffled about and had made herself appear as comfortable as possible, then leaned back against the side wall and smiled.

David had explained that their mother was going to ride the little closet down into the darkness and stay down there. Then, each of the children was going to have the chance to follow her and stay out of sight, too. Maxine took one more look about herself before giving David an enthusiastic thumbs-up sign. She gave her family an excited wave and David pressed the controls that began to lower her out of the sight of her children.

Dona and Trevan watched their mother slowly disappear; the excitement of the moment was quickly replaced with worry then fear. It was one thing to see toys and books ride the closet, it was quite another to watch their mom vanish into the darkness. The children's fear grew and became something almost tangible by the time the tiny room came back into view without Maxine. David had been explaining the entire time that nothing had happened to their mother but when that little room reappeared without her, the children were definitely not happy!

Trevan examined the dumb-waiter from within the safety of the den, then turned to his father his face resolute and announced, "I want to find mother!"

David smiled proudly at his young son, "Get in, son, like you saw your mother do."

Trevan hesitated for only a moment before he clambered inside the space his mother had occupied just minutes before. Without a moment's pause, he looked about himself and gave his father a much less enthusiastic "thumbs up". He nervously waved at his sister as the little closet slowly descended out of sight.

As soon as her brother was out of sight, Dona announced, "Now it's my turn, Papa." She had not taken her eyes from the vacant space where her brother had only just disappeared from view.

David had been studying his watch but he looked at his daughter and answered with a wink, "Let's just give them a minute, shall we?"

Dona met her father's look with a defiant look of her own. She folded her arms across her chest and shifted her weight to one foot, "How long will I have to wait?"

Again David smiled proudly at his first born. "I'll tell you what, if you bring the dumb-waiter back up all by yourself, you can get in and leave just as soon as it locks into place."

Dona rushed to her father and gave him a quick hug then reached to receive the controls from him. She took a deep breath and, without hesitation, set the device to bring the little room back to the den. This time when the closet came into view, it was not empty. Her mother was smiling and waving and her brother had his arms wrapped tightly around her. Trevan opened his eyes and with a shout began to explain the adventure to his sister, "You should see it, Sis, there's a whole 'nother room down there and it isn't dark at all!!!"

Maxine had started to pry herself loose from her son but, as soon as the dumb-waiter stopped, Trevan bounded out to hug his big sister. "You just gotta go down there" he said enthusiastically. "Papa, can Dona go now?"

The situation was different this time and Dona knew it. The memory of that family meeting faded away as Dona retrieved the control board and handed it to her mother. Trevan had already released the lock and had nervously opened the doors to the dumb-waiter. Maxine motioned for Dona to get in first. Dona obediently placed her baggage into the little room and quickly followed inside. Max smiled as she watched her daughter look about herself to ensure all was in place before giving her the thumbs up sign.

Only Dona's wide, anxious eyes exposed her apprehension of the sudden turn of events as she disappeared slowly into the darkness. She knew what to do; she would exit the dumb-waiter and switch on the life support system that their mother had done just a few months ago, then, send the closet back to the den. She also knew that this time it wasn't a game. This time there were hostile people outside and her father was not at home.

Dona pressed the switch that poured power into the hidden shelter and breathed a loud sigh of relief as the flood lights forced the darkness away. Her hands were still shaking as she reset the dumb-waiter and set it back to her mother and brother.

Trevan just as quickly pushed his 'stuff' into the closet as soon as it locked back into place. He dashed inside and gave his mom a 'thumbs up'. Maxine looked at her son with her eyebrows arched high on her forehead. Temporarily abashed, Trevan frowned for a moment to consider the situation. With a start, he quickly looked about himself and cleared a stray strap away from the closet opening. Then, settling back against the wall in mock calmness, he gave the signal to his mom. Maxine obediently set the controls to deliver him into the shelter waiting for him beneath her.

Maxine pushed her bags into the closet and sent them down to her children. Dona and Trevan hurriedly cleared the dumb-waiter and sent it back up to their mother. In the meanwhile, Max quickly searched the room to make sure there were no telling traces as to where they had gone and entered into the closet with the controls. From inside the tiny room she pulled the façade doors closed and locked them into place. Finally, hoping she had not forgotten anything, she sent the closet down for the last time.

She heard the steel panel slide into place that would block the entry into the dumb-waiter or was it the plate that sealed the path to the shelter sliding into place that she heard? Dona and Trevan were sitting at their own consoles watching the crowd from the monitors. Max was impressed. Sure, they had practiced the escape a number of times but she was surprised that everything had gone exactly according to plan. Except for one thing, where was David?

* *

I have to keep reminding myself that this is not, officially, an interrogation, David said to himself. He was in a board room on the top floor of the Mayoral complex and there did not appear to be a sympathetic person in the room.

David had been escorted into the facility under heavy guard. He had been thoroughly searched and every piece of electronics in his possession had been taken away with the dubious assurance that everything would be returned to him at the end of the meeting. He knew from the moment he entered into the room that he was in trouble. Pictures of various portions of the canyon project were displayed around the room in chronological order; some of the pictures, in David's mind, made it pretty obvious that some extensive, extraneous construction had been completed that did not appear to have a purpose associated with the new capital of York-City, the Citadel.

"I've told you already", David began again, "those are merely stress walls that have been placed throughout the base of the city in order to stave off soil erosion and possible shifting of the city's base." *That sure sounds good*, he thought. Looking around the room however, it was clear that these people were looking for a different answer.

"We have taped confessions that actual, subterranean levels exist under this city", Captain Brose countered. She gestured pointedly at the photos lying on the table in front of David, "From these photos, I would have to agree that there is something else down there other than some garden-variety terrace walls!" The mayor had ordered the Captain to study the construction photos and find someone that could explain the purpose of the formations that seemed to be built and buried in an extraordinary short period of time.

David merely shrugged his shoulders and tried his best to appear as perplexed as the Mayor's head of security while steadfastly studying the pictures hoping to think of any plausible explanation to tell them other than the truth. *Right now*, he thought, *silence may be my only option*.

"Fine", Captain Brose finally said after waiting what certainly appeared to be plenty of time for David to come up with an answer. She pressed the intercom and spoke clearly into it, "Arrest them. Do it now and bring them to our interrogation offices."

David heard a crisp acknowledgement before the communication went dead. To his surprise he heard what sounded like true regret in the Captain's voice, "We will have your family in our facility within the hour." Susan Brose glanced briefly towards the Mayor to see the contented smile on the city leader's face. Her eyes flickered back and locked with David's, "We will have the truth" the tone of her voice and the disgust in those eyes did not match the harshness of the words she spoke, "no matter what it takes."

David dropped his head in horror. He uttered a brief, fervent prayer in his heart, "Please, be safely away." After a deep breath he raised his head and looked to the heavens, "Please, please protect my family!"

✶ ✶

Max climbed out of the dumb-waiter and locked it into place; the only way it could be utilized now would have to be from this shelter. She heard her daughter take a quick snatch of breath before she softly spoke, "They are here."

Max gasped and walked over to the monitors. Dona was absolutely correct; a small group of individuals had broken away from the street mob and were even now beating on the door, demanding entrance.

David's family watched from the safety of their shelter as the small group suddenly backed away from the front doorway to their home. Moments later that entrance to their home was gone. A small explosion could be seen but not heard from their underground hideout. The crowd immediately rushed into the home. Another small mob had gathered at the back door to no doubt grab them as they attempted to flee from the intruders.

Room after room was first searched then wantonly destroyed as the professional thugs tried in vain to discover the whereabouts of Maxine and the children. There were cries of distress from Dona and Trevan as they watched their possessions be first torn apart then torched by the hired mob. More than one tense instant was felt by the family as the mob's destruction included the monitors that gave them a view to what was happening in their home. The worst moment came when the intruders placed small explosives around their fireplace. After the smoke cleared, Max breathed a sigh of relief that the steel plates had covered their exit. The dumb-waiter was completely destroyed and, with luck, so was their chance of discovery.

The house was completely engulfed in flames but not a neighbor had come out to investigate or offer assistance. A brief conference was held out in the middle of the street. Apparently it had been decided to dismiss most of the crowd and leave a small force to watch the house burn to the ground.

Every monitor that had been attached to or built into their home was now useless, not a single one had escaped the destruction. Maxine and the children had no way of knowing what was happening to their home or if the crowd was still gathered in the street outside. The small family, blind to the outside world, huddled together and offered a prayer of thanksgiving that they had been kept safe from the attack. Even during this time of tribulation, Maxine smiled at some of the words offered up by her children, "Please let Papa be safe, too." Not a word was spoken against the attackers or the loss of their personal treasures. They were happy to be safe with their mother and they were worried for their father. Max added some final thoughts, "Yes, Lord", she said, "Please keep David safe and help us all meet together again, soon."

Trevan looked up and searched his mother's face, "Is Papa going to meet us here, Momma?"

Maxine reached out and pulled her youngest child to her side and hugged him for a long moment. Quietly, she finally answered him, "I don't think we will see Papa here, sweetheart. I am hoping he will catch up to us on the road."

Dona looked at her mother quizzically, "What are we going to do, Momma? Where can we go?"

She reached out and flicked a few strands of hair away from her daughter's eyes before replying, "First, we will get some sleep. Tomorrow, we will have a nice breakfast and, if all goes well, we will leave to meet up with your father."

The answer did not satisfy Dona. "But we don't know where Papa is", she spoke plaintively. "How will we find him?"

"Do you remember where Papa told you to go if you ever needed a place to hide?" Max looked intently at her daughter. With a knowing look in her eyes and just a hint of teasing in her voice she hinted, "You said that you could find it with your eyes closed and that it wasn't THAT far to walk . . ."

Trevan stirred at his mother's side and murmured sleepily, "We're going to Uncle Skip's barn."

CHAPTER NINTEEN

"You're telling me that you have no idea where they are", Mayor Kourie growled at his security chief. He suddenly shouted and slammed his hand on the highly polished table top "Is that what you are telling me?"

His theatrics had the desired effect on nearly everyone that was seated around the table, nervous jumps, uncomfortable shifting in chairs, and even a small yelp from his mousey public relations clerk. There was a reaction of some kind from everyone in the room except his intended target, Captain Brose.

"As I said, sir", Brose calmly repeated, "They were not in their home as your informants had disclosed. My security teams are out searching for them. I am confident that they will soon be found." Captain Brose had weathered stormy outbursts like this from her boss in the past and she had never approved of them. She considered this kind of communication to be quite unprofessional as well as a waste of her and the committee's time. Still, she was careful to not let the disdain she felt reach her voice nor show in her actions.

"You better find them", Posin snarled menacingly, "and it had better be soon!" The Mayor glared ominously at his security chief while Ms. Brose remained tight-lipped waiting for the storm to pass. The Mayor's facial expression suddenly changed to benevolence, perhaps even a hint of humor as he cocked his head slightly to one side and began a new conversation, "Oh, by the way, we are done with your other two prisoners."

Captain Brose eyed the Mayor suspiciously for a moment, *my other two . . .* Suddenly, she knew of whom the Mayor was referring; Carol Brunson and Trish Vonner had been picked up by one of the Mayor's special teams just two nights ago. Their abduction was made under much quieter circumstances than the attempt on Mrs. Kendal and her children. Brunson had been guiding her transport and Trish Vonner was a passenger when they were discreetly hijacked and forced into the Mayoral compound. Susan had made sure that they had been treated as hospitable as possible once she had found out that they were locked up within her cellblock. But she had no idea why they had been arrested in the first place. "Done?" she asked Posin.

"Yes, of course", at which Mayor Kourie smiled, "They were only just released a few minutes ago", he tapped his earphone knowingly. "They should be leaving my complex any time now."

Susan felt sick to her stomach as the Mayor watched her closely for a reaction. Kidnapping persons of interest was somewhat of a specialty of the Mayor's special unit, but so was getting rid of those people. Despite the opticals that Kendal Enterprises had caused to be placed in every transport built, the accidents involving pedestrians and other vehicles had nearly tripled in the past two years. She was quite sure she knew what the Mayor had meant when he said that he was 'done' with them.

He must have seen what he wanted because he turned brusquely away to address the next person sitting attentively around the conference table. The smile was gone and his voice was once again a familiar growl, "Now, why hasn't my new mansion been completed, yet?"

Before the nervous council member could even begin to respond, Brose casually cut into the Mayor's tantrum, "I would like to question David Kendall, sir. He—"

The Mayor was speechless. It was almost beyond his comprehension that someone would actually interrupt him. He turned to his security chief in amazement but before he could blast her for her brashness, she continued her explanation, "He would have the best idea as to where his family would be."

Mayor Kourie was furious, "YOU—"

The head of security continued to speak while rising from her chair, completely overriding whatever the Mayor was beginning to say, "They are scared and hiding. No doubt they are someplace known to David and expect him to arrive at any time." Captain Brose walked to the conference room door and brushed the gaping security guard aside, "I will bring you results within the hour, sir."

Brose walked out the door and shut it firmly behind her. With a smile she gestured for the security guard standing outside the room to remain at his post and walked over to the nearby bank of elevators. As the doors closed, and she punched the button that would bring her down to the lobby and out of the Mayor's building, she released a deep breath and sagged back against the marbled lift wall.

By the time the elevator doors opened to the plush lobby, Susan Brose had a plan and knew she didn't have much time. She exited the lobby, again brushing the guards aside, and pulled her audio from its holster. "Savish? Get Kendal ready to travel." She listened for a few seconds and with a snarl that would have made the Mayor proud spoke harshly into the unit, "I don't care what you think or what you have been told. Get him ready and keep this quiet. I'll be there in ten."

Her transport pulled up and came to a hushed stop directly in front of her. The guider hurriedly began to exit the craft but Brose instead opened the passenger door and clambered in next to the driver. She casually smiled and spoke lightly, "Get me to the office, please."

The guider relaxed and smiled back. The man expertly raised the craft from the tarmac and sped across the darkened grounds. His superior officer punched in a message into the transport's communications console and the dispatcher quickly acknowledged. Her personal transport should be parked outside of her office long before she would require its use.

"Good evening Mr. Kendal", the security guard spoke politely as he approached David's cell. "Please stay away from the door", he continued and, once it was plain that David did not have any intention of leaving his small bed, he pressed the switch that caused the ironed-bar door to slide silently open.

David watched the proceedings with interest. He had never been incarcerated before and had no idea whether this was a normal activity or not.

The guard pointed at the silver collar clasped around the prisoner's throat and then held up the small device he held in his hand. David merely nodded in understanding.

He had received a short demonstration concerning the power and the control the collar had over Captain Brose's prisoners. He had been brought to a small, empty room where the collar had been unceremoniously attached about his neck. The guards had then left him alone for nearly an hour where he had, cautiously at first, then when no one had come to stop him, with great energy tried everything he could think of to get the collar off.

Finally, he had sat down on the floor and leaned against a wall in frustration. A voice piped in over the intercom, "Now that you understand that you cannot remove it, please accept that you must do whatever you are told while you are wearing it." Skepticism must have been clear on

David's face because the voice continued, "Yes, we understand and have anticipated that you would need convincing." With that announcement, the door to the room opened and a small security guard quietly entered holding a small device in his hand out in front of him so that the prisoner could easily see it.

The voice spoke again, "I will give you a command for which you must carry out immediately. If you do not instantly do what you are told, the guard in front of you will press a control and you will honestly regret your decision. If you comprehend what I have said, please raise your right hand."

David continued to watch the guard carefully and nodded his head in understanding for which the guard lightly pressed a button on the device. David suddenly screamed in pain as sharp tendrils of electricity seemed to sear the flesh about his neck. He grabbed at the collar trying valiantly to strip if from his body when the torture suddenly stopped. Without realizing when it had happened, David found himself stretched out on the floor, flat on his back, and lying in a pool of his own sweat.

"That was the first of three settings", the voice spoke again. "Please listen carefully. If you do not wish another demonstration, raise your right hand."

David used to wonder why so many people couldn't seem to learn lessons by watching others make mistakes or why some people needed to make the same mistake over and over again before they would finally 'get it'. David immediately raised his right hand and left it high over his head until the voice quietly thanked him and told him he could now lower it back to his side.

The guard had kept his eyes on his prisoner the entire time he was in the room. For the first time, he spoke to David. "Most people need two lessons before they truly understand that they must follow any orders given to them." He once again held the device so that David could easily see it, "I would very much like to believe that neither I, nor any other guard, would need to use this on you again."

So, when the guard opened the cell door, casually displayed the control device, and motioned him to follow, David was only too willing to be led from captivity while carefully maintaining a discrete and respectful distance from the otherwise unarmed man. He conducted David down a short hallway and up three flights of stairs before he stopped in front of what was probably the only unlabelled door in the entire complex. With hardly a pause, he rapped lightly on the door and, after hearing a muffled disengagement of the lock, opened the reinforced door and gestured for David to go on inside.

David walked carefully inside and heard the door shut quietly behind him. He waited a few moments for the next order to be given, then, turned slowly around to find himself apparently alone in the foyer of a small, darkened room. Panic suddenly filled his thoughts as being set up as an escapee flooded his mind. He had only just worked up his courage to try the door when he felt rather than heard movement further inside. Warily, he walked slowly forward fully aware that the effects of the collar would quickly disable him if this was not the expected or correct thing to do.

As he entered into the room, a quiet voice instructed him in short, concise sentences, "Sit down in the chair in front of you." The voice was gruff but feminine, "Do not make any sudden movements. We do not have much time."

Without looking to the right or left, he walked directly across the small room and sat down in a surprisingly comfortable chair. His eyes were already beginning to adjust to the dim light and he could see a woman leaning against the counter across the room.

She stepped forward a couple of steps before continuing, "I do not want any trouble from you. Do you intend to cause me any problems?"

What is going on here, David thought but, aloud, he only answered, "No ma'am."

"What about now?" she asked as the collar released with a soft click and dropped into David's lap.

David stared at it stupidly for a moment, then, picked the collar up and studied it distractedly before he answered the question. "I don't intend to cause anyone problems", he spoke slowly. He looked up from the collar and glared at his would be captor, "Where is my family?"

Susan nodded in understanding, "I do not know where they are. Posin's men did not find them in your home even though I know they were in there. You are here", she paused for a moment, "because I want you to take me to them."

He stared at her in disbelief. His jaw worked as he tried to formulate words to answer her unusual request. Yet, reason worked against emotion as he considered her behavior in the conference room, her seeming abhorrence to the command she issued that should have resulted in the capture of his wife and children, and even the surprising release from the shock collar. Instead of speaking out in retaliation, as was one of his first impulses, he instead leaned forward in his chair and simply asked, "Why?" For all his exertion to remain civilized, his voice was as icy as it was menacing. "Why would I do this?"

Her hand had been holding her loaded and cocked service revolver since the knock on the door heralded David's arrival and she had been fully prepared to kill him if he had even started to lunge out of the chair. Now she pulled the gun out for him to see it and gently brought the hammer to rest before she reached back and set it on the counter behind her. She was very much surprised and quite impressed with his emotional control especially under the present conditions. "I . . .", again she paused, "I have studied what you have created and I do not mean just the construction of the Citadel. I have seen many of your invoices, shipment schedules and manifests", Brose indicated a folder lying on the in-table next to David. "I have seen enough to know that there is more beneath us than stabilizing walls to prevent the shifting of soil", she finished with only a hint of sarcasm.

David picked up the folder and quickly leafed through its contents. He had become increasingly alarmed as Posin's security chief continued to describe the information that made it clear that there was definitely something more substantial beneath the Citadel than to what he had confessed. David suddenly stood up. Susan had been so caught up in her explanation that the movement had completely caught her off guard. Flustered, she stumbled back to the counter groping for the weapon. David paid her no mind, however, as he was pacing in front of his chair trying to grasp the security officer's intent.

Maxine and the children mean more to me than my life, he thought, *but those people who have entrusted their very existence to me . . .* David stopped pacing long enough to look up at his captor and was surprised to see the revolver pointed evenly at his chest. He shook his head and sat back down heavily into the chair. "I cannot . . ." he paused, the distress he felt made it painful to continue. "I will not save my family at the expense of the city." He looked Mayor Posin's security officer in the eyes, defiantly and defeated, "I will not."

Susan blinked her eyes in confusion for a moment and fought the desire to laugh out loud in relief. "No", she said quietly, "you do not have to. I want to join you and your family in your city."

David searched her face uncomprehendingly. "But . . ." he stammered, "Posin . . . the files", here he held up the incriminating pictures and manifests. "How . . . ? Why . . . ?"

Before Susan could even begin to explain, her audio board lit up. A quick glance told her that time was most likely a precious commodity of which was rapidly running out. "We will have to continue this on the ways", she stated suddenly. "We must get out of here." She holstered the pistol and motioned for David to follow her out into the hallway. Just as she reached the door, however, she stopped, turned to him and said, "You will need to put that back on."

David looked down at the narrow, silver collar, "I don't think so", he said as he started to back away from her.

Susan handed him the control device before explaining, "You need to appear to be under my direct control", she said, "and the collar is all the explanation that is required." She signaled to him to give up the collar, "Just don't press any buttons and you will be fine."

David did not look convinced and shuddered when she clasped the collar loosely around his neck. Susan smiled at him comfortingly and pulled the revolver from the holster. Then, she gestured with the gun for David to walk out the door in front of her, down the steps, and outside to the former security chief's waiting transport.

The transport had been refueled and readied for travel just as she had requested through dispatch. Once inside, Susan immediately disabled several electronic controls, "Tracking devices", she said over her shoulder as she climbed into the guider's seat and powered up the sleek machine. However, before she pulled away from the prison quarters, she told David to get the weapon from the satchel beside his seat, "I hope you won't have to use it", she said with a sad grimace. "Anyone we would have to shoot would probably be friends of mine."

David searched the satchel and pulled out a small, semi-automatic machine gun along with several clips of ammunition. He fit the magazine into the weapon, pulled the charging handle to release a bullet into the chamber then set the safety switch to 'on'. There was a small slot to hold and secure the weapon beside his seat and David inserted the weapon as Susan pulled away from the buildings.

The security guard executed a swift salute as Susan sped past the first checkpoint. "That should mean that there is no alert out for me, yet", she said with a short sigh of relief. She indicated the collar control in David's hand and told him to press the button at the bottom of the device. With only a moment's hesitation, he found and pressed the control and was immediately rewarded as the hated collar quietly released from around his throat. Before Susan could stop him, he threw it out the window of the fast moving vehicle and into the darkness. David leaned back into the seat cushion and breathed deeply before he twisted in the seat to more fully face his former warden.

"Just this last checkpoint to pass and we are off Posin's facility", Susan said matter-of-factly. "Where do we go from here?"

David slowly pulled the machine gun back out of the transport holster and laid it on his lap before quietly answering, "I am grateful for being released from your compound and you probably have no idea how relieved I am to have that collar off, but you will have to do some more explaining before I take you to my family."

Captain Brose returned the salute to the final gate guard and continued guiding the transport away from the Mayoral complex. After a few minutes, she slowed the vehicle and guided it off of the ways until it could not be seen by anyone traveling to or from the compound. The dark, sleek craft landed within a sandy depression surrounded by a substantial amount of discarded flex-stone. "I understand your reluctance to trust me", Susan said with a sigh, "but, like I keep telling you, we don't have much time."

David merely shrugged his shoulders and said, "Convince me."

A hint of a smile touched her lips as she described how she had come by the photo intelligence and made sure that Mayor Posin had never seen them. The written correspondence like the manifests and invoices had been carefully obtained and painstakingly concealed from anyone other than her. Most of the photos that had lined the conference room walls had not been seen by anyone else until that very moment. Even those pictures were chosen with care so as to not reveal any more than what had to be seen by the Mayor's council members. She cocked her head ever so slightly before continuing, "I know how your family escaped when Posin's men attacked your home and I know all about the underground shelter that they used to hide themselves."

David gripped the weapon more tightly before grimly replying, "So, since you know where they are. Why, exactly, are we playing this game?"

Emotion, for the first time, was heard in her voice as she rushed to explain, "I know about the dumb-waiter. Why do you think my people set charges to destroy the fireplace? I did not want Posin's men to discover where it led. My men only followed my orders—to destroy the fireplace and chimney in order for the home to be utterly destroyed. No one else knows about the shelter under your house—I made sure of that!"

The weapon was still lying across his lap but David had listened intently to everything Posin's security chief had explained. She had not reminded him but he vividly recalled that she had told the Mayor, in front of his entire council, that there was no one in the home.

Finally David placed the weapon back into its holster, "I believe you", he said at last.

Susan let a short sigh escape her lips, "we don't—"

"Yes, I know, we don't have much time", David said with just a little exasperation. Do you need directions in order to guide us to Jonathan White's home?"

Susan fired the transport up and deftly raised it from its hiding place before replying, "Skip White's place? No problem." She guided the dark transport back onto the ways before turning abruptly left and turned up the speed. Exactly at that instant an alert sensor on the vehicle's dashboard ominously lit up. Her lips formed a tight smile, "You don't have to worry about me saying it anymore", she said cryptically. "If I am not mistaken, an alert has just been issued for my arrest. We are now out of time!"

CHAPTER TWENTY

"Momma", Dona asked quietly, "Where is papa?"

Maxine smiled at her daughter not wanting either one of her children to know just how worried she was becoming. It was amazing that they had made it a third of the way across the Citadel, walking at night and hiding during the daylight hours, to arrive just before dawn at the home of Skip White. Dona was the first of them to recognize the gateway. With a quiet shout of excitement, she had forged ahead of her mother and brother only to stop short just a little way up the driveway. It was not the darkness of the estate that had brought her to a stop nor was it the ominous silence that blanketed the area.

Once Maxine and Trevan caught up to her, she pointed at the home and simply said, "That doesn't look right."

The problem was fairly obvious once they all stopped and studied the shape of the house. The silhouette should have been imposing, even in the semi-darkness of pre-dawn. Instead, the stars revealed what appeared to be a huge camp tent where the middle pole had been removed causing the entire structure to sag and lean precariously.

Max's shoulders slumped for a moment, *when will this end*, she thought to herself. "You are right, Dona", she said with a rueful shake of her head. "Come on", she continued after looking up at the slowly brightening sky. "We better get off of the road."

"I guess that's the barn over there", Trevan pointed to a ruined structure to the left of what was left of the house.

Maxine herded her two children towards what was left of the rendezvous point where they will have to wait for their father. The three travelers approached the barn with both caution and a heightened sense of dread. The barn doors were crumpled beneath a large section of the upper hay loft while broken and splintered timbers were haphazardly scattered about their path. There was a fairly large entrance hole around one side that Trevan was able to walk, almost without ducking, into the darkness. Dona followed after him being careful not to disturb any of the devastated lumber and, knowing full well what kind of animals Uncle Skip had kept in the barn, even more careful where she placed her feet on the soft, warm straw.

They made their way far enough into the barn to feel secure that they could not be seen from anyone outside the building. Maxine broke open one of the bags and took out enough food for everyone to have a small celebration breakfast for reaching their objective. As the sun slowly rose on the horizon and dusty light began to drive away the darkness, they started to search for someplace better to hide.

"Perfect", Trevan announced from somewhere further back in the recesses of the barn where darkness still reigned strong. Max and Dona followed his voice and found a small stack of partially shattered hay bales that had been blown down from the hayloft above. They saw his hand stick out of a small opening between some of the bales, "Through here", he announced.

They dragged their luggage to the gap in the hay and handed everything, one by one, to Trevan. He moved the items against the wall when, finally, Dona and Max joined him inside the little fort. 'Perfect' indeed was an excellent way to describe the small, hay-walled room that Trevan had discovered. As long as they were inside the musty shelter, they would be save from all prying eyes unless those eyes got close enough to look inside their fort.

The weary travelers had scrunched and molded the hay to create the most comfortable beds that they had slept in since they had been driven from their home. Sleep, the kind of slumber that only comes when accompanied with a feeling of security, had quickly enveloped them.

But, now, they were awake and the question on everyone's minds was finally asked out loud, "Where is papa?" The heavens answered with an ominous, growling rumble that was heard, or maybe it was felt, from somewhere off in the distance.

* *

"I don't think we are being targeted", Susan shouted over the din from the latest explosion that had landed close enough to spray dirt and debris across the windshield of the transport.

"Oh, really?!", David shouted back. They had only driven a couple of units from the point they had seen the alert flash on the instrument panel when explosions had begun to reshape the landscape not too far from their transport. For the next several hours, small rockets had exploded much too close to them for comfort. Brose had abandoned the ways for more unpredictable terrain and, although the detonations had continued, it did seem as though they were no longer a target.

"Yes, really", Susan shot back. "Take a look at the pattern", she initiated a holograph that displayed a large area where their transport was located within the center. Nearly every discharge had occurred to the east of where the transport was now parked; with the one exception of the explosion that had just rocked their vehicle. "We're pulling out", Susan announced. "I think we should stay west of this ridge until we get to this point", she indicated an area within the holograph that was well north of the barrage, "then we should be able to get back on the ways."

Sure, David thought, *why not?* Aloud he said, "At this rate, we won't arrive at Skip's house until sometime this afternoon."

Susan countered, "If you can think of another route then by all means tell me about it." She pressed the controls that raised the transport from its latest shelter and slowly guided it north across undeveloped land. It did not take long before they realized that the further they traveled from the Mayor's governmental complex, the fewer rockets and explosions they encountered. Finally, with a small shrug of her shoulders, she pulled back onto the ways and sped towards the Jonathan White estate.

Just after noon, Susan's craft glided quietly up the driveway outside of Skip's home. David shook his head in disbelief, "What happened here?" He searched Susan's face for answers, "This isn't from the rockets we just left behind."

The transport settled slowly to a stop and settled in the ruined front lawn. They waited a few minutes to see if their arrival would attract attention before they opened the doors and exited the vehicle. David's first impulse was to shout Skip's name but just as he put his hands to his mouth, Brose touched him on the arm and shook her head to the negative. Susan drew her weapon and motioned for David to retrieve his from the front seat of the transport. She pointed to him and motioned the right side of the house. Then, she pointed to herself and gestured towards the left side. "If you see ANYONE", she whispered pointedly, "call me." She pressed a small audio into his hand then walked stealthily towards the left side of the destroyed home.

David watched for a moment before, mimicking his companion, he made his way to his assigned part of his friend's house. He could not help but believe that Skip could not have possibly survived this attack. It appeared that some kind of explosion had completely obliterated the middle of the home while the outer-most sections of the home were leaning precariously towards the center, like a small house of cards ready to crumple. Without actually entering into the unstable rubble, he peered and poked into every crevasse he could find. As he crossed around to the back of the house, he saw Susan gesturing for him to join her. He broke into a slow jog but kept scanning for any signs of life. He stopped examining the home when he saw the only partially visible body through the crushed window and collapsed wall of what used to be an upstairs bedroom.

David stared dumb with shock at the senseless death of his friend. Without taking his eyes from the body, he quietly asked aloud, "Why? Why was this necessary? Skip has never, ever hurt anyone his entire life. This man was the most hard-working and compassionate man I had ever known." He turned to Susan and his voice growled, "Why?"

Susan shook her head sadly, "This was not my doing." She met David's glare, "This is why I want out" she said with finality. "I cannot stop the corruption and it will probably get worse before it gets better." She broke eye contact to look toward the horizon and to where the sounds of explosions could still be heard in the distance. "I have no idea what that is all about but I am glad I am not in the middle of it."

Now Susan's eyes grew compassionate and her voice much quieter as she gently asked "Was your family was in there, too?"

"They should not have been", he answered brusquely. David turned to face the ruined barn, "The staging level could only be accessed from Skip's barn. Max and the kids were supposed to wait for me in there." He nodded his head towards the damaged structure. Full daylight showed that the barn had been damaged but not destroyed as the home had been. Still, he did not bother to hide his concern while he eyed the broken and twisted timbers lying between the house and barn.

Susan motioned with a nod of her head and said, "Lead on."

David walked cautiously toward the barn with his weapon held at the ready position while Susan followed quietly behind him. He found a large gash in the back wall of the barn as if someone had driven a tractor through it that had most likely caused the collapse of the rearward hay loft. Susan gestured towards what was left of the hay lofts but David shook his head to the negative. Instead, he pointed towards a small glint of metal that shone dimly through the murky, filtered sunlight.

They worked their way quietly over the strewn and broken bales towards the surprisingly untouched back corner of the barn. David searched for a few minutes before he found the control board and, after only another couple of moments, gauges and sensors that had automatically been set into a sleep mode blinked into life. He set the board on a nearby table and whispered to Susan, "This is our way out." Then he turned back to the interior of the barn, "Now, all we have to do is find our passengers." David called quietly just as another, distant explosion rumbled in the distance, "Max? Dona? Trevan? Where are you?"

* *

Everything had worked perfectly so far, thought Alican as she had made her way from her apartment to the security lifts in her quadrant of level three. A few people had passed her by; some people had acknowledged her when they crossed her path while most were busy enough with their own affairs to not even bother to even notice her. She knew that she was dressed a bit conspicuously as her more formal outfit was acceptable for attending a business board meeting above the caverns. The light backpack strapped across her shoulders tended to help her appearance seem more casual, which was the normal dress code within the levels. A letter of passage was gripped tightly in her right hand as she approached the lift site. Two uniformed guards standing at either side of the lift doors smiled as she drew close but their smiles froze into place as they read that she intended to travel to the staging level.

One guard snapped up his audio and attempted to reach first Boston, then Skip, and finally David Kendal. The other guard questioned the traveler as his companion tried to gain authorization for someone to leave the canyons.

Alican Sykes answered every question quietly and sweetly, after all, she had come this far, all she needed to do now was to get topside and she would be set for life! "Yes, I am David Kendal's personal secretary. Yes, I have video of the caverns as that document explains that I was sent to take pictures as well as collect information of the progress of the colonization effort."

The guard continued to itemize every article within her backpack and made copies of every document he could find. Everything looked legitimate but his orders were clear: ANYONE LEAVING THE CITY OF

DAVID NEEDS TOP LEVEL APPROVAL. He looked to his partner for help but the other guard only nervously shook his head; he could not find anyone who had the authority to approve the transit. Yet, this was the chief administrator for Kendal Enterprises; they certainly did not want to get on the wrong side of her!

Finally, the first guard put down the audio and politely asked if she would please come inside and sit down while he found someone, anyone who could verify the lift usage. Alican again smiled sweetly and entered into the small security shack. She asked the guard if she could have her computer and, once she was comfortable, asked each guard for their names and immediate supervisor while she prepared a report of the experience. *Patience*, she kept telling herself. If the plan was being executed as it was outlined, there would be no one left that the guards could reach. Sooner or later they would let her up, *Patience*.

* *

"Papa!" exclaimed Trevan as he hurled himself from the window of their straw-bale structure. If there was anyone else close by, their presence was now clearly broadcasted to them.

Dona's head popped up from behind the bales of hay. Her eyes first showed concern and disbelief then she, too, flew out from their small shelter, "Papa!"

Maxine clambered out of the stacks of hay and, laughing with relief, worked her way between the children to give her husband a big hug and kiss. She suddenly pulled away from him and slugged him on the bicep, "What in heaven's name took you so long?!"

"Yes, Papa", Dona and Trevan exclaimed in unison. "Where have you been?"

David rubbed his arm in mock pain and grimaced at his wife. When she doubled up her fist and began to advance towards him again, he quickly changed tactics and raised his hands in surrender, "All right, all right! Give me a chance to explain."

Max folded her arms across her breasts and leaned back on one foot tapping her other foot soundlessly in the soft straw. Dona mimicked her mother but Trevan walked over and stood at his father's side. David reached down and took his son's hand in his before he stretched out his other hand towards Susan, "I would like you to meet Susan Brose."

Maxine noticed the woman for the first time and stared at her in surprise before she broke her pose to walk over and shake her hand. After only two steps, Max suddenly froze, "Captain Brose", she said quietly and looked at David in alarm. She looked at the weapon in Susan's hand and backed away to stand with David. Dona quickly abandoned her stance of defiance to join her family, not quite sure what had just happened but could tell that the introduction of this stranger had caused no little amount of distress to her mother.

Susan gave an encouraging smile and quickly holstered her revolver, "Good afternoon Mrs. Kendal, we are sure glad to have found you and the children unharmed."

Max turned to David, "If this is your explanation, I may have to slug you again."

David opened his mouth to explain but Susan cut him off, "He was imprisoned for the last several days", she began. She continued to describe how she and David were able to escape before Mayor Posin could arrest them both. Susan gestured vaguely towards the grumbling sounds of distant thunder as she described the explosions that they had evaded while on their way to find them and how they had searched Skip's home before they had entered into the barn. "You, young man", Susan startled Trevan with a withering look, "scared us half to death when you shouted and jumped out of that hay stack!"

Trevan looked up at his father with a worried expression but he tousled his son's hair and told him, "We are glad you did. It took a lot of pressure off of us once we found out that there was no one else around." David turned to his wife, "Am I off the hook, now?"

Maxine gave him a light kiss on the cheek, "I guess we are even," she said innocently. She looked past David back to the point where he and Susan had entered the barn, "So, where is Skip?"

Dona and Trevan looked anxiously towards the same place, "Yes, where is Uncle Skip?"

David knelt down by his children and beckoned with his hands for them to come close, "Did you see what had happened to our home?" he quietly asked them.

"Oh papa, it was terrible", Dona answered. "We could see it in the moonlight as we left. Even in the darkness we could tell it was burned to the ground and it was still smoking."

David nodded in understanding, "Uncle Skip's house was burned, too, but not all of it. Those people didn't find you but they did find him."

Max covered her mouth with the back of her hand, "Oh no!"

Tears began to run down his daughter's face but she looked to her father for answers, "Is he dead, papa?"

David hesitated for a moment as he steadied his own emotions. He quietly cleared his throat and looked into her eyes, "I am afraid so, honey."

Dona nodded unhappily, "We", she said as she pointed to herself and her brother, "had hoped that he had escaped like we did. But, when we saw his house, we thought . . ." She paused for a second, "we were afraid that . . . he . . ."

Trevan took her hand in his and finished the sentence, "We kept hoping . . . but we knew he would come to see us in the barn . . . if he could." The two children looked at each other, "But he didn't come."

David hugged his two children and Maxine knelt to join them in the musty hay and straw. Susan watched from a short, discreet distance but wanted to say something to bring comfort, "He was a brave man." Dona and Trevan looked up at her and she continued, "They found him and hurt-killed him but, he didn't say anything about this!" She gestured towards the machinery that David had briefly checked before his family had come out of hiding.

"We were running for our lives", Maxine started by looking at her children, then looked at David, "and you thought you were going to stay in prison—or worse", she continued, "but, for Uncle Skip . . ." Max paused for a moment, "His trials are over. He has gone 'home'." She looked around the barn uncertainly and shivered, then looked from Susan to David, "And, now . . ."

"Now", David said as he nodded towards the awakened machinery behind them, "now we see about going to the caverns."

David walked over to the small computer station to the left of Skip's personal lift and brought up security screens similar to the ones that Boston had manipulated only 24 hours earlier. "Strange", he muttered aloud, "the staging level has been sealed."

"Sealed?" Susan asked.

"Everything and everybody must go through the staging level. It doesn't matter how important you think you are you still must get clearance from the security staff in staging. Yet," David paused while he executed more commands on Skip's console, "that level has been shut down—sealed. Whenever the staging level is sealed no one can get in or out of the caverns—the lifts won't transport to a sealed level."

David continued to work the controls while Susan helped Max and the children gather their belongings. It was only a matter of a few minutes before everyone that was going to the caverns was standing behind David anxiously waiting to enter the lift.

Finally, David stopped typing and swung around to face his family and the latest addition to the colonists. "There is something wrong on the staging level", he began. "I've unsealed the level but not only is no one answering the audio but Boston's console is offline." Concern was obvious on his face as he continued, "Max, Susan, I will send you down with the children. You only need to walk straight out of Skip's lift and get to the first lift down the right hand side of the corridor. As soon as you are inside and ready for transit," here he paused to look at Trevan, "just give me the 'thumbs up' sign—I'll be able to see you in this monitor."

Now he alternated looking from Max to Susan, "Once you are safely in the caverns, I will re-seal the staging level from here and join you before the lifts no longer operate from Boston's level."

"But David, you said the lifts won't transport to a sealed level." Maxine did not like the plan and didn't want to lose her husband again.

"I won't have much time", David continued, "but I cannot leave this lift operational when I leave. I'll set a destruct for this lift, get to the staging level and then use the same lift that you used." He said the words as nonchalantly as he could muster but he knew he had not disguised the worry in his eyes.

He drew his wife and Susan aside and dropped his voice almost too low for them to hear him, "Boston's security offices have been hit." His eyes darted back to his children who were busy repacking their possessions for the next journey. "There is nothing alive on that level", he continued, "I don't think there is anyone but us alive above the Caverns that know about the city."

Susan looked quizzically at David but Max looked like she might be going into shock. He turned to Susan, "Keep your weapon drawn. I don't know what has happened down there but if anyone tries to stop you and Max doesn't recognize him," he paused for a moment and pointed at her revolver on her hip. Susan nodded resolutely.

David turned to his wife and tenderly cradled her in his arms. Finally, he pushed her gently away from him, "you must get to that lift! Do you understand?" He looked into those beautiful eyes that were already showing defiance, already fighting their way back to reality. "Stay as far from Boston's offices as you can."

Max nodded reluctantly just as the lift cover slid silently open, pushing a couple of stray hay bales aside and Skip's personal elevator rose from its silo. The lift sat quietly in front of the little band before a soft click was heard and the lift doors shushed open. After a nod from their father, the children excitedly entered the small room and Susan followed them inside with the bulk of Maxine's baggage.

Maxine hesitated outside the lift to give her husband a long hug and a soft kiss goodbye. "I don't want to lose you again", she said quietly. She gave a small shrug of her shoulders, "Look around", she continued, "this time there is no one left to rescue you."

David smiled and touched her gently on the nose with the tip of his finger, "I'll be right behind you, I promise!" He kissed her once more before he reluctantly released her from his embrace.

Max entered the lift, closed her eyes briefly, and gave Trevan a slight nod. Trevan looked gravely at his father and gave him the signal. Moments later, the small lift was bringing its passengers underground towards Boston's staging area while the sound of explosions in the distance began anew.

The moment the lift doors closed, David went back to the computer console so he could monitor his family's movements. He saw Susan staring at the information displayed on the elevator monitor concerning the blueprint of the staging area they would soon be entering. Their monitor suddenly switched to show the area immediately surrounding the landing zone of the lift. The passengers noted that there was no one in sight while David utilized other security cameras within the staging level to confirm that the floor was, indeed, empty.

Susan pulled her weapon from its holster and held it at the ready position as the doors silently opened to a still very cold staging level. She exited first, swinging her weapon to the left, then right to make sure the area was clear before she motioned everyone out of the lift. Susan reached for one of Max's bags while holstering the revolver but Max only shook her head and told her to keep the gun out. "I don't know what David was worried about, but I would feel better if you continued being the guard rather than the porter", she said quietly.

Captain Brose smiled grimly and nodded as the small party left the lift and made their way down the corridor as David had suggested and entered into the first waiting lift they came across. Susan was the last to enter so it was she who gave Trevan the nod this time. Trevan nervously gave the 'thumbs up' sign to the silent monitor screen and the lift doors closed quietly in front of them.

Almost there, Maxine thought to herself. *Almost there.*

CHAPTER TWENTY-ONE

Finally, Alican thought to herself as she tried hard not to show her relief to the two security guards. She quickly shut down her computer and re-packed her backpack in preparation of her immediate departure.

The guards, however, were more concerned with the sudden appearance of a lift from the staging level. They had not been notified that anyone was coming down from the staging level and, according to their monitors; the passengers were none other than Mrs. Kendal and her children. They were riding the small lift, unescorted, along with another woman who was carrying at least one drawn weapon.

The lift came to a gentle halt and, after a short pause, the doors opened. This time, the first one out was Maxine Kendal followed closely by her children. Susan Brose hung back as if she knew that her sudden appearance was likely to cause trouble. Besides, the look on the guards' faces and their drawn weapons told her that she was probably not far wrong.

Maxine was quick to explain Susan's presence as the guards cautiously gestured for her to exit the lift and hand over her weapon when Max noticed Alican sitting quietly inside the guard shack. Her brows furrowed, *what is she doing down here*, she thought. Alican, as soon as she caught Max's gaze, immediately picked up her pack and left the shack to join the new arrivals.

"Hello Maxine", she said as friendly as possible, "David did not come down with you?" She displayed her most concerned expression to Maxine before she continued, "I have the reports that he requested and would have already given them to him if it wasn't for those fine fellows", indicating the two guards that were patiently interrogating Susan Brose. *Captain Brose!!! She shouted to herself, what on earth is SHE doing down here?*

"So THIS is where you have been hiding these past few weeks", Max answered just as cheerfully. "It's no wonder no one could find you and

David didn't even tell me!" Maxine exerted all the energy she had left to placate the person that stood so casually in front of her. She and David had tried valiantly to find her over the past couple of weeks to no avail. The problem was that she was probably telling the truth and that she did indeed have reports and video of the underground city.

Alican nodded her head secretively, "Only Boston, Skip and David knew I was here", she said quietly, "and I am very late getting back." She threw an exasperated look towards the guards.

"Let me reset the lift for you so you can be on your way", Max offered, "Give me just a minute." Maxine entered the lift and pressed a couple of buttons before stepping back out. *I hope David is still monitoring the lift*, she said to herself. She smiled at David's secretary and motioned her to enter the lift. *But, even if he is not, he should run into her in the staging level. That's a meeting I would have liked to see*, she thought.

Alican glanced at the guards for a moment but since the surprising arrival of Maxine and her obvious vouching of Ms. Sykes, they no longer cared if she left the caverns. She entered the lift while Max smiled and waved good-bye. One of the guards disengaged the lock and the doors silently closed. Alican breathed a sigh of relief knowing that she was one step closer to freedom and wealth. She folded her arms quite satisfied with herself and leaned against the back wall of the lift.

* *

David leaned back in the dusty chair and blew a big sigh of relief. His family was finally safe. He had watched them exit the staging level from Boston's cameras and noted that the lift had arrived on level one. He had begun the process of re-sealing the staging level when he noticed that Skip had several high-priority messages in his queue.

He suddenly jumped out of the chair as a rocket detonated close enough to the barn that hay bales that had not been dislodged during the earlier destruction fell from the upper level and landed much too close for comfort. After a brief wait for the dust to clear, he pressed the controls to play the messages aloud while he continued to set the process in motion that would put the staging level back into a deep-freeze state. A written message from Boston flashed onto the screen and David froze and stared at the words in disbelief, "Alican is in the Caverns. Captives are her body guards."

Alican? In the caverns? Why would she be . . . ? Suddenly he understood. The board members had been trying to figure out how the breakdowns in security kept happening whether in the Citadel or in the underground city but no one could figure it out. Alican had made it clear that she had wanted nothing to do with the caverns yet now Boston had discovered her IN the caverns. What else had she been doing? Memories of demonstrations where the rioters knew when and where to arrive and cause destruction before a security force could arrive flashed through his mind. He suddenly slammed his fist on the desk, *Asman, Skip and Boston!!*

It was at that moment David noticed the flashing security alarm on the lift that had just docked within the staging level. Boston's cameras were still focused on the lift his family had used so he merely needed to wait until the lift had locked into place and the doors opened to find out what was wrong.

Alican Sykes strolled casually out of the lift and into the staging level. She looked expectantly around before, with a surprised shrug of her shoulders, began to walk towards Boston's security office.

David shook his head violently as if to clear his mind but kept the cameras focused on this one person that had been available, even enthusiastic, to keep the records of his business while inconspicuously hanging around and no doubt hearing interesting tidbits concerning the caverns. The anger that continued to build inside him seemed to match the sound of the explosions that were beginning to sound much closer than before.

Alican's almost carefree stroll suddenly slowed to a halt and her brow furrowed while she looked at . . . something. David swiveled the cameras around in order to also see what had caused his secretary's unexpected concern when the blackened walls of the security office suddenly came into view. He quickly switched to other cameras only to find many of them around the office had been rendered inoperative. It was clear that some kind of a battle had taken place, walls had been destroyed, and the security stronghold had been breached. *This may explain why the staging level had been sealed*, he thought. *Boston would have done whatever was necessary to protect the caverns*.

Alican slowly appeared within the view of the closer cameras and it appeared that she was speaking to someone. David suddenly remembered to turn on the audio sensors. "Gustav?" she called quietly. "Hardin?" Alican continued to approach the ruined office before she finally called the name of someone for whom David, too, was interested, "Boston?"

Alican shivered and wrapped her arms about herself before she entered into the office and out of the view of David's monitoring cameras. She ducked under a ragged portion of a wall and, turning slightly, saw the Kendall Enterprise's Security chief pinned under rubble and lying in his own blood. She clucked her tongue with regret but continued cautiously forward a few steps until she noticed that there was another body lying close to Boston's. "Hardin" she muttered. Alican turned slowly in a circle, noting the destruction of the computer systems as well as Boston's personal security lift while looking for her other body guard.

She gasped suddenly as she spied who must be Gustav leaning against a wall bundled up to protect him from the cold and wearing an oxygen mask. "Gustav", she called, "Wake up. We've got to get out of here." When he did not move she walked several small steps to bring him closer to her sight in the dim office light. "Well", she finally announced, "I guess I won't have to worry about splitting up the profits." She chuckled at her own joke and shivered again. "Why is it so cold in here?" she asked her dead guardian. "And, where did you get that coat?"

David had been trying to figure out what to do with her. Thoughts of revenge kept coming to his mind and he kept pushing those thoughts aside. He knew that she was pretty much trapped on the security level unless she happened to find the only lift that was still operational. "Of course, that lift would bring her directly to me", he said aloud. *Besides*, he thought, *in another few minutes none of the lifts will operate, up or down, and she will have to stay there until someone*, he smirked at the thought, *unseals the level*.

Another explosion, this time David was pretty sure that Skip's home had been utterly destroyed. Debris from the house slammed into portions of the barn and the last section of the hayloft above David suddenly gave way dropping heavy bales to the floor all around him. He scrambled away from the console trying to escape the unintentional missiles but one caught him on the shoulder and slammed him to the ground while a second one pounded heavily into his back.

He was not unconscious for long. The darkness slowly receded but when he tried to move, pain stabbed violently down his right side. The bales had done their damage when they struck then rolled off of him after they had broken his shoulder, a couple of ribs and who knows what else. David craned his head to look about himself and after only a glance towards the lift knew that his brief flirtation of revenge had cost him his future. A large number of bales had fallen on top of the lift silo creating small mountains of heavy fodder that would have taken him half the day to clear off even if he had not been injured. But now, given the pain that kept him from being able to move much more than his head, he was more than likely going to stay right where he was until someone happened to find him.

All David could see was that the lift was blocked and he would need help before he could ever use it again. What he could not see were the shattered timbers that had broken loose from the loft and had fallen on and around the computer console. The last operational lift had just been destroyed—which had been his plan, but it wasn't supposed to happen until after he had safely joined his family in his city.

The irony is rich, he thought. *Alican will be dead in hours unless the sealing process of the staging level is stopped and reversed. I am the only person left in the Citadel who can reset the controls but unless someone stumbles into this barn soon . . .* Warm blood dribbled from his lips into the hay beneath his head as he wearily closed his eyes. "I'll be right behind you", he said softly. His raspy breathing was all that could be heard for a few minutes. "I promise", he gasped as he drifted back into unconsciousness.

CHAPTER TWENTY-TWO

The first two explosions that were heard within the Citadel were reported to have happened on the same day and at exactly the same time. According to the official reports from the city's Vision Services, the two transports had been built and serviced at the same plant and both vehicles contained a flaw that had been left undetected through the years. Apparently, a charge that had built up in the power packs finally sent a surge through the system that caused a chain reaction of explosions that completely destroyed the two vehicles. The investigators were at a loss to explain why they exploded exactly at the same time except that it must have been a freak accident. The owners of the transport plant had announced that they would cover all the costs of the funeral and burial of the two ladies that had been killed as a result of the explosions. They also announced that Ms. Carol Brunson and Ms. Trish Vonner would be laid to rest alongside their former employer and friend, the late Robert Kendal.

Although the citizens residing in old York-City didn't really notice or care about the destruction of the two transports, the explosions did cause quite the stir amongst the populous of the Citadel. Then, other detonations were heard and felt within isolated sectors of the Mayor's Internal Capital as well as within many of the industrial areas of the old city. At first, everyone wanted to know what was causing the explosions. It did not take long, however, before panic took hold within the two cities and the people were desperately trying to find safe havens for themselves and their families and escape the destruction.

In the meantime, the Mayor's staff desperately tried to figure out from where the rockets were coming. Mayor Kourie suddenly burst into the room, "What do you mean this isn't another riot attempt from the radicals of the old city?" he thundered.

Colonel Cushman was just as confused, "The rockets are not coming from anywhere in the city", he did not bother to make eye contact with Mr. Kourie. Instead, he continued to read the reports that were rapidly coming off of the printers. "We . . ." he paused in surprise, "are under attack . . ."

"We are WHAT?!" For the first time that the Colonel could remember, the self-assured veneer that always surrounded the Mayor showed signs of cracking. "How? Who?" he began, then stopped long enough to take a deep breath and steady his nerves. "What are you talking about, Cushman? Why would anyone attack us?" Anger was clearly written across his face but not because his city was under attack, it turned out, "How could anyone marshal weapons of destruction against us without you knowing about it?"

The colonel did look up, now. The Mayor was not thinking about defending the city or even launching a counter-attack in hopes of ending or at least deflecting the barrage, he was interested in placing blame! Colonel Cushman ignored the barb and, instead, concentrated on the damage being inflicted within the city and from where the attack was originating. "The attack has been concentrated in areas of known industrialization production and governmental presence", he began, "we were very lucky that you had ended your inquisition when we did and were traveling to separate destinations when this attack began."

Still not making eye contact with the Mayor, he used a holographic image of the Internal Capital and a pointer to display where the rockets had landed and had caused the most destruction. The top five floors of the Mayor's office building had been seriously damaged and many areas within the building were still burning. Captain Brose's security complex had been utterly destroyed from several direct hits. Several other buildings had taken salvos as well as several sections of the ways to and from the Mayoral complex. "These people had some decent intelligence but they definitely had not obtained anything particularly recent." Cushman indicated their abandoned offices in the old part of the city, "It is obvious that they had hedged their bets; they bombed both areas of the cities in order to have the best chance of disrupting our chain-of-command and communications."

"They?" Mayor Kourie asked hotly. "Who, exactly are 'they?"

"You had nearly all of our resources trained on the old city in order to identify the people that were perpetrating the incidents against your Internal Capital", the Colonel tried to explain. "Once we refocused and launched our defense and intercept rockets, the barrage was halted."

Colonel Cushman hesitated for only a moment, "We . . . I don't know who the attacker is, sir."

The Colonel snatched the latest intelligence report that had just been released from a printer and eagerly scanned its contents. His brow furrowed in frustration as he quickly handed it to the Mayor. "Our resources have been placed back into their international tracks but, since the barrage has stopped, we still have no clue as to who launched the attack."

"So, someone caught you with your pants down, is that what you are telling me, Colonel?" Now that he understood that the initial attack had been thwarted, the Mayor wanted to find someone for whom he could hold accountable for this terrible tragedy.

Again the Colonel did not take the bait, "I believe that the attack has been only temporarily halted, sir. I believe that the quick response of our intercept rockets and the redeployment of our satellites have temporarily stopped the launch of more rockets. I also believe that whoever has instigated this attack is evaluating the damage inflicted upon us. If they decide that, despite our armament being put back into service, they can complete their plan, they will resume the attack."

The Mayor narrowed his eyes in thought before asking, "So, what would be YOUR determination?" He caught and held the Colonel's eyes, "If you were the enemy and could see the damage that had been inflicted, what conclusion would YOU come to?"

Colonel Cushman folded his arms across his chest and met the Mayor's gaze, "They do not have real-time knowledge of our condition so they will have to rely upon their satellite images. We know that, except for a few officers, our leadership corps is intact. We also know that our communications have been damaged but not destroyed. If I were them, I would not consider resuming the attack until I had concrete evidence one way or another."

"Are you suggesting that I make a public appearance? NOW?" the Mayor asked incredulously. "You want me to become an exposed target to whoever has attacked us?

Colonel Cushman's answer was as calm and rational as the bite in the Mayor's words was sharp, "I am only suggesting that you broadcast from a secure environment and give as positive an outlook to the populous as possible so that this enemy will know, not guess, that the surprise attack did not cripple the city."

This was not the Colonel's position of expertise. Under normal conditions (as if a surprise attack from outside the city could be considered 'normal'), Captain Brose would have launched the counterattack as well as given war-time advice to the Mayor. However, because Captain Brose's facility had been utterly destroyed along with anyone within her buildings, he had to step up and cover both posts. The Colonel continued, "As long as they believe that our satellites are still operative and we are capable of launching a counter attack, they will not resume their attack."

Mayor Kourie considered the advice for the moment. *This may not only be an effective way of staving off another attack, but I may be able to already start building the blocks of belief among the citizens that I was blameless.*

A dishonest man believes that everyone else is also a thief and a liar. Thus, the mayor believed with all his heart that he needed to protect himself from others faulting him for the attack and he needed to put the culpability in motion before any of his staff had a chance to act first. "I think that is an excellent idea, Colonel Cushman" the Mayor unexpected announced. He turned to his communications officer, "Set up for a broadcast within the hour", he commanded. "I'll broadcast from my primary defensive bunker."

Posin Kourie smiled as he left the war room. *Yes, that was an excellent idea Colonel,* he thought. *An excellent idea indeed!*

A waiting transport picked up and delivered the Mayor to his reinforced broadcasting room and, while he spent his time with his speech-writer to perfect the message to his waiting constituents, his personal vision crew reconfigured the room to make it appear as if the Mayor was braving the elements of war for his interview.

"Sir", one of the radar men interrupted the Colonel's thoughts.

"Yes?" Cushman asked and turned towards the small bank of monitors that now displayed not only the international sights but several of the closest former U.S. cities.

"We have incoming." The servicemen in the room were scurrying around, verifying altitudes and trajectories with the waiting defense satellites. The stress in the room was already thick but, with the likelihood of reengaging the enemy seemingly imminent, somehow the tension managed to increase to a breaking point.

The Colonel approached the screen the radar man indicated and there was indeed a large force in flight with the apparent destination of York-City. The aircraft approaching the beleaguered city were more high-altitude support transports. Obviously, there could not be enough soldiers within those ships to commence an authentic ground attack.

"Shall we attack, sir?"

Colonel Cushman frowned for a brief moment, "Absolutely not, Captain!" he snapped.

The Captain looked at the Colonel, "A welcoming committee, then?"

Now the Colonel smiled, "Yes, a welcoming committee." Cushman winked at his fellow officer, "Do you know where we want them to land, Captain?"

The Captain stood up from his console, "Yes sir" he barked, then, gesturing for several men to follow him, exited the room. Only a few minutes later, the captain and a growing number of men began to gather outside the Mayor's broadcasting bunker.

The tension in the room had changed to confusion. Many of the servicemen were still at their consoles but they were no longer sure what they were supposed to be doing. The Colonel glanced at the clock on the wall, *right on time,* he thought. "Hey!" he suddenly said aloud and gestured towards the large video-screen, "Get the Mayor's address on the screen."

The Colonel was obviously in better humor but the reason for his sudden change in attitude was not clear to anyone else left in the war room. Cushman leaned against a table as he watched a very serious Mayor describe how the incompetence of his intelligence officer had caused in the misdirection of York-City's defense satellites which resulted in another country trying to take advantage of the temporary blindness to attack. Fortunately he had ordered the satellites to be retrained to their original targets in time to stop the attack. "Obviously", he went on to say, "I will have to re-evaluate the members of my staff to ensure this kind of tragedy can never happen again. In the meantime, let me assure you that my chain-of-command is intact, our defenses are totally operational and we are prepared to do whatever is necessary to protect our city."

The smile remained on Cushman's lips during the entire time that the Honorable Posin Kourie slandered the Colonel's good name. The Mayor continued to reassure the people that he was ever ready to protect their good city and was doing everything in his power to ensure their safety and well-being. The broadcast was coming to a close just as the first of the incoming transports landed within the mayoral compound. On a whim, the Colonel checked his watch, "This should be good", he muttered. *The Mayor should be exiting his defense bunker just as the first of the troops disembark from their ships.* Aloud he ordered, "Make sure we are getting this recorded."

The first airship landed in the exact center of the parade deck in front of the still-burning buildings. The dirt and dust had not even begun to settle before the disembarkation doors swung open wide and troops spewed out of the craft and set up an armed perimeter of defense. As each successive transport landed, the troops readjusted their perimeter to include the latest airship. More troops disembarked from the ships and joined the already positioned soldiers until a formidable force was assembled within the mayor's complex.

It was this sight that met the Mayor as he emerged from his fortified bunker. No sooner had the barricade doors swung open wide and the Mayor's entourage entered into the courtyard did a small platoon of soldiers rush forward with shouts of "Stand where you are!" and "Surrender!" An impressive array of weaponry was trained on the small group and the Honorable Mayor, Mr. Posin Kourie, immediately raised his hands in defeat.

The Colonel rubbed his hands in satisfaction. The surprise attack got rid of both Captain Brose and David Kendal, two people that had been a pain in his side for way too long. And, although the same attack should have killed the mayor, he much preferred this ending of York-City's political ruling class.

The communications officer signaled for attention, "I have the Kendals on the audio, sir."

"Excellent", he smiled. *This is turning into a good day*, he thought. "Transfer the call to my office." Without waiting for an acknowledgement, the Colonel spun on his heel and walked out of the war room. *I have seriously underestimated those two*, he thought while he walked down the hallway. *Jocelyn should have knuckled under the pressure the mayor put on her but, instead, she thrived. She not only participated in the demonstrations, she had come up with information that had been instrumental with the planning and the removal,* at this thought he smiled, *of his biggest pain—the Mayor.*

He entered into his private office and immediately switched on the audio, "Good afternoon Jocie, Sunis."

Sunis nodded his head politely while Jocelyn grimaced but returned the greeting, "Good afternoon, Colonel."

"You've been keeping up with the news, haven't you?" the Colonel's smile broadened at her obvious dislike to the nickname and gestured vaguely towards the large screen behind him. The monitors displayed the former mayor and his closest staff being loaded into one of the airships while a small group of dignitaries were just leaving the last transport to be carefully escorted into the former mayor's command center.

"It's everything you wanted", Jocelyn said guardedly. She looked directly into her accomplice's eyes before continuing, "What about me? When do I get what I want?"

The smile stayed intact on Cushman's face but then some of the pleasure faded from his eyes, "Everything is set up" he said, "The Citadel will be yours. Just get over here right away and we'll head over to the command center. You know the drill", he continued, "The two of you have papers to sign."

The Colonel cut the connection, stood up, and stretched before he confidently signaled his aid to join him. "Go get ready to meet the new boss", he said lightly and watched him abruptly turn and leave. As the leftover pieces of the old leadership prepared to meet the new Mayor and staff, the rest of the populous watched the vision screens show York-City and its new Internal Capital fall to a foreign power without a single shot fired by the ground troops.

CHAPTER TWENTY-THREE

The seas of level four were a beautiful sight that only continued to grow more spectacular as the interior seas continued to age. The confining walls had been cut ragged to help cause the breakers to form and the resulting soft roar could be heard from the man-made beaches. The purification beams continuously scanned the water for bacteria and known contaminants but it had been decided to allow as much of the natural marine life to grow and flourish as possible. Water fowl had been introduced as soon as the seas had become stable and the variety of transplanted fish had proven to be able to thrive in their subterranean conditions. There was already talk of commissioning a crew to construct a new wharf that would allow easier access to boats and watercraft.

The engineers had spent plenty of time and effort to help cause a somewhat controlled weather system to transpire within the enormous water chambers. The high ceilings allowed water to evaporate and 'rain' back into the seas while the recycling of oxygen from the other levels helped to create breezes and waves to the delight of the tourists visiting the beaches. Fishing was allowed and even encouraged, which resulted in a water industry that included fish and bird wardens as well as fishing and boating tournaments. Going to the beach had not been an activity the people of York-City were able to participate in since before the radiation wars. But now, the underground twin seas were an easy commute and a pleasant pastime for anyone who had the time and inclination.

The subterranean seas existed exactly in the center of the entire city and the level was divided into two enormous chambers so as to ensure that if there was a serious problem or malfunction with any of the maintenance machinery it could only affect half of the internal water source. The walls, floor, and ceiling had been constructed to handle more than twice the amount of water that could be contained within and the array of sensors that fed data to the engineer level was almost sensitive enough to tell the engineers how many fish existed at any given time. The people didn't care about any of the engineering feats, however. They were really only interested in the serenity and the clean, fresh air and water—so much water!

It was interesting that a great many discussions had been held to argue the pros and cons of yet another water source within the confines of the underground city, especially with the slowly expanding reservoir being created by Asman's dam. However, when any of the hydroponics farms were visited, especially the main facility on level seven, one of the first questions that always came to mind was how could there ever be enough water to grow so much food! Since the always available artificial sun light from the lower ceilings helped to provide four well-controlled growing seasons, an available and abundant water supply was of the utmost importance. The water that was extracted from the underground seas and augmented from Asman's dam provided plenty of nourishment for the farms while still providing the necessities of life for the growing population of the city.

The vast corn and wheat fields that were conscientiously tended and harvested within the level seven hydroponics farm could be compared to the (very) old pictures of some of the substantial Nebraska and Kansas farms. Sweet potatoes, green beans, corn, name the vegetable and, if it can be grown underground, it was produced and supplied to the rest of the city. When the City of David was new, the level seven hydroponics farms lay mostly fallow as many of the crops were being grown on each, separate level. But, as the demand increased and the city's population continued to grow, the enormous agricultural area that had been set aside by the city's founding architects began to justify its existence with an abundance of excellent agricultural products.

Acres of meticulously tended fruit and nut trees shamed the Citadel's small, terraced orchards. An interesting consequence from growing orchards within the confines of an enclosed, albeit enormous, indoor structure was that the heavily reinforced ceilings could be extensively utilized for pruning and harvesting. A complex system had been constructed to allow the harvest and maintenance crews to be transported and lowered into the trees instead of or in addition to accessing the forest from the ground. There was almost no waste of the delicious produce and the orchards could be kept pruned and maintained like they never could be in an open-air environment.

Maxine and her family had remained on the first, administrative, level for a longer time than was really necessary. Max had no idea what had happened to her husband and, at first, harbored the hope that he had merely been delayed. She wanted to make sure that the family would be on hand to immediately greet him when he arrived. As time passed without word of any kind, she grew more despondent and she made fewer trips to the security monitors. All the security officials were able to tell her was that the lift that they had taken to the caverns had become disabled and that the staging level had, once again, been sealed. Max and Susan had forced the issue to the head of security within the caverns only to find out that all upper-world communications had been disabled.

Dona and Trevan went back to school while Maxine haunted the security offices hoping for word of David. Susan shadowed Maxine on every trip to the security offices to the point that she learned how the security teams were set up and how they operated within the underground city. She was astonished at the amount of information that was available within the confines of the administrative level. The sensory and auditory equipment that was utilized on every level of the city provided incredibly accurate information. What fascinated Susan was that the data was not used for gathering incriminating evidence against the people as it would undoubtedly have been under the rule of Mayor Posin. Instead, the information identified possible problems; traffic congestion, temperature or humidity anomalies that needed correction, machinery malfunctions, even suggestion of poaching. The departments within the administration level would identify every issue as a potential crisis and proactively address the trouble by sending out the appropriate work crews or security forces.

Susan was offered, and she accepted, employment. It wasn't long before she was once again promoted to Captain Susan Brose, one of several security leaders. It was Captain Brose who was finally able to convince Maxine that she needed to get on with her life; that her husband, for whatever the reason, was not going to join them in the subterranean world that he helped to create. Maxine moved herself and the two children to level three with the hope of encouraging Dona and Trevan to once again excel in their education. She also encouraged her children to resurrect their dreams, change them as necessary, and to find new goals that could come to fruition in their new home. Meanwhile, Susan encouraged Maxine to consider putting her considerable analytic Y-CR skills to work within the administrative level.

Level three had been designated as the housing area of which the most pre-built apartments and houses were constructed before colonization had even begun. The next most populated area was, predictably, the administrative level. Various sized apartments had been built in order to free up as much property for later development as possible. Parks, biking and running trails, and various shops and malls were built or designated for construction in order to make these two levels the most family and people-friendly of the entire city. Even though there was some habitation available on every level, the amount of accommodations allowed and accessible was in direct relation to the number of people that were expected to live in each level. For instance, less abundant housing and apartments had been constructed for the farm crews that worked on level seven. Even level four had a small housing area that was situated somewhat ominously between the two underground seas.

David's City had been designed for internal expansion so, even though a lot of construction had been done to make sure the first colonists would be more comfortable than travelers of long ago, the Board made sure that there would still be plenty of room for growth, even restructuring, should the original design prove to be faulty. The habitation levels had areas set aside for small markets and strip malls interspersed within the subdivisions even though most of the significant industry was located on other levels. Police and fire departments had been built and more were entered into the overall master plan for future development as the population grew. There were small medical clinics as well as hospitals on every level so that care would be available for anyone with the least amount of time possible wasted in transport of the sick or injured.

The educational facilities on level three easily rivaled the best teaching institutions that had ever existed above-ground. The colonists selected the best teachers and professors that could be depended upon to teach truth and facts while encouraging the students to utilize the information in practical applications. It was very likely that Dona had thrown herself into her studies as an intellectual escape after losing her father. She still excelled in theatrics and drama but her finest performances were no longer the positive, exuberant roles. Dona flourished best when she portrayed the underdog, the hard-working downtrodden person who overcame great odds until the hard fought victory had finally been won.

Perhaps the theatrical roles that she played assisted Dona to stick to her original goals of helping the less fortunate people of the world. More than likely it was the steady influence of her parents, her mother in particular, especially during this delicate time of her life that kept her focused on the needs of others rather than dwell on the loss of her father. Dona took advantage of her mother's decision to work within the administrative offices to learn the pulse of her new home. She loved this new environment where people could learn a new skill and seek employment anywhere for which they showed an aptitude. It was exciting to discover opportunities and match them to people who were actively looking for that type of employment. This was so different from the officiously controlled agency that had been in effect in York-City. Here in the caverns, the people had the prospect of going where they wanted and earning a living in a career that they had chosen for themselves.

Trevan changed his goals. He already had an exceptional work ethic but, without his father to channel his energy, Trevan no longer had much of an interest in academics. Instead, he found that focusing on his physical talents gave him the release he needed to deal with his new life. The coaches loved the sudden appearance of this young athlete that seemed to have a near-fanatic devotion to whatever sport he decided to play. Trevan enjoyed the attention and accolades that came freely to him for doing something that seemed to be easy and natural. The world of sports was suddenly a live thing that he knew he could subject to his will and would repay him by distracting him from the hole he felt in his heart whenever he thought of his father.

There were two mammoth stadiums, one on each of the levels two and five. Anyone with enough talent and effort could put themselves in a position to play their sport within their stadium. Every year the top teams of each stadium would compete for city honors. Trevan was the perfect age to feel the exhilaration of victory and the idol worship most young men experienced for the warriors he watched battle within the confines of his stadium.

The two stadiums, as most huge facilities built in an area with limited space available, was constructed for multiple purposes. Another purpose for such a large edifice was its use as a civic center and concerts and other events that could predictably draw a large crowd of people. Trevan had attended an event of which his sister had performed and even though he had always thought of a stadium as a place for sports, he was also intrigued with the fanfare and the adoration that attended the political figures as they emerged from their favored box seats to congratulate the performers.

There really were not that many people in leadership positions within David's city. The city had been designed as a self-governing organization that encouraged discussion and cooperation within each level as well as cooperation between the levels. Because the early colonists had followed and taught a strong adherence to the ten laws that David and his board members had drafted and tested while the city was being created, a solid base of morality had been formed among the settlers. The still too recent memories of the upper-world's corrupt leaders and their decisions helped to keep David's fledgling city from falling into the hands of dishonest people.

Boston had originally selected the underground city's Chief of Security but he set up the office such that this person had limited authority unless granted by the two councilors assigned to him. Even though the security chief may choose his own councilors, these two people were tasked to keep their leader in check should that person try to overstep his or her authority. The department of agriculture had been arranged in a like manner with the Chief of Agriculture having the same level of authority as the Chief of Security. All other departments that had been or would be created to assist in the administrative needs of the city were to follow this same method so that no one person could have absolute power and control.

The design of internal leadership had been constructed with the unsophisticated concept that the number of good people voted into positions of power will always outnumber the bad. Even if evil or misguided people should obtain the level of support that allowed them legislative power over the entire city, the city had been physically built to further complicate the misuse of power. The usurpation of the overall power and authority of the city would still need the cooperation of the leadership of each level before that control could be made absolute.

The sensory equipment seemed to be working perfectly, Captain Brose thought with a nod of approval. She had been assigned the oversight of the integrity of the borders. That meant that no one was allowed access into the city or, even more rare, the permission to leave without authority from every department chief. It had not taken her long to realize that the border task was mostly academic; every precaution had been taken to program the lifts such that, without the myriad of needed electronic signatures, the border elevators wouldn't budge. Instead, Brose took to scanning the sensors that monitored the massive walls that separated each level from the outside world.

Susan marveled at the forethought that David and his engineers had put into the construction and placement of the sensors. The monitors were continually updated with data from the outside world with information from temperatures to seismographic readings and how any of the causes of the thousands of readings may have affected the strength and integrity of the level walls. She was, however, most intrigued with the interior sensors that were interlaced throughout the walls that lined the inside perimeter of each level. These sensors were continuously scanned for the unpardonable sin; someone attempting to create an opening from within the city to reach the outside world.

The reasons to do so were mostly because of the development of the survival instinct that had been cultivated while living in old York-City. These people were used to fighting for every possession and every advantage only to have it taken away from them. All the damage to the structure of the borders had always been because someone had tried to hide a prize within the secure confines of the flex-stone walls. Any destruction or vandalism was quickly identified, stopped and repaired before any real damage was done. Susan was quite certain that it would probably be quite some time before anyone would actually want or try to escape this underground fortress. She was also quite sure that, sooner or later, someone would attempt to circumvent the sensors and breach the thick walls. She knew that for the safety of the future generations, she needed to put into place everything possible to protect David's city.

Maxine typed in a few commands into her console that caused her software to once again check for new employment postings. She smiled as she watched the results scroll across her screens. Level by level she saw a wide variety of prospects for the colonists and the potential for the business owners to get a more firm standing in the communities. Many of the people that lived in the caverns had been the very same people that had existed without hope in the upper world. A whole new world had opened up for them and nearly every one of them was working as hard as possible to make something of their lives. Her shoulders slumped for just a moment as she thought again of her husband and their friends on the board that had given up so much; some had given more than what they had to give. With a slow shake of her head she pushed away her melancholy thoughts as her board lit up with inquiries to the latest employment postings. A sad smile tugged at her mouth as she once again contemplated what her husband had sacrificed in order for these people to have a better way of life. She shook away the tears and bent to the task of assisting the people of the City of David.

Edwards Brothers Malloy
Thorofare, NJ USA
August 21, 2012